MATCH
Penalty

MATCH *Penalty*

KENNA KING

ANYA

Anya
An Imprint of Meredith Wild LLC

DEDICATION

"...and last but not least, the wonderful crew at McDonald's for spending hours making those Egg McMuffins, without which, I might never be tardy."

—*Clueless* (1995), directed by Amy Heckerling

PLAYER POSITION & NUMBER

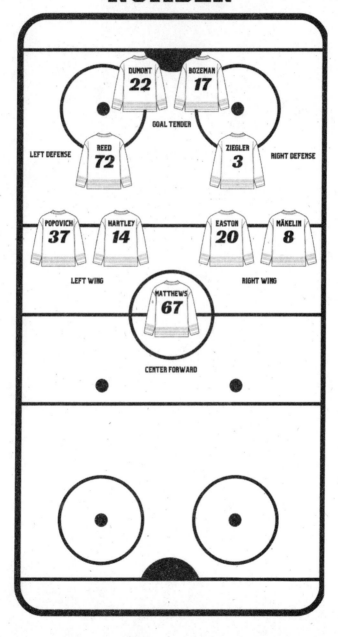

PROLOGUE

Cammy

"Damn sun," I mutter at the early morning light streaming through the expensive blackout curtains, landing squarely on my face. It's the kind of light that demands you wake up, even when you don't want to.

I groan softly, stretching my arms above my head as I try to burrow deeper under the silk sheets. The smell of his deodorant and a hint of me still cling to the bedding, along with the faint smell of sex from last night and then again early this morning before we fell asleep.

Three years of saying no to Jon Paul Dumont, to avoid being another notch on his bedpost, and here I am, completely worn out yet deliciously sated in the guest bedroom of his teammate's beach house. I allow myself a brief, blissful moment, letting myself sink into the mattress, soaking up the tenderness of my nipples from his teeth and the beautiful soreness between my thighs where he took me—over and over again.

Trying to also forget that he's the reason my team, the Seattle Hawkeyes, was bumped out of their spot in the championship, beating them out of contention three weeks ago. Though, watching him play against my dad was something else entirely. Goalies on opposing teams—on opposite sides of the rink.

It's been three years since I caught him staring at me from the ice, his face hidden behind his mask, except for the sharp curve of his smirk. He tossed a puck over the plexiglass, scribbled in silver sharpie... *Dinner?*

I shook my head no, assuming he thought I was just another puck bunny and feeling insulted by it, but JP didn't stop there. Every game after that, every charity event, every time our paths crossed, he'd toss another puck my way or drop a smooth comment walking past me in the hallway during post-game media interviews, that perfect cupid's bow pulled tight.

JP came with a warning label—his reputation preceding him. Though, not the same reputation as his father's, which I'd heard whispers about in hockey circles. The great Jon Paul Dumont Sr., whose drinking had cost him everything—his career, his marriage, his relationship with his son. JP never talks about it, but I'd seen the way he tensed up whenever someone mentioned his father's name.

Three years of saying no. Three years of trading barbs at charity events and all-star games, pretending I don't secretly look forward to the start of a new season when we'll be pushed back into proximity because of our jobs. Because I do.

And now, he's the same man who whispered French in my ear last night—words I didn't understand but melted for anyway—who looked at me across the ice as he won another playoff game, like I was the only thing that mattered.

For once, someone in my life means what they say.

I let out an audible groan at the idea that I can't stay in bed with the sexy goalie a little while longer. After all this time—all those moments where we talked for hours, where he found excuses to linger longer before getting on the team bus, and all those times I pretended his attention meant nothing—I finally gave in. And now, ordering breakfast and partaking in a few more rounds under these silk sheets with JP would be more fun, but the reality of today hits me like a slap.

I have to get up.

My flight home leaves this morning, and I need to return my rental car. What was I thinking, coming to a Blue Devils' playoff win celebration? If anyone from the Hawkeyes' front office found out that their general manager's assistant spent the night with the rival team's goalie, I'd never live it down. If my dad found out... I push the thought away.

Besides, last night was supposed to be a quick appearance at Danny Cooper's house—the Blue Devils' right winger. But the second JP's eyes met mine from across the room, his gaze dipped to the puck in my hand—the one he'd tossed me before second period with Cooper's address scribbled on it—and his smile spread. Not the cocky grin I've spent years brushing off, but something real. Genuine. And all at once, I wasn't thinking about the reasons I'd been saying no.

When he suggested we escape the chaotic celebration downstairs and order Chinese food to one of the guestrooms, my usual defenses crumbled. Instead of my typical witty rejection, I found myself following him up the grand staircase, my hand in his, my heart racing with every step.

But one of the biggest reasons I usually decline crosses my mind this morning. The Hawkeyes and the Blue Devils share the longest rivalry in NHL history—a fact neither of us ever let the other forget.

Suddenly the lack of sound and movement on the other side of the bed feels off. I reach across the bed, and my hand brushes cold sheets.

My eyes snap open.

The spot where JP was lying just hours ago is cold, the silk sheets pulled back like he got out of bed in a rush. My heart stutters as I push myself up onto my elbows, scanning the room.

There's a sleek dresser in the corner, his suit jacket still draped over the chair beside it. His stuff is still here, besides his keys, wallet, and cell phone that he had on the nightstand before we fell asleep, evidence that I didn't dream last night into existence.

But no JP.

Wherever he went... he took them with him.

On the dresser, five empty Chinese takeout containers from last night sit next to an untouched glass of water. The sight brings back memories of sharing spring rolls and laughing about all the times I've shot down his dinner invitations. Though, I reminded him that he sucker-punched my dad three weeks ago in their head-to-head and might not have the warm welcome he thinks he will.

I listen for him, but all I hear are muffled conversations from downstairs, doors opening and closing, and the occasional burst of laughter as the mansion slowly wakes up to its post-game hangover.

He's probably just downstairs brewing coffee. Maybe ordering breakfast in bed.

Dread pools in my stomach anyway. My gut is warning me to lower my expectations and prepare for the worst.

I reach for my phone, scrolling quickly to his number—the one he programmed last night with a confident grin and a promise to keep in touch. He even winked and said, "The season's over. If I come to Seattle, will you see me, mon petit oiseau?"

The way my heart leaped at the thought of him already making future plans with me has me hoping that my gut isn't right, but my past experiences with my family, specifically my mother, tell me to expect disappointment.

I press *call.*

The line doesn't even ring before it goes straight to voicemail.

The sinking feeling worsens.

I hit *redial.*

Still voicemail. Panic begins to heat under my skin, but I try to shake it off. This isn't the time to jump to conclusions. Maybe he forgot to plug in his phone last night. After all, his hands were a little preoccupied... with me.

But my stomach doesn't buy it.

I sit on the edge of the bed, with only a pair of panties on, pulling the silk sheet up and around my chest, feeling more naked now than I've ever felt in my life. More exposed than all those times I felt his eyes on me across a crowded room, more vulnerable than when I finally let him kiss me last night.

I would have pulled on a T-shirt last night—I usually can't sleep without something on—but his request made my whole body flutter. "No clothes, Cammy, please? I want to be able to feel your bare skin against mine," he whispered against my neck.

I guess there were a lot of things he said, and yet, he's not here.

I grab my dress off the floor. It's crumpled, the fabric wrinkled from where he tugged it off last night, his voice a low growl as he spoke French into my ear. I squeeze my eyes shut against the memory.

I take a steadying breath and head toward the door. I crack it open, peering into the hallway. The mansion is already alive with movement. Across the hall, a woman in a cocktail dress, just as wrinkled as mine, steps out of another guest room, fluffing her hair as she turns to the player inside.

"You'll call me, right?" she asks hopefully.

"Yeah, totally," he says, but the bored tone of his voice tells me he won't.

The woman doesn't seem to notice as she struts down the hallway in last night's heels.

I glance back at my phone clutched tightly in my hand. As I'm about to step into the hallway, it dings.

A news headline flashes on my screen like a gut punch:

STAR GOALIE JON PAUL DUMONT
GETS DUI AFTER PLAYOFF
CELEBRATION.

My chest tightens as I tap the notification, skimming the story quickly in disbelief.

JP Dumont, star goalie for the Blue Devils and son of Hockey Legend Jon Paul Dumont Senior, was in a car accident early this morning. Reports say Dumont was driving under the influence with an unnamed female passenger. The couple left a post-game win celebration shortly before the crash in his Ferrari. Dumont hit a guardrail and was later taken into custody by the sheriff's department, while his female passenger was taken to the hospital for non-life-threatening injuries.

The couple.

The room spins as the implications hit me. The "unnamed female passenger" wasn't me.

A door creaks open, and footsteps echo down the hall. I glance up and freeze as two players step out of a room. One of them has his phone in hand, shaking his head with a laugh.

"JP was busy. Two girls in one night—epic," one player snickers.

The other player elbows him, grinning. "Yeah, and I think one of them is still in the guest room."

My throat tightens.

Another player's wife walks past, phone pressed to her ear. "Did you see who he left with? That blonde attorney that's been hanging around the team all season—Angelica Ludwig. Looks like she finally landed herself a player."

I step back into the room, closing the door to just a crack, and then realize I'm forgetting something. I look around for my bright green hairband. The one that JP had taken out of my hair when things started getting heated last night. He wanted to see my hair down and then slid the hairband over his wrist.

It was the last thing I saw before I fell asleep—my bright green hairband stretched over his tanned wrist as he held me. How stupid it feels now, thinking it meant something.

I hear more voices in the hall. "If Angelica was really all that smart, she should have gone for one of the other single players instead. JP takes after his old man. She wouldn't get more than just one dirty fuck," one of them snickers.

"His dad's that retired all-time hockey hall-of-famer from Montréal, right?" another asks.

"Yep," a deep voice chimes in. "His dad was a player on and off the ice. That apple doesn't fall far from that tree, if you know what I mean."

The heat of humiliation rushes through me as their laughter fades down the hall. I clutch my phone, the weight of everything crashing down at once: the story, the whispers, the realization that I was just another conquest.

I should have known better.

No... actually, I did know better.

My face burns as I hurry down the grand staircase, past the remnants of the celebration—empty champagne bottles, red Solo cups, the faint smell of stale beer, the women slipping out with the same dazed expressions I must be wearing.

By the time I reach my rental car in the circular driveway, my humiliation has hardened into anger. And then I remember the stupid thing I sent Brynn, my stepmom, when she texted last night to check in.

> **Brynn: Did you have fun tonight?**

> **Cammy: Yeah, and I take back what I said last week. I think you're right about happily ever after's coming from the most unexpected places.**

I cringe, my eyelashes fluttering closed at my error. I never should have sent that. I shouldn't have believed a word he said as he held me close to him, his lips against my temple.

"I don't want this to end after tonight. My contract is up with the Blue Devils. I'll tell my agent to get me a deal with the Hawkeyes... whatever it takes to sign me."

I'd been warned about guys like JP Dumont. Everyone in hockey knows the type: talented, entitled, and fully aware of both. Following in their fathers' footsteps, making the same mistakes, breaking all the hearts. But I thought I was different—I thought I was different *to him.*

I grit my teeth, gripping the steering wheel as I start the engine. Through the rearview mirror, I can see the mansion that housed the Blue Devils' game win celebration, now the site of my biggest mistake.

"Hope I never see that asshole again," I mutter under my breath as I pull away.

And I mean it.

CHAPTER ONE

Cammy

Present Day

"Everett Kauffman is coming in today," Penelope announces as she breezes past my desk, clutching her dirty chai latte like it's the only thing keeping her upright, her long blond hair swishing behind her in a low ponytail. The sharp click of her heels against the dark wood floors of this Hawkeyes' suite echoes through the space before she disappears into her office.

I glance at the contracts spread across my desk—returning player contracts and professional tryout players, helping to make sure everything is ready for the talent coming back in to start the season—and then at her office door, left ajar for me. The smell of cinnamon and espresso from her usual drink mingles with her vanilla perfume, a familiar scent that usually brings comfort, but today it only heightens my sense that something's off.

My phone buzzes with a text.

Dad: Still on for lunch?

I smile, typing back quickly.

Cammy: Wouldn't miss it.

These lunch dates with my dad started as his way of making up for lost time, but they've evolved into a weekly check-in that we both look forward to.

Four years ago, I moved to Seattle for an internship with the Hawkeyes—the same team my dad used to play for. Since then, I've worked my way up, determined to prove myself beyond being Seven Wrenley's daughter. And these lunches with him were everything I missed growing up, thinking his older brother "Eli" was my father.

Penelope Matthews, the youngest GM in the NHL, is usually rock solid, but the way she barreled through without her normal cheery "good morning" or even a passing smile tells me that whoever is coming in today has her rattled.

Pushing back my chair, I grab my notebook and follow after her. She's already perched on the edge of her desk, fingers drumming against the to-go cup from Serendipity's Coffee Shop down the street. The moment I step inside, she comes around her desk and heads for the door, softly clicking it shut behind me, the sound low but ominous, like the calm before a storm.

"Everett Kauffman?" I prompt, sliding into one of the leather chairs across from her as she returns to lean against the desk. My pen hovers over the fresh page of my notebook, ready to take notes like I've done countless times in this office over the past four years, working my way up from intern to executive assistant under Penelope. "As in Everett Kauffman? Oldest of the billionaire Kauffman brothers? Didn't *The Seattle Sunrise* just do a piece on him and his family?"

"Yep, the very one," she says, taking a sip of her drink. "And Phil just signed a deal to sell the Hawkeyes to him."

My notebook slips from my fingers, landing on the floor with a dull thud that seems to echo in the suddenly too-quiet room. "Wait. Phil Carlton is selling the team? Phil, who swore on his mother's grave he'd die before letting anyone else own it?"

I lean down to retrieve my notebook.

Penelope sighs, her fingers tightening around her cup until her knuckles whiten. "Phil thinks it's time for a fresh vision, new energy. He believes the Kauffmans have the resources and connections to take the Hawkeyes to the next level."

"And you're okay with this?" I ask, watching her closely. Penelope Matthews doesn't rattle easily—I've seen her handle trade deadlines, playoff pressure, and media storms without breaking a sweat—but the tension in her shoulders and the way she keeps adjusting her grip on her drink tells a different story.

Her gaze drifts to the framed photo on her desk—her, Phil, and her father, Sam Roberts, taken at her first game as GM, when she stepped into her father's shoes, taking over the General Manager position. The glass reflects the morning light, highlighting their proud smiles.

"Phil's decision caught me off guard," Penelope admits softly. "We had a system, and now everything's changing—Phil's gone, Slade's retiring, and Coach Haynes is still finding his footing. It's a lot to juggle."

My chest tightens at the mention of Slade Matthews—her husband, the team's captain and center, and the last of the original players. This season is already shaping up to be one of transition, and I can feel the weight of it settling over the room like a heavy blanket.

I nod, keeping my tone gentle. "The Hawkeyes are strong. We've weathered change before. If Phil's selling to Everett, he must feel confident about it." I flip through my notebook to the section where I've been tracking potential roster moves. "Besides, we've got solid prospects coming up, and the new training facility plans are already approved."

Now I'm beginning to wonder if the new practice rink that was announced earlier this summer is actually part of Everett's big offer to show Phil that he intends to take care of a team that Phil holds dear. But then it has me wondering what other changes are on the horizon for the Hawkeyes.

Penelope smiles faintly, though it doesn't quite reach her eyes. "That's what I love about you, Cammy. Always thinking three steps ahead. You're going to run this place someday, you know that?"

"That's what Dad keeps saying." I laugh, but the compliment means more than I let on. The truth is, Penelope is my idol, and I would love nothing more than a chance to prove that I can follow in her footsteps. "But for now, I'd settle for getting through this transition smoothly. Is there anything I can do to help?"

Her expression brightens slightly, and I know I've just volunteered for something big. "Actually, yes. The Kids with Cancer charity auction is in six weeks. I promised Autumn I'd handle the player donations and memorabilia now that she's on bed rest with her pregnancy, and Briggs doesn't want to leave her side. But with everything else on my plate..."

"I'll take care of it," I say quickly, straightening my spine at the chance to prove myself. The foundation holds two events each year: an auction and a gala. I've attended both over the last four years, with Autumn giving me several projects to help with setup. Since Juliet, Coach Haynes' wife, is the Hawkeyes official party planner handling the event set-up, all I need to take care of are the auction items. "Whatever you need."

"You're sure? Everett wants to host it here at the stadium instead of the convention center like usual. Juliet is looking forward to the challenge, so I'm not concerned with the set-up, but Autumn is hoping to double the silent auction's donations to fund the condos for families going through treatment near the cancer center. That's going to require a lot more donors to show up and bigger ticket items for the silent auction."

I'm already making notes, mind racing with possibilities. "Actually, that could work in our favor. The stadium gives us more space, better atmosphere. We could do interactive elements, maybe even something on the ice—"

My words cut off when I notice a folder on her desk with a name written on it. A name that I've tried to forget over the last year and a half, with little to no success.

My pen stalls on the page, a drop of ink bleeding into the paper.

"JP Dumont," I utter, unintentionally saying it out loud.

Suddenly, I'm drowning in memories: JP's cocky smile, the puck with Dinner? scrawled in sharpie, the way he always seemed to find me in crowded arenas, as if drawn by some unshakable pull. And then San Diego—the night I thought maybe, just maybe, there was more to him—until I woke up alone, realizing how wrong I'd been.

I still remember that night—his calloused hockey player hands caressing every inch of me, the intensity of his blue eyes, the way his laugh sounded, carefree and easy... Only to find out I'd been played by one of the biggest players in the league.

Worse still—I knew better.

My dad has always warned me of hockey players—especially players like Jon Paul.

"Cammy?" Penelope's voice breaks through my thoughts. "You okay?"

"Fine," I say quickly, forcing my eyes back to my notebook. But my imagination quickly conjures up the image of JP in a Hawkeyes jersey—an easy confidence in his stride as he walks through my stadium, imagining the way he'll carry himself in here like he's already part of the team. Like this is where he's meant to be.

I shake my head, breaking the thought from my mind.

The words hit me like a cold plunge. Three years of him pursuing me from behind enemy lines, only to leave me in that guest bedroom to wake up alone, and now he's here. In my space? The professional distance I've carefully maintained suddenly feels paper-thin.

"When did we—" I start, but Penelope's already nodding.

"Coach Haynes confirmed him for a professional tryout, a

PTO contract a couple of weeks ago to see how his knee holds up and how he does with the team," she says, her tone cautious, watching me like she's waiting for me to crack. "He's been practicing with the team for over two weeks."

Two weeks?

He's been in this building for two weeks, skating on our ice, and I didn't know? The betrayal cuts deep—not just from him being here, but from my own father keeping it from me. Dad's the special team's goalie coach, so he's been working with JP this whole time. We've had lunch twice since then, and he never said a word. Not that my dad knows the extent of our history, but he warned me about JP the first time he saw him stop to talk to me at a Hall-of-Fame induction party that we were both at years ago. JP wasn't subtle with his flirting, and my dad wasn't subtle about mentioning that he doesn't want me anywhere near any Jon Paul Dumonts—junior or senior.

If my dad knew about the night I spent with JP in San Diego, there's no way he would have let Coach Haynes go through with signing him—PTO or otherwise.

"Right." I nod, fighting to keep my expression in check. "Wasn't there some controversy with his DUI case in San Diego? I'm surprised that Phil would have approved JP with the 'family-friendly' clause in the contract. And his knee injury was bad enough that his old team didn't re-sign him, right? Can a goalie even come back from something like that?"

"Phil didn't make the call—Everett did. And that whole DUI thing was a mess." Penelope waves her hand dismissively. "The charges were reversed two weeks later. Some activist lawyer proved his blood alcohol was well below the legal limit. Plus, he should have gone to the hospital, not jail. The judge and local law enforcement were trying to make an example of him. I'm surprised the Blue Devils dropped him over it, but his knee injury would have put him on the Long Term Injury list, and he was one of their most expensive players. Even if he had gotten the medical treatment he deserved, he would have been out the following season. I think they wanted to unload expensive talent anyway." She pauses, studying me. "Are you okay with this? Him being here? Especially after that fight with your dad at the charity game?"

I force a smile, even as my stomach twists. "Why wouldn't I be?"

Penelope glances down at JP on the ice. "Because the bad blood between Wrenley and Dumont started with your fathers before either of you were born. Not to mention that your dad ended up with a bloody lip, and it wasn't exactly your typical run-of-the-mill fight. Seven's never lost his cool on the ice like that before."

The memory of that fight flashes through my mind—JP didn't look much better after either, favoring his left leg after my dad took him down to the ice. I had a front-row seat to the whole thing, sitting with Brynn behind the home bench. What started as both of them trying to separate their teammates during a late-hit brawl somehow ended with them trading blows. The image of my usually composed father losing it on the ice still unsettles me.

"A bloody lip is nothing to a hockey player, right?" I keep my tone light. "And anyway, a year and a half is practically ancient history."

Penelope licks her lips. "Sure. Most players have to move past these things. The league isn't that big. A lot of them will end up playing together on a team or at least train together at off-season camps," she says, setting her coffee cup down with a gentle tap against the desk. "Can you get JP set up with an apartment in The Commons? He needs to be settled before regular-season practice starts tomorrow. He's been living in a hotel these past couple weeks during tryouts, and a hotel room won't work long-term."

I nod quickly, willing myself to stay professional, even as my heart races at the thought of having to interact with him. "Of course. I'll call the property managers for The Commons and ask them to get him set up."

She studies my face carefully. "I thought you knew, given..."

"Given what?" I ask, perhaps too sharply.

"Given that your father's been handling his training

personally, working to strengthen his knee. With Olsen Bozeman on LTI until next month when he gets cleared, JP is starting this season—assuming he makes it through the pre-season." She pauses, then adds more gently, "And given your history with him."

I force my expression to remain neutral. "There is no history."

But even as I say it, memories flood back to three years of careful distance punctuated by moments of almost-something—moments he'd steal in quiet corners of event centers or stadiums... all leading to that one night after a playoff win that changed everything. The smell of salt air brings back every sensation of those hours spent under him.

"I'm not sure what happened between you two, but there's a big elephant in the room."

"What elephant?"

"JP's attention was obvious to everyone, Cammy. The way he'd wait for you in the halls, always tossing you pucks with that grin—it was impossible not to notice. He did everything short of spray-painting *I Heart Cammy* in the middle of the rink on game day. And now, ever since he got in that accident after the playoff win, your face practically turns green like you're about to be sick whenever anyone utters his name," Penelope says, leaning forward. "You're going to have to work with him. Charity events, team functions, media days—your paths are going to cross, especially if Coach Haynes officially signs him onto the team."

I had no idea she had noticed all of this. I guess I should have, but I was preoccupied with JP's attention, not realizing how obvious he might have been in front of team staff. I knew my dad had noticed, but I didn't realize that Penelope had too. I guess since our paths haven't crossed in a year and a half since he's been training in Montreal, I figured people had forgotten about all of that—the way I thought I had up until seeing his name on a Hawkeyes file folder.

At least he's only on PTO. Maybe I'll get lucky, and he'll end up with another team. It's all I can hope for.

My stomach twists. "I'm a professional, Pen. I can handle it."

"I know you can. But this isn't just about professionalism." She taps her fingers against her desk thoughtfully. "JP Dumont carries a lot of weight in this league. His comeback story is going to be media gold, especially with Seven coaching him. Not only because Seven and his dad used to play on the same team, but also because they were widely known to clash. Not to mention that the media has caught him tossing you pucks on numerous occasions in the past. And though he's silenced them before, this time things are going to be bigger than him. The pressure's going to be intense."

"And you think I can't handle pressure?" The words come out almost juvenile, and I shrink into myself. This is not how I prove I'm ready for more responsibility—I know that.

"No," Penelope says calmly. "I think you handle pressure better than most, but this is different. This is personal and professional colliding in a very public way."

She's right, and we both know it. Every interaction with JP will be scrutinized—by the team, by the media, by my father. One wrong move, one slip in professionalism, and everything I've worked for could be questioned. My father has already threatened enough of the press not to run a story about the two dynasty families uniting with JP and I dating, when they caught JP tossing a puck to me in that first game: *The Wrenleys and the Dumonts, a hockey fairytale.*

More like a tragedy... like Romeo and Juliet.

But I'm not stupid enough to drink the poison twice.

It's almost as if JP tried to garner the attention—get the media talking about us to build more buzz around his career. I wouldn't put it past him, and I had already fallen for it—showing up in San Diego to watch him play in the playoffs.

"I've worked too hard to prove I'm more than just Seven Wrenley's daughter. I won't let JP's presence undo that."

"No one doubts your capabilities, Cammy." Penelope's voice softens. "But maybe this is about more than just work."

"It's not," I insist, but the words feel hollow. "This is just another challenge to navigate. Nothing more."

Penelope studies me for a long moment before speaking again. "You know, when Slade first joined the team, everyone thought I'd have trouble maintaining professional boundaries. The GM's daughter dating the star center? It was practically a scandal waiting to happen."

"That was different," I argue, but she holds up a hand.

"Was it? Because from where I'm sitting, I see a lot of parallels. Talented player with something to prove, complicated family dynamics, the weight of everyone's expectations..." She trails off meaningfully. "Sound familiar?"

I resist the urge to squirm in my chair. "JP and I aren't you and Slade. We're not anything."

"Maybe not," she concedes. "But that tension between you? That's something, Cammy. And if you don't decide how you're going to handle it now... it might come out in a way you can't control."

"I can handle it," I say, though I'm not even convincing myself.

Penelope nods. "I know you can, which is why I'm giving the project to you."

My phone buzzes again.

> **Dad: About lunch, kiddo. Can we reschedule? Drills are going longer than expected. I don't want you to have to wait for me.**

> **Cammy: Yeah, No problem.**

The thought has me wanting to slip out and look out of the windows of the corporate office on the third floor, down to the rink below to see if the drills going late are with JP.

Dad: I owe you.

"You're overthinking this," Penelope says, reading my expression. "Take a breath. Focus on one thing at a time."

"Right," I say, straightening in my chair. "The auction. That's what matters right now."

I try to push back the thought of Dumont coming back after getting kicked off the Blue Devils after his DUI and subsequent injury.

"The media's going to love that JP is making his comeback on the rival team," I mutter.

"They already do," Penelope confirms, sliding a newspaper across her desk. "Look."

The headline from The Seattle Sunrise makes my stomach churn:

DUMONT RETURNS TO SEATTLE: A STORY OF REDEMPTION AND SECOND CHANCES

Redemption for him, maybe. For me, it's a reminder that the man who shattered my trust gets to rewrite his story while I'm left cleaning up the pieces. My fingers tremble as I push the paper away, determined not to let it get under my skin. But the words linger, each one a thorn pricking at the edges of my carefully constructed composure.

The article goes on about his journey—the playoff win in San Diego, the accident that nearly ended his career, the long road back. But there's one quote that catches my eye.

Seattle feels like the spot I've been trying to get to for years, JP is quoted as saying. *Training under Seven Wrenley? That's been the dream since I was a kid. Sometimes life puts you right where you need to be, and this is where I need to be—with this team.*

I push the paper away, ignoring the way my hands shake

slightly.

"We should focus on the auction. Autumn is expecting something big, and I want to deliver for her."

"One more thing," Penelope says as I stand to leave. "The auction's closing event—we need something special. Something interactive that'll get people talking and get donors to stay the entire time."

"I've got some ideas," I say. "I'll think about it and get them to you by the end of the week."

As I head back to my desk, my mind is already spinning with possibilities. A skills challenge. The spotlight on JP this coming season. The tension between us on display for everyone to see.

A flash of memory hits me—two years ago at the All-Star Game, before everything fell apart, JP found me: "Just five minutes," he'd said, hands up in mock surrender. "Then you can go back to pretending you don't like me." Those five minutes turned into thirty, and by the end, my cheeks hurt from laughing. When Brynn interrupted us, I remember thinking maybe, just maybe, there was more to JP Dumont than his player reputation suggested.

God, I'd been so stupid.

He doesn't belong here—not in my building, not on my team, and definitely not in my life. Not after how thoroughly he made it clear that those three years of pursuit were nothing but a game to him. The ultimate conquest: the coach's daughter who kept saying no.

But the universe doesn't care what I want. It's decided to drop him back into my orbit, and I'll have to deal with the fallout. Because no matter how much I've tried to forget him, there's one thing I know for sure.

You can't outrun your past.

And mine just came skating in, wearing a Hawkeyes jersey.

CHAPTER TWO

JP

For the last year and a half while rehabbing my knee in Toronto, I've been dreaming about this ice. This is where I convince everyone I'm more than my father's son, more than the headlines. More than the guy who left her.

Coach Wrenley's standing at the boards, arms crossed, watching my every move with the same intensity that made him a legend. The same intensity I used to study in game tapes as a kid, learning every technique, every nuance of his style.

"Again," Seven calls out, his voice echoing through the empty practice facility. "This time, watch your left post. You're leaving it exposed on the transition."

I nod, resetting my position. My knee twinges slightly—a reminder of why it took me two weeks on PTO to get signed instead of just signing with one of the other two teams that wanted me. A PTO here was better than signing anywhere else, and it paid off. It was tense between Coach Wrenley and me on day one, but the moment we're back on the ice, it seems like all of that fades away—both of us knowing we have a job to do out here.

After everything.

The fact that Cammy's here, just a few floors above us in the corporate offices, makes my heart race in a way that has nothing to do with the drills Seven is running me through. It's been four and a half years since the first time I spotted her sitting across rivalry lines, three years of finding excuses to linger after games just to see her smile, of tossing pucks with dinner invitations she always turned down. Then finally—one perfect night that ended in disaster, followed by a year and a half of silence.

"Focus, Dumont," Seven barks, pulling me back to the present. "You wanted to train under me? Then train. Leave everything else outside the rink."

If he only knew that "everything else" was his daughter. That I've been trying to get to Seattle since the DUI and my knee injury. To explain. To make things right.

But Seven Wrenley isn't just my childhood idol anymore—he's Cammy's father and my goalie coach. And after what happened in San Diego, I'm pretty sure he'd sooner break my other knee than let me anywhere near her.

"Better," Seven says as I make another save. "But you're still thinking too much. Let your instincts take over."

My instincts. Right. The same instincts that got me into this mess in the first place. That night in San Diego cost me everything—my contract, my reputation, and most importantly, her. And no matter how much I want to explain, I know it might not be enough to fix what I broke.

The practice session stretches on, each save bringing a new correction from Seven. His coaching style is exactly what I expected—demanding and precise. It's everything I've wanted since I was six years old, watching him shut out Montreal in Game seven of the playoffs.

"You've got the raw talent," Seven says during a water break, his tone thoughtful. "Always have. But talent isn't enough in this league. You need focus."

I take a long drink, buying time before I respond. "Is that

why you agreed to work with me? To see if I could focus?"

He studies me for a moment, his expression unreadable. "I agreed because Haynes asked me to. Because every goalie coach in the league knows you've got something special. But mostly?" He pauses, and I can feel the weight of what's coming. "I agreed because I wanted to see for myself what a year and a half off the line would do to you. What kind of player it would make you. If it would shake the arrogant Dumont genes out of you."

The words hit like they intended, like a punch to the stomach, but I don't let it show. He'll be watching to see if I keep my cool or fly off the handle like my father. "I'm not him."

"Prove it," Seven says simply, then skates back to position. "Again. This time, focus on your glove side. You're dropping it too early."

I reset, trying to push everything else aside. The memory of my father's drinking, of the night he got in a bar fight and my mother stepped in to stop it. She ended up taking the hit that was meant for my father. That night was her last straw with my father's drinking and fighting. She filed for divorce soon after, moving me to Toronto.

The weight of my father's legacy has followed me my whole career. The constant comparisons, the whispered expectations. Bouncing from rich stepdad to rich stepdad, as my mom remarried another three more times, every one of them expecting me to turn out like my father—hiring nannies so they never had to interact with me.

Movement in the corporate windows above catches my eye. Cammy's there, watching. Even from this distance, I can feel the electricity between us. Four and a half years of wanting her, three of those years I spent trying to prove I was worth her time, of fighting against my reputation and her hesitation. Then one perfect night where everything felt possible, followed by the worst morning of my life, and then the last year and a half trying to give her space, not being able to tell her the real reason I left that night...

"Eyes on the puck, Dumont," Seven barks, and I snap back to

attention just in time to make a save.

But it's sloppy, and we both know it.

"That's enough for today," Seven says, his disappointment evident. "Hit the showers. We'll pick this up tomorrow."

I nod, gathering the pucks. "Yes, Coach."

He starts to skate away, then pauses. "Why the Hawkeyes, JP? You had other options—New York, Texas—I heard Toronto wanted you. Teams that would've signed you outright instead of the work you've had to put in the last two weeks. Why here?"

This is the question I've dodged from everyone who's asked. I could avoid the truth and say it's about wanting to be part of a winning organization. It wouldn't be untrue, but it's not the full reason. I'm here to prove to Cammy that I'm not who she thinks I am, and I'm here to prove to Seven that I'm good enough to play for him. So, I give him a partial truth.

"Because I have something to prove, and I have to do it here," I say finally.

Seven's expression shifts, something like recognition flickering across his face. "Just remember why you're here. To play hockey. Nothing else."

The warning in his tone is clear. He might not know it all, but he can see it in my eyes—he knows I'm up to something, and that it might not be something he'll like.

I shower and change quickly, my mind racing. It took a year and a half to get back here, confirming my knee is solid, training with a rehab sports specialist, convincing teams I wasn't the screw-up the media painted me as after San Diego. A year and a half of missing her, of carrying her bright green hair tie on my wrist like a goddamn rosary, wondering if I'd ever get the chance to explain.

The elevator doors open on the corporate level, and I step out before I can talk myself out of it. The office suite is quiet, most people out for lunch.

My knee twinges in pain as I walk down the third-floor hallway of the Hawkeyes' corporate office.

Everything here feels sleek and polished—brass nameplates,

espresso-stained wood floors, floor-to-ceiling windows overlooking the rink below, and memorabilia in shadow boxes on the walls to pay homage to the long history of players who have all skated here before me.

It feels quiet for a Monday afternoon, but I'm not complaining. I'd rather be here than sitting in my hotel room, watching more sports media on TV.

They've been having a field day since the Hawkeyes announced my PTO signing—former all-star goalie Jon Paul Dumont attempting a comeback after a career-ending injury and his run-in with the law. It's all a little dramatic if you ask me. The headlines are mixed for *The Seattle Sunrise*:

HAWKEYES GAMBLE ON DAMAGED GOODS AND HOCKEY LEGEND JON PAUL DUMONT SENIOR'S PRODIGAL SON RETURNS TO THE ICE.

Some want a good comeback story, others want a dumpster fire, but what they can all agree on... they hope my first season back on the ice brings in high ratings.

As if they couldn't do worse, they put my father's name in the headline. It will only spur his "tough love" text even further, reminding me not to fuck up my second chance. But mostly, he just doesn't want me to embarrass the family name—his name. Not that I'll answer him back. I haven't in over a decade. Sadly, it hasn't stopped him from coming to my games for the media attention—looking like the doting father supporting his protégé son.

I pause at the nameplate on the door: *Penelope Matthews, General Manager*.

My hesitation isn't because I'm about to walk into the GM's office. I've met Penelope before, and as long as I do my job, I don't see us having any issues. It's the woman sitting just outside Penelope's door who has my pulse hammering.

Fuck it—here it goes.

I twist the handle and push through.

My vision seeks her out, landing on her instantly.

Cammy Wrenley.

I pause at her desk, memories flooding back—her rolling her eyes at that first puck I tossed her, the way she'd try not to smile when I'd find her at charity events, how she'd pretend to be annoyed when I'd speak French just to get under her skin. Three years of pursuing her, of learning every little detail I could—how she takes her coffee (three raw sugars, splash of cream), how she bites her lip when she's trying not to laugh at my jokes, how her eyes light up when she talks about hockey. Three years of wanting more than just one night, of trying to show I'm capable of more than the reputation that I might have earned.

She's bent over her desk, her dark caramel hair cascading down over her shoulders, typing furiously, a pen caught between her teeth. Her hair is longer than the last time I saw her, but the sharp focus in her deep hazel eyes is the same.

She hasn't noticed me yet, so I take a second to drink her in. Cammy Wrenley—coach's daughter, my unresolved past, and the only person who's ever unsteadied me.

"Bonjour, chérie," I say, walking up to her desk. Her head snaps up, and I watch the recognition flicker across her face.

She straightens in place behind her desk, clicking the top of her pen twice in rapid repetition, and then sets it down, probably convincing herself that stabbing me in the throat with it wouldn't be worth the jail time.

"Jon Paul," she says, knowing full well that I hate my full name. A nugget of information I told her when she was wrapped in my arms in my teammate's guest bedroom. Her voice is short, professional, but laced with ice. "I wasn't aware you started today."

Somehow, I doubt that's true. I guarantee she knows every player signed on the roster, but I'll play along. No need to get on the administration's bad side if I can avoid it.

"Just signed the PTO paperwork," I say, leaning a thigh

against her desk. "Looks like we're on the same team now."

"Not exactly," she says, turning back to her work, dismissing me. "The administrative office and player facilities are in different levels of the stadium for a reason. And besides, PTO isn't a confirmed spot on the roster. You still have to prove yourself to Coach Haynes."

I expected the cold shoulder after the dozens of texts and voicemails that I sent her after I got bailed out of jail went unanswered. But experiencing it firsthand feels heavier than I imagined it would.

I cross my arms over my chest, noticing how she tenses at my movement. "Come on, Wrenley. A year and a half is a long time to hold a grudge."

"I'm not holding anything," she says, shuffling some papers on her desk, still not looking at me. "But unlike you, I still have work to do today."

"Have you always been this bad at lying?" I ask, unfolding my arms to pick up a photo frame from her desk—her with a toddler, her half-brother, Milo—Coach Wrenley's son. Wrenley's wife, Brynn, and Milo have been out to watch practice since I started skating with the team. "How's the little guy?"

She snatches the frame back. "Milo's fine. And you can stop pretending to care about my family."

There's a fire in her eyes. She's fiercely protective of them. But that's something she told me herself, in San Diego, sitting on a king-size bed, eating chow mein and potstickers out of a to-go box that I ordered in to get her away from all the noise downstairs. The second I saw her walk into Cooper's place in that dress, I knew all the hard work of trying to get her attention for years had finally paid off.

Little did I know that I was minutes away from having the best night of my life, and only hours away from fucking it all up.

"I've always cared, Cammy." The words slip out before I can stop them.

Her eyes cut from mine to the picture in her hand. I see past her carefully constructed walls. There's hurt there—the kind I've caused and the kind that makes my throat tight.

She sets it back down, the mask of perfect professionalism put right back in place. I can't blame her. We're standing in our boss's office after all. And she still thinks I left her for someone else. A truth I can't completely tell her without hurting someone else in the process and potentially earning us both a ten-thousand-dollar fine and up to four years in jail.

"You must be here for a reason. What can I do for you, so that we can both get back to work?"

I clear my throat. She wants to pretend that there isn't history between us.

Fine.

For now.

After seventeen months, two days, and nine hours of time between us, I'm finally standing in front of her, and yet, she couldn't be further away.

"Just here to pick up my apartment keys," I say with a small grin. Inside, though, the tension in her voice claws at me. "The property manager was supposed to send a courier here with them."

"Right," she says as if she just remembered—relieved that I have a real purpose for my visit. She pulls open a drawer, retrieving an envelope. "The Commons, unit four fourteen. Don't worry, I made sure they didn't put us on the same floor," she says, holding out a simple white envelope with my name written on it in her loopy cursive *Jon Paul*. The same handwriting she'd left on a note with no thanks stuck to a puck I passed her years ago. Still, seeing it brings back memories.

"What a relief. Being on the same floor with you would have been a nightmare," I tease.

Her eyes narrow. The easy laugh I used to get from her all those years ago is nowhere to be heard.

"A two-year lease? That's a lot of commitment for you, isn't it? Figured you'd like to keep your options open... you know, in case a better apartment calls you in the middle of the night asking for a ride home."

And there it is, the truth of what she thinks I did. Told with the Cammy Wrenley edge: purrs like a kitten, cuts like a razor blade.

I still remember the first thing we said to each other in Cooper's kitchen, before I ordered Chinese and took her upstairs to have her all to myself—no more interruptions.

"You flew all the way down here to watch me play?" I asked, a smirk spread across my lips.

Someone tapped my shoulder to ask if I wanted to take a shot with them, but I couldn't have cared less if anyone else was in the house. Cammy was the only one I wanted to celebrate with.

"Are you kidding? I'd never do that. I just flew down here to tell you that my dad says he still owes you a fat lip for that sucker punch three weeks ago. Want me to pencil you in for next season?" she teased, taking a sip from her red Solo cup to hide her grin.

That's the moment I knew I was a goner. If I didn't know it before, I knew it then. Cammy Wrenley is it for me.

No second choice—no runner up—no contingency plan. Only her.

"Trying something new," I say with a shrug, wanting to address the "apartment knocking on my door" as being Angelica. But I know she won't be open to me asking for another chance to prove it right now. Our boss's office isn't the best place to have this out anyway. And I shouldn't enjoy this back and forth with her, but fuck, I'm just glad she's speaking to me. "The team wants me close to the arena for physical therapy, and my hotel room doesn't have a coffee maker," I counter.

I don't drink coffee—I hate the stuff.

An energy drink and a candy bar between game periods is more my style.

Her brow arches, unimpressed. "Good luck with that."

"You don't sound convinced," I shoot back, leaning in just enough to see if her hazel eyes are green or honey brown. An indicator of how pissed off she is at me right now.

Something I picked up on over the years in short moments of close proximity.

To her credit, she doesn't lean back away from me. She stands her ground. Which earns me a better view.

"I don't have to be." Her tone is smooth, dismissive, an eyebrow cocked.

I should let it drop, but I can't resist. "Tu ne sais pas à quel point tu m'as manqué," I say, keeping my voice light.

Her eyes narrow further, suspicion flaring. "What did you just say?"

"Nothing you'd care to hear," I reply, leaning back as if I hadn't just bared a fraction of my soul.

Her glare could cut through diamond, but before she can retort, Penelope's door swings open.

"JP," Penelope says brightly. "Did you get your key from Cammy?"

"Just about to," I say, reaching for the envelope.

Cammy, ever the professional, hands it over without another word, her focus already shifting back to her computer.

Penelope glances between us, and for a moment, I wonder if she notices the tension. But she just smiles. "Cammy, did you get the list from Autumn this morning? We'll need everything ready by next week for Everett's first big event as the new owner."

"Yes, I printed the list earlier, and I'm already making notes for Brynn and me to meet up and brainstorm," Cammy replies, her voice neutral.

I glance at the printed sheet on her desk, reading the list out loud.

"Kids with Cancer Foundation Auction—Item Collection List. What's that?" I ask, glancing at Cammy and then Penelope.

"We're helping Briggs Conley's charity to raise funds for family condos near the cancer center. The Hawkeyes have been heavily involved with the charity since Briggs started it years ago, and Cammy volunteered to head up the auction item collection," Penelope explains.

"Sounds like a big project," I say casually.

"Not your concern," Cammy says under her breath but loud enough for me to hear, her tone colder than the rink three floors below us.

Penelope nods. "It is. Everett Kauffman is expecting this to be the biggest fundraiser that the charity has ever seen, which means Cammy could use some help."

My ears perk up. "What kind of help?"

Cammy shoots me a look that says if I volunteer, she'll change her mind about that prison sentence and stab me with the pen after all.

"Just someone who could help facilitate between the locker room and our office. Someone who knows the players and can convince them to participate with more than just signed gear and cash donations. Not that we don't appreciate those," she adds quickly.

"Like a liaison?" I ask.

Penelope lights up. "Exactly!"

"I could pitch in if you need," I offer.

It sounds easy enough, and it's for a good cause.

Cammy shakes her head instantly, her eyes darting from me to Penelope. "That's really not necessary—"

"Really? Are you sure? Having someone on the team would be a huge help for Cammy," Penelope says, the sound of hope in her voice.

"Whoa, hold on..." Cammy jumps in, "The season starts soon, and he should be focused on the season opener... right?" she asks, looking between us. "Besides, Brynn and I have it covered. I promise."

Penelope's lips purse in disappointment, but then nods in agreement.

"She's right," Penelope says, causing Cammy's shoulders to relax a little. "You have a lot on your plate as it is. And the team needs you more than we do. I'm sure one of the assistant coaches would be willing to help out."

A cell phone rings inside Penelope's office, cutting through the tension. She offers a quick goodbye and disappears inside, the door clicking shut behind her.

Cammy might be right about one thing: my focus should be on the ice. It's been over a year since I've played at a professional level, not since the Stanley Cup—a moment that feels both like yesterday and a lifetime ago. But I know her suggestion wasn't for my benefit. Cammy doesn't want me in her orbit, let alone involved in the auction project.

I should be laser-focused on my comeback, proving to the Hawkeyes that signing me wasn't a mistake. Solidifying my place within the Hawkeyes gives me two things:

One, proving to everyone—including myself—that I belong here.

Two, staying close to Cammy. If I can't find a way to get her to trust me while still keeping what happened that night in my Ferrari from coming out, at least I can be near her.

Her sharp gaze makes it clear she'd rather I stay in the past where I belong.

"You're still here?" she finally bites out, sitting back in her chair and typing up an email.

"Just soaking in the warm welcome," I say, flashing her a grin.

Her eyes narrow, her jaw tightening, but whatever snarky comeback she'd like to say, she's biting it back.

I push off her desk, slipping the envelope into my back pocket. "For what it's worth, Cammy..." My voice drops just enough to soften. "It's good to see you again."

Her expression flickers—confusion, maybe doubt—but she shuts it down just as quickly. "Save your charms for your female fans, Dumont. They're the only ones buying it."

A call comes in on her desk phone, perfectly timed to end the conversation.

I watch her turn away. Everything's changed—my career, my priorities—but being in the same room with her still stirs something I can't quite name, something I'm not sure I'll ever find anywhere else... with anyone else.

The headlines are already writing my eulogy—*Dumont's Last Stand*. Maybe they're right. Maybe this is my last chance to prove I'm still the player I used to be. Or maybe I'm chasing something I'll never have again.

I force my feet to move, pushing through the door and out into the hallway. My knee aches with every step. I need to get moved into the new apartment and get ice on it. It's a brutal reminder of how far I've fallen and how much further I have to go. Rehab, practice, the media circus waiting to devour me—it's all waiting outside this office, and it's all on me to survive it.

Cammy doesn't look back, her voice steady and calm as if I'm not even here. It's like I don't belong in this office—or her life. Maybe I never did. But as I leave, the ache in my chest tells me one thing hasn't changed: she's still the only thing worth fighting for.

CHAPTER THREE

JP

"That's the last of it."

I hear Hunter Reed, the Hawkeyes' left defenseman, drop a moving box onto the laminate wood flooring of my new apartment in The Commons.

Most of the players live here since it's only a couple of blocks from the Hawkeyes' stadium. From what I've heard, Penelope Matthews, the current GM, worked out some deal with building management to keep units available for players during the season.

"Vittu," Aleksi Mäkelin mutters out a curse word in Finnish as he walks through the door with another box. He drops it with an exaggerated groan, rolling his shoulders back. "What the hell did you pack in there? Cement blocks?"

I grin. "It's just my gaming system. It doesn't weigh that much."

I walk over and slice open the box, revealing the console and a few neatly packed wires.

Hunter's brows shoot up. "A PS3?" he barks. "You're still carrying this thing around? Why?"

"Because my college coach said that gaming is good for hand-eye coordination." I shrug, pulling the console out completely.

Aleksi, who's suddenly a lot more interested, shoves Hunter out of the way with his shoulder to peer inside the box. "It's true, Reed-man. It's science."

Hunter raises a skeptical brow. "You're kidding. Where'd you hear that crap?"

"On a podcast," Aleksi says, pulling out the controller with an expression of reverence.

Hunter scoffs. "Everything's a podcast with you, Mäkelin."

Aleksi doesn't even look up. He's too busy inspecting the cables like they're fragile artifacts. "Podcasts are very educational. You should try them sometime. Expand your mind."

Over the short time I've been here, I've learned a few things about Aleksi.

One, he takes comfortable silence as a personal offense.

Two, he's weirdly loyal to any random fact he finds on podcasts, and if you challenge it, he will bury you under citations until you give up.

Three, he has a nickname for every player on the team. Reed-man for Hunter Reed, Popeye for Luka Popovich, Hart for Trey Hartley. The list continues. Monty is the only name he calls me.

Eh. I've been called worse.

"You believe this guy?" Hunter snorts, turning to me.

"Actually," I say, biting back a grin, "he's not wrong. There's a study about surgeons who game. Better precision, fewer mistakes."

Aleksi points at me without lifting his eyes from the controller. "See? Even Monty knows. Science."

Hunter groans, raking a hand through his hair. "Whatever. I still don't trust anyone with suspicious facts he got from some dude in his makeshift podcast studio in his musty basement."

Aleksi finally looks up, lips twitching. "Careful, Reed-man. It's scrimmage tomorrow, and we play against each other. You don't want me to beat you at your own game, do you?"

Hunter grins, grabbing a bottle of water from the counter. "You mean you'll beat me on the ice? Or on that prehistoric game console that Dumont's got?"

"Hey, watch it. She's a classic," I say, feigning insult.

"Both," Aleksi replies smoothly.

Hunter laughs, shaking his head. These two can go rounds and often do. "You're all talk, Mäkelin. But I'm too tired to deal with this Finnish brainwashing tonight." He tosses his empty water bottle into the trash and heads for the door. "Good luck setting up your grandma's PlayStation, Dumont. Night, boys."

"Night," I call as the door swings closed.

He's kidding. A hundred bucks says he's over here tomorrow night playing against Aleksi in the new NHL game that I just got after preordering it months ago.

Aleksi doesn't say anything. He's too absorbed in arranging the wires on my coffee table like it's a sacred ritual. I don't stop him. I'm too tired to argue and, honestly, I'm half-tempted to play a round just to clear my head.

Aleksi's phone rings, cutting through the quiet. He glances at the screen, his expression softening instantly. "Sisko," he murmurs.

Sister.

He answers in rapid Finnish, his voice dropping an octave as he paces to the other side of the room. I catch only bits and pieces—nothing I can decipher—but his tone is gentle. Protective. After a couple of minutes, he hangs up, tucking his phone into his back pocket.

"Everything okay?" I ask, even though it's none of my business.

He nods, but there's a faint crease between his brows. "Yeah. She needed to talk about something. Nothing serious."

"You sure?"

Aleksi waves me off with a tight smile. "Family stuff. You know how it is." He tucks his phone into his pocket and heads for the door. "I'm heading out as well. See you at practice, Monty. Don't open the new NHL game without me."

I smirk. "I'll try not to."

He grins faintly, the door clicking shut behind him, and suddenly, the apartment is quiet. Too quiet.

The silence feels heavy once they're gone, like the quiet is daring me to sit still with my thoughts. And that's the last thing I want to do right now.

I drop onto the couch, grabbing the remote to turn on the TV, and then crack my neck from side to side as the screen comes to life. Quickly I find the sports channel and stop when I see the Hawkeyes logo in the top right corner of the screen—they're talking about my team. I stare at the few boxes stacked against the wall. Unpacking can wait.

I turn up the volume, and like I thought, they're talking about us. A banner runs across the bottom of the screen:

HAWKEYES' NEW SEASON BEGINS
TOMORROW—ALL EYES ON DUMONT.

"Of course," I mutter under my breath.

I used to live for being the center of attention before the Blue Devils let me go. But now, my name is never in the news for anything to be proud of.

I twist Cammy's neon green hairband around my wrist absentmindedly. The elastic is starting to stretch out now. It's the same one I've worn every day since that night with her. No one knows why I wear it, and I don't explain it. It's just a piece of her, a reminder of everything I'm trying to fix—my game, my reputation, myself.

"In other Hawkeyes news"—the TV anchor's voice cuts through my thoughts—"controversial new PTO signing of Jon Paul Dumont in Seattle, ahead of tomorrow's first official practice of the season."

Perfect timing. I position my thumb over the power button to turn it off but then stop.

"The former Blue Devils goalie, whose promising NHL career

ended after a DUI accident and knee injury a year and a half ago, has been signed to a PTO contract by Coach Ryker Haynes, despite concerns from fans and sports analysts alike. Sports director Tom Summers weighs in."

The screen splits to show a middle-aged man in a suit too tight across the shoulders. "Look, Dumont was a rising star—rookie of the year contender, three shutouts in his first season. But with that accident, the drinking and the party reputation he had, not to mention the female passenger who ended up in the ER... There are too many red flags. Coach Haynes is biting off more than he can chew as the new coach for the Seattle hockey team. The question remains: can Dumont overcome his past, stepping out of his father's shadow, or is this a mistake for the Hawkeyes?"

I switch off the TV, letting out a slow breath. They love dragging up ancient history, especially when they don't know the whole story. Not that I can tell them the truth about that night—I made a promise, and I plan to keep this one. Even though it's costing me everything I've ever wanted.

My phone buzzes on the kitchen counter. I get up off the sofa to retrieve it and then see Angelica's name flash across the screen.

Right on cue.

Somehow, she always knows when I'm feeling beat down... and then likes to rub salt in it.

"You're in Seattle?" Her voice is sharp, worried. "Are you insane?"

"Good evening to you, too," I say, running a hand through my hair. "And, yes, I'm in Seattle. On a PTO with the Hawkeyes. You know, the one you got me."

Angelica Ludwig, one of the only people on earth I trust, and my temporary sports agent... though the last one is against my better judgement. I have to hand it to her; she pulled a rabbit out of a hat with this one. Getting me onto the Hawkeyes ice for PTO. It wasn't an easy feat. Nor was getting my DUI expunged, but she managed both.

I should be grateful, but I know she's doing all of this out of guilt. Guilt that I wish she'd let go of to focus on her own life.

"Yeah, I know I got it for you, but I didn't think you'd be stupid enough to take it when you had teams ready to sign you immediately," she says, her voice gruff with annoyance.

"Stupid? Jesus, Ang, don't hold back–tell me how you really feel."

She lets out a dramatic sigh. "JP, this was supposed to be a quiet rebuild, not a spectacle." Her frustration is evident through the tightening of her voice. For some reason she thinks she holds superiority over me just because she tutored me in high school a whole lifetime ago. "You're playing for your ex-team's biggest rival, under a coach who has every reason to hate you—and your father. The media's already circling, and you're giving them front-row seats to your mess. This is exactly what we were trying to avoid. Remember what I said?"

"Fly under the radar—yeah, I know," I say, though I already regret mocking her.

"This isn't flying under the radar, JP," Angelica snaps. "You're training under Coach Wrenley—the guy you fought weeks before the crash and split his lip open. The guy who used to play with your dad, and *hated* him. You know what kind of attention this is going to bring? You're putting a target on your back—and on mine. If they start digging back up the DUI case..."

Angelica's been like a dog with a bone about getting me back into the pros, and she made it happen. I'll give it to her; she's been impressive as my stand-in sports agent after mine dropped me a year and a half ago when I lost my NHL contract. If she wasn't committed to saving the world with her lawyering skills, she could kill it as an agent for pro athletes.

"I know. We had a plan. I didn't stick to it," I confess.

She lets out another deep sigh that tells me she's already coming to terms with my decision. "How's the apartment?" she asks, changing the subject. "Better than that shoebox in Toronto?"

"Hey," I say, feigning insult. "For the record, I never complained about my shoebox. You're the one that pulled me out of it, remember?"

I wasn't sure if I was ready to try out this year, but Angelica pushed me to do it, and once she sent me the PTO for Seattle, she didn't have to do any more convincing.

I glance around at the floor-to-ceiling windows, modern furniture, and empty walls. The place screams temporary, like everything else has been since the accident. But I'm determined to stay this time.

"That's great. You'll have plenty of time to live in a shoebox after you secure your place as the best goalie to ever play the game." she insists. "Speaking of? How's it going with Coach Wrenley?"

My stomach tightens at Seven's name. All Cammy would have to do is tell her dad what happened between us that night at Cooper's beach house, and I'm sure he'd find a way to get me benched for life. "He didn't break my nose the day I skated out onto his ice, so I'd say he doesn't know about me and Cammy."

"Wait. You didn't take this PTO contract just because of her, did you?" Angelica asks suddenly.

"Who?"

"Don't play dumb with me, Dumont. I already know that you're too smart for your own good. You let your stepdad waste his money on paying me to tutor you because you sure as hell didn't need it." She pauses. "Cammy. Seven's daughter. The girl you've been chasing around for the last four plus years—the girl from Cooper's post-game party. Ring any bells? The one who made you stop being such a player and pull your head out of your ass."

"Yeah, okay, I get it. You have a good memory of my greatest failures. By the way, that's your worst trait."

I turn to the window. It's dark out now, the lights of Seattle glittering outside my window. For a moment, I'm back in that guest room, the glow of the moon outside the second-story window casting a blue hue over Cammy's skin as she told me about her dreams of working in hockey, of carving out a place in the Hawkeyes family like her dad.

"JP, she could blow our secret—"

"I'm not going to tell her anything. I made you a promise that we are in this together. There's too much at stake for both of us. But as soon as I can... " I say finally.

"One and a half years, JP," Angelica says, her voice softening. "After that, the statute of limitations runs out, and no one can touch us."

"I'm not sure I have that long," I say. "Coach Wrenley's looking for a reason to cut me, and Cammy..." I trail off, gripping the neon green hairband around my wrist. "She hasn't forgotten about San Diego. She's barely speaking to me."

A laugh bubbles out of Angelica. "Wait. You actually thought she might have forgotten? Women don't usually forget the guy who slept with them and disappeared, only to show up in the news hours later getting arrested with another woman."

"Thanks for that stellar recap of the worst morning of my life." I move to another box by the island and pick it up off the floor—plates and silverware. "Any other highlights you'd like to revisit? Maybe that time I got food poisoning at my mom's third wedding and threw up all over you and the dance floor during the Macarena?"

"Gross. Did you really have to bring that up? I'm still trying to erase that night from my memory. And don't bother blaming the food again. You were absolutely wasted and only seventeen years old. Your mom was furious. Don't you remember?" she asks. "And for the record, it's a true testament of my love and loyalty, because I don't know many friendships that could survive being puked on."

"I know, you're a good friend, Ang," I tell her.

She clicks her tongue, like she's about to cave—because she always does with me. "Fine. If this is what you want..."

What I want is to go back to that morning, and change everything. I'd leave a note for Cammy, tell her why I had to leave instead of letting her wake up alone. But I can't. Instead, I raced out of that room to help Angelica, dragging myself into the crash that ruined everything. And now, Cammy thinks I abandoned her for another woman—and I've got no way to prove otherwise without implicating myself and Angelica, for something I still believe I made the right call on.

But I can't change the past. And after weeks of calls, texts, and even a desperate flight to Seattle, trying to track her down after she blocked my number, I finally gave up. That's when I knew that my chances with her were gone. All I can do is take it day by day, hoping I'll get an opening to show her that I'm not who she thinks.

In the meantime, I'll focus my efforts on getting signed with the Hawkeyes.

"We don't always get what we want. What I need right now is to focus on proving myself to the team," I tell her. "To Coach Haynes. To Coach Wrenley."

"What are you going to do about Cammy?"

I stare at the hairband around my wrist, worn and stretched from a year and a half of trying to figure that out. It's my only tether to her—and the reason I made it through tryouts. My lucky charm, or a reminder of everything I wrecked. Maybe both.

"I don't know yet," I admit. "But I know one thing—I have to sign with the Hawkeyes. If there's even the slightest chance she'll give me another shot, I need to be here. I need you to do everything in your power to make this deal happen. No negotiations, no counteroffers. If they put a contract in front of me, I'm signing it."

"JP, that's not how negotiations work."

"I don't care about the contract, the money, or the starting line. At the end of the day, I'm here for one thing. I'm here for her. The Hawkeyes are my way in, and a nice bonus, but none of it means anything without her."

Making it back to the NHL felt impossible a year ago. But losing Cammy again? That's something I know I wouldn't survive.

Tomorrow, I'll be back on the ice, Seven breathing down my neck, waiting for me to screw up. Every drill, every block, every second in the net—none of it will matter if I don't get this right. Because no amount of pressure, no contract, no championship win will ever compare to what's really at stake.

Her.

A second chance with Cammy is the only goal that matters. And signing with the Hawkeyes? That's just how I'll get there.

I hear Angelica take a deep breath. She's getting the point now. Cammy doesn't want anything to do with me. She made that clear this morning when I went in to get my key.

"Okay, you made your point. I won't twist arms to get you a mega signing deal. Though you're killing all my fun," she says begrudgingly. "Good luck tomorrow. Show them what you can do." She pauses. "And JP"—her voice softens—"I never meant for any of this to happen. If I hadn't been so upset that night, if I hadn't called you—"

"You're my best friend, Ang," I say finally. "You needed help. End of story. And if the truth about that night comes out, it won't just cost us fines and jail time. It will end both of our careers. I'll lose my shot at Cammy all over again, and you'll lose everything you've worked for. I can't let that happen."

"So, what do you need to do now?" she asks.

The only thing I can do. Take my last shot.

"I need to stay on the Hawkeyes' team. I'll play for free if that's what it takes. But I can't leave that team--not until I know Cammy and I are done for good." I tell her knowing that it pains her to leave money on the table, but Cammy is worth more than any contract in the NHL.

"Then play your heart out and get them to send me a contract. Good luck," she tells me.

After we hang up, I stare at my reflection in the window. By morning, I'll be back on the ice with Seven, so for now, I need to get some sleep.

My phone buzzes again—a text.

> **Seven: Early practice. 5:00 a.m. Don't be late.**

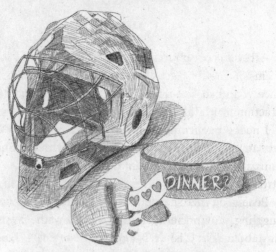

CHAPTER FOUR

Cammy

The rain drums softly against Serendipity's front window, but inside, the café hums with warmth and familiarity. The smell of cinnamon rolls and freshly brewed espresso drifts through the air, and our usual corner table is just as crowded with breakfast plates as it is with opinions.

"Everett is impossible!" Aria groans, dropping her head onto her arms. Her dark auburn hair falls forward like a curtain. "For the third time this week, he made it clear he doesn't need two assistants. I'm just excess baggage leftover from Phil Carlton's reign."

"You're not baggage," Kendall says firmly, her coffee cup hovering just below her lips. "You're probably the only thing keeping his life together, and he'll figure that out soon enough."

"Maybe once the stress of the transition settles," Penelope adds with a small smile, though the sharpness in her voice makes it clear she's making a mental note to step in if Everett doesn't shape up soon. "You're too good at what you do for him not to notice."

Aria sighs but offers a faint smile. "Thanks. I just hate feeling like I'm waiting for the axe to drop." Then she turns to me. "Any chance you need help with the auction-planning? I could use a distraction."

I nudge her arm with my elbow lovingly. "No offense, but I think you've got enough on your plate without adding auction-planning to it. You're always taking on too much. I've got it under control."

Penelope's gaze sharpens as she sets her cup down. "Speaking of juggling, how's the auction coming along? Everett's already asking about donor lists. Oh, and maybe take JP up on his offer to help. He seemed... eager."

The name hits like a slap, but I force my expression to stay neutral. "It's fine. I'm keeping it professional."

"JP?" Kendall perks up, her brows shooting skyward. "Jon Paul Dumont? Our new goalie?"

Penelope smirks knowingly. "The one who couldn't stop staring at Cammy when he came by for his apartment key."

Heat rises to my face. "It's complicated."

"Complicated how?" Kendall asks, leaning forward.

I swirl my coffee cup, trying to distract myself from the women staring at me. "It's a long story, and it's not worth telling. I promise."

"We've got time. My first appointment this morning is with Aleksi, but not until after morning skate, so I'm wide open." Kendall gleams, settling back into her chair, clutching her hot black coffee.

"And wine later if needed," Aria adds, momentarily distracted from her own drama.

I sigh, knowing they won't let it go. "Remember how I went to San Diego for the last playoff game before the championship two seasons ago?"

They nod.

"Well... I might've run into JP after the game. And I might've ended up at Cooper's afterparty. We spent most of the night talking about family stuff and eating Chinese food..." I start, debating whether to spill the rest of the embarrassing story.

"Oh, this is getting good," Kendall says, leaning forward.

"That sounds like one hell of a party. Are you sure there isn't more you want to share with the group? Safe space and all," Penelope says, bringing her cup up to her lips.

Why fight it... They'll get it out of me eventually.

"Then I woke up *alone* a few hours later, with headlines hitting my phone that he was arrested on a DUI charge, and the woman he was taking home went to the hospital. The woman he must like enough to keep around because she's his sports agent now. So, yeah, that's the end of that story."

A beat of silence falls over the table before Kendall blinks a couple of times and then finally says, "Damn."

"Yeah." I agree.

"But that was a year and a half ago. Do you think he's changed?" Penelope asks.

I cut a piece off my sticky bun with my fork but don't eat it right away. I glance at Kendall to answer this one... because she has firsthand experience. "I don't know... Do players ever change?" I ask her, already knowing her answer.

Kendall's lips purse as her eyebrows rise. "Not in my experience."

Then I turn back to Penelope. "I doubt it. But if he has changed, I wish him all the best... with anyone other than me."

Penelope shakes her head. "It just seems so hard to believe he'd do that. The tension between you two has been building since you started interning here. He's been trying to get your attention for years. Everyone saw it at those league events."

I shake my head, remembering the sting of waking up alone. That's an experience I only need to try once to know that I'll never put myself in that position again. "Maybe he was after the chase—or maybe he was just trying to get under my dad's skin. I don't know, but I do know that whatever he wanted, he got, and then moved on pretty damn quickly. I've been used as a pawn before by my own mother. Whatever game JP wants to play this time... I'm sure he can find a willing opponent within his many female fans."

Thinking of my mother sends a familiar ache through my chest. Fourteen years of believing Eli was my father, only to learn my mother had lied to trap him—and to hurt Seven in the process. Even now, years after telling Seven the truth and building our relationship from nothing, it still feels raw.

"Look," Penelope says, her GM voice slipping through, "I'm not saying trust JP blindly. But maybe give him a chance to explain? People aren't always what they seem at first glance."

"Like Slade?" Aria pipes up, managing a smirk.

We've all heard their love story, and honestly, after everything that happened between them, I'm surprised that she was able to forgive him. But I also can't imagine Penelope and Slade not being together. They're completely in love.

"Exactly." Penelope grins. "Though the jury's still out on that one," she teases.

We all laugh, and I'm grateful for the subject change. But as the conversation shifts to safer topics—Kendall's new condo she just bought, Penelope and Slade's babymoon vacation they're planning for the end of the season—I can't stop thinking about what Penelope said about JP changing.

With all my trust issues and family drama, it's hard for me to give people second chances. Changing that view means risking my heart again, and I'm not sure I'm ready for that.

Not even for the guy who still makes my pulse race every time he struts in with that air of confidence and bright smile.

"I hate to run, but I'd better get back so I can hit the treadmill in the stadium gym before the guys take over after practice."

Next Aria stands. "Yeah, and I need to get back and make myself irreplaceable to the new boss so that I can keep my job," she says, rolling her eyes.

"It's all going to work out. You'll see," I tell her.

Penelope pushes back her chair next. "Cammy and I will walk back with you girls. Brynn's meeting us at the stadium. We're headed to morning skate this morning," she tells me with a wink.

That's definitely a change to our schedule, and I have to wonder exactly what she has up her sleeve.

∂

The rain has eased by the time we step into the stadium, but the chill lingers in the air. Brynn lifts Milo from his stroller, wrapping him in a blue dinosaur blanket as we head toward our usual seats behind the home bench.

"How do you think JP's doing so far?" Penelope asks, her heels clicking against the concrete steps as we ascend.

"I'm not sure yet. This is the first time I'm seeing him practice with the team," I say.

Brynn glances at me, then back at Penelope. "Well, if Seven's working with him, he's doing fine. Your dad doesn't put in this kind of effort for nothing. They've been meeting early—before practice."

I absorb the information, keeping my focus on the rink.

Sitting in the cold seats of the Hawkeyes stadium, I stare out at the ice as players in turquoise, white, and black jerseys run shooting drills for morning skate. My dad stands at the boards, his signature stance as commanding as ever. But my attention drifts to the far end of the rink, where JP is in the crease. He's dialed in, his movements sharp and precise, though I can tell from the tension in his shoulders that Seven's been pushing him hard.

"How are you doing there, champ?" I ask while bouncing Milo on my knee, wrapping his tiny frame in the blanket that Brynn made for him. Milo gurgles and points toward the ice, where our dad stands with his arms crossed, watching practice with his signature intensity.

The empty arena feels so much bigger without the fans who'll pack it in just a couple of weeks once training ends. Right now, it's just Penelope, Brynn, and me sitting in our usual seats behind the home bench. I try to focus on Milo's warmth instead of the figure gliding between the pipes at the far end of the rink.

But my eyes betray me, drawn to JP, despite my better judgment.

He moves through his warm-up routine with the same fluid grace that made him the NHL's hottest college rookie prospect five years ago, at the age of twenty-two. Each stretch, each adjustment of his pads, each tap of his stick against the posts—it's muscle memory honed to perfection. Watching him settle into position stirs the kind of discomfort I'd prefer to avoid.

"How's it going with the new owner?" Brynn asks Penelope, passing me a Ziploc bag of goldfish crackers for Milo.

Penelope exhales, her gaze flicking toward the owner's box high above the ice.

We crane our necks to see Phil Carlton, the current owner, standing with several figures against the glass. One of them is Everett Kauffman, the billionaire who just signed to take Phil's place as owner of the Hawkeyes.

"It's... going well," Penelope says carefully. "Phil's showing Everett around today. He wants to ease the transition."

"You don't sound thrilled," Brynn observes, her sharp gaze not missing a beat.

"It's going to be fine. Cammy is taking over the auction-planning, so that's huge."

Brynn grins. "I know. I'm so excited. We're meeting in a couple of days so that I can help."

"You've got a manuscript due to your publisher next month," Penelope counters, with a smirk. "This better not be you finding an excuse to procrastinate. The last thing we need is your agent calling me to complain."

Brynn laughs, holding her hands up in surrender. "Fair point. I'm just going to get Cammy on her way, then I'll back off, I swear."

We fall into a comfortable silence, watching as puck after puck flies toward JP. He blocks most of them, diving and lunging with precision, though there are close calls. My dad's voice cuts through the arena, sharp and precise. JP doesn't flinch, doesn't argue, only adjusts his stance like he's been waiting for this criticism his whole life.

The same way I used to...

"Your dad's not making it easy for him," Penelope observes, her sharp eyes tracking every save and miss.

"He never makes it easy for anyone," I reply, keeping my tone neutral.

But as JP lunges for a low shot, his mask tilting up to glance at the stands, my stomach twists. Seven's high standards are nothing compared to what JP and I left unsaid.

I force out a hum of agreement.

I shouldn't care. I shouldn't even be watching.

JP glances up, his eyes locking on mine through the plexiglass. Even from here, I feel the pull—the same magnetic force that made me say yes in San Diego, the same one I swore I'd never feel again.

His mask hides his expression, but his posture stiffens. He missed a puck by Luka Popovich. The Russian Olympian Left Winger taking over for Lake Powers, after Lake retired last season to move to Aspen full time with his wife, Tessa.

Brynn whistles low. "Well, that was interesting."

"What was?" I ask, feigning innocence as I bounce Milo on my lap.

Penelope smirks. "The way JP just missed that shot because he was too busy staring at you."

"I have no idea what you're talking about." I shove a handful of goldfish crackers into my mouth, hoping they'll absorb the flush creeping up my neck.

Brynn leans in, smirking. "That shot he missed? It's your fault, you know."

I glare at her. "I'm pretty sure Luka's slap shot is what beat him, not me. Or maybe he's just rusty." I grumble, bouncing Milo on my knee.

"Mmm, sure," Brynn hums. "It has nothing to do with the way he keeps looking up here like a puppy who lost his favorite toy."

As Brynn reaches for Milo, and Penelope's phone buzzes with another notification, I can't help glancing back at the ice.

"Bozeman!" I hear my dad's voice echo in the stands. "You're up!"

JP's skating toward the bench, his shoulders tense. Olsen Bozeman, the Hawkeyes starting goaltender who was signed to take Reeve Aisa's place when he retired last year, skates past JP, heading for the goalpost. He hasn't gotten cleared for games yet, but he's back to practicing with the team.

My dad meets him at the boards, his expression unreadable as they exchange a few words before JP steps into the home bench and takes a seat.

Brynn's voice pulls me back. "Whatever happened between you two in San Diego, seems more than a one-night stand to him. Why don't you just ask him what happened and why he left with her?"

Brynn knows our history. She got it out of me the night I came back from San Diego.

The text about happily ever after really tipped her off.

I freeze. "It was nothing. I should have figured that one night was all he wanted. It was a misunderstanding."

Penelope raises an eyebrow. "It was more than a misunderstanding. I've never seen a player go to the lengths he went to in order to get your attention."

I grit my teeth, forcing my tone to stay neutral. "It doesn't matter. Like I said before, it's ancient history."

And as long as I have something to say about it, that's how it will stay.

CHAPTER FIVE

JP

The smell of sweat clings to the cold air as I walk through the players' tunnel, the sound of guys chirping at each other echoing off the cement walls. For most of them, this is just another day at practice. For me, every moment feels like I'm one mistake away from losing everything I've fought to rebuild. The mistake I made out there was unacceptable and could have been prevented if I would have had my eyes where they should have been.

That mistake didn't go unseen. An entire hockey team and several coaches saw me miss a puck headed straight for me. Then they all saw Coach Wrenley trade me out for Olsen, who's still on the long-term-injury list for another six weeks, at least. Humiliation doesn't begin to describe it. I have to do better if I ever want to earn a spot out of PTO.

"Dumont. A word."

Seven's voice slices through the noise, stopping me cold. I figured this was coming.

I turn, and he's standing at the edge of the tunnel, arms crossed, his presence as commanding as it was when I was a kid watching his highlight reels.

"Sure, Coach."

I follow him a few paces into the hallway, the locker room door swinging shut behind us. The tunnel feels colder somehow, the fluorescent lights of the stadium beating down on the hard features of his face. He's not happy—that's easy enough to see from the deep scowl, and sharp lifted eyebrow.

"You've got talent, Dumont," he starts, his voice calm but cutting. "Maybe more than your old man ever did. But distractions? They'll end your career faster than any injury."

I swallow hard, knowing exactly what he's getting at. This isn't about just any distraction. This distraction has a name, a killer smile, and happens to have half his DNA.

"And staring into the stands during practice?" His tone sharpens. "That's a distraction you can't afford."

Cammy. Her name hovers on the tip of my tongue, but I don't say it. Innocent unless proven guilty.

Seven steps closer, his voice lowering. "I know what you were looking at. And let me make one thing crystal clear: Cammy deserves better than a player who's looking for something to play with and then toss out with the trash on one of his nights off. Cammy's no puck bunny, Dumont, and I'll never let anyone treat her like one."

His assumptions about what I want from Cammy couldn't be further off base.

"Coach, about Cammy—"

He cuts me off with a raised hand, his expression hardening. "Stop. Whatever you think you're about to say, don't. If you want a future here, keep your eyes on the puck and off my daughter."

His footsteps echo as he walks away, leaving me standing there, his words settling like ice in my veins.

The locker room hits me with a wall of noise as I push through the door—guys laughing, gear being tossed, the sharp snap of towels, and the underlying tension of a team finding its rhythm.

"Dumont!" Luka Popovich calls out, his Russian accent thick with amusement. "That was some save out there. Oh, wait, no it wasn't—guess you were too busy taking in the sights, eh?"

"Rafters needed inspecting," I shoot back, forcing a grin, heading to my stall. "Just making sure this place isn't falling apart around us."

"Maybe check the boards next time," Luka quips, earning chuckles from the guys around him. "They're closer to eye level."

"Or the back of the net," Hunter adds, tossing me a towel. "You know... where the puck ended up?"

Luka grabs the puck sitting next to him and lobs it my way. I catch it in one hand. "Oh, look, you left this in the net. Want me to autograph it for you?" he asks with a smirk.

I roll my eyes but laugh anyway, the tension in my chest easing slightly. The chirping is relentless, sure, but I'd take a little smack talk in the locker room over Coach Wrenley warning me off of his daughter, any day. And after a year and a half off the ice, not knowing if a team would take a chance on me again after the DUI charge, I'm just happy to be back in the locker room.

"Yeah, sure," I shoot back. "With your chicken scratch, I might be able to convince some sucker online to buy it. Maybe I'll get enough to buy a hot dog at the street vendor out front."

"Jesus Christ, Dumont," Scottie Easton, one of our left wingers, says as he strolls back from the showers, a towel slung low around his waist. "Don't let Popeye sign that biscuit. He'll devalue it down to nothing more than a glorified paperweight."

Laughter ripples through the locker room. Luka says something in Russian, his tone sharp but amused, though none of us understand a word. He smirks anyway, which only makes it funnier.

As a three-time hockey Olympian for Russia, Luka's got the résumé to back up his swagger—two bronze and a gold medal all before he turned twenty-five. This is his first season in the NHL, after coming back from retirement, and while it's fun to flick him shit, we all know that a signature from Popovich would fetch more than just a hot dog.

Slade Matthews, our captain, appears at my stall. His presence commands attention without him even trying. "Cheer up, Dumont. It's just practice. You're allowed to screw up once in a while," he says, loud enough for everyone to hear. "Just don't make a habit of it during games. And keep your eyes off my girl." He grins. "She's up there, too, and I don't need her thinking she can trade me in for someone younger. I'm well aware I married up," he says, elbowing my bicep lightly.

"Thanks for the pep talk, Captain," I reply, earning a few more chuckles.

But Slade isn't done. He leans closer, his voice dropping. "By the way, you're telegraphing your moves. And I don't mean on the ice."

I glance at him, brow raised. "That obvious, huh?"

He grins, but there's wisdom in his eyes. "Only to someone who's been there already—GM's daughter," he says, reminding me that he used to play college hockey for Penelope's dad back in the day. "Get your head straight first. The rest will follow."

Before I can respond, Coach Haynes steps into the room. The chatter dies instantly, like someone hit mute.

"Good work today," he says, his tone even but commanding. "Keep it up, and we'll hit the ground running come season opener." He pauses, scanning the room. "One more thing—the charity auction's coming up. Kauffman's expecting full participation from the team. Don't make me chase you down for donations."

A collective groan rises from the guys, but it's good-natured. Coach Haynes nods once and leaves. Half the team grab their gear bag and heads out while the other half heads for the gym.

I change quickly, an idea forming. If I can't prove myself to Seven on the ice today, maybe I can show him another way. Show him I'm not the same guy who screwed up two years ago.

The hallway outside is quieter now, most guys having cleared out. I spot Penelope Matthews walking toward her office, her heels clicking against the floor, tablet in hand.

"Penelope," I call out, jogging to catch up. "Got a minute?"

She turns, her sharp eyes assessing me instantly. "JP. What can I do for you?"

I take a breath, steadying myself. "The charity auction—I want to help."

Her eyebrow arches. "I love the enthusiasm, but didn't we already discuss this and decide it would be better for you to focus on the ice?"

"Yes, but I can do both. And it's for a good cause."

Penelope studies me for a long moment, then a small smile tugs at her lips. "This wouldn't have anything to do with what I saw at practice today, would it?"

I suck in my lower lip. It figures she didn't miss that. "I screwed up before. With Cammy. I want to make it right. And this isn't all about her. The Hawkeyes are giving me a shot. The least I can do is pitch in where I can. Prove to Coach Wrenley—"

"Ah... now I see," she says with a soft smile. "The coach's daughter is a tough one. Slade can tell you all about it. He gave up the NHL and spent four years on the Hawkeyes farm team to gain back my father's good opinion of him. Are you sure you want to go down this road? There's no guarantee."

"I just need a shot—one shot at the second chance."

She studies me for another moment, then nods. "Okay. But, JP?" Her voice hardens, reminding me that before she was GM, she was a player's wife who knows exactly how this world works. "Don't make me regret this. Cammy's not just my employee—she's family."

"I understand."

"Do you? Because if you hurt her again, you'll have more than just Seven to deal with. I know I'm not technically supposed to have a favorite on the ice, but no one said anything about the administrative staff. I'd really hate to have to kick you off this team for causing her any more pain."

I meet her gaze steadily. "I won't hurt her."

"For your sake, I hope you don't." She glances at her watch, a mischievous glint appearing in her eyes. "She and Aria are helping out the legal team today, but she'll be back in my office tomorrow."

A voice calls out to Penelope—Dr. Kendall Hensen. The Hawkeyes in-house doctor.

"I was just coming to see you," Penelope says, beaming at Kendall, then turns back to me. "Good luck, JP. You're going to need it," she says with a smirk.

I nod and then head for the exit.

First order of business—ice this knee.

Then tomorrow, I'll convince Cammy to give me a second chance... at helping her with the auction.

Here goes nothing.

CHAPTER SIX

Cammy

Penelope's door clicks open as she comes out of her office after a call with Legal on some new potential player trade deal. She stops at my desk before heading out to lunch.

"How's it going out here?" she asks. I was on a roll sending out emails when she walked in this morning, so she didn't stop at my desk for small talk like she usually does.

"Good," I say, and then hit the send button on my keyboard. "That's the last email to the sponsors from previous years that Autumn gave me." I shake out my hands that are threatening to cramp after sending over a hundred emails all before lunch. "Now I'm waiting on Everett's assistant to send me Kauffman Corp's usual list of charity donors. From what I've heard, it's about three times the size of Autumn's email list. And I still need to head over to merch and get the boxes of gear down to the locker room for the guys to sign tomorrow morning after practice."

Penelope leans against my desk, a knowing smile I've come to dread when it's aimed at me plays at her lips. "Well, then I think you'll be happy to hear that I had a player volunteer to help take a little bit of that load off your shoulders."

I wrinkle my nose at the thought of having dead weight in the form of a player "volunteering" out of obligation or duty. Honestly, I'd rather do it myself than deal with a hostage-like situation. "Like I mentioned before, I don't need help. Brynn and I are getting together tonight to go over the list, and I'm sure that Aria would love nothing more than for me to call her from down the hall and get her out of Everett's office. No need to force feed a player to me."

She shakes her head. "No, no. That's the best part—he offered. I didn't even ask for participation," she says. "He came to me."

"A player offered to help me with the auction on his own free will?" I ask with a furrowed brow, not in the least bit buying her story.

Something's up.

"Yep." She grins. "And why wouldn't they? It's for a great cause, and you're a joy to work with."

"*Ha!*" I give a dry laugh—now I know she's lying.

Not because the charity isn't doing amazing things for families—it is. But because never in my life has anyone called me "a joy to work with."

I mean, I'm not tough to get along with or anything; I just take a few minutes to warm up. Like an old automobile.

You have to prime the engine a little before you just jump in and take me for a spin. I like to feel out people's motives before I fully trust them. I can thank my mother for that.

Basically, my hot mess of a family gave me trust issues.

Then, Seven and I reconnected, and the Hawkeyes took me in as one of their own.

"All I'm saying is, he knows the guys." She adjusts her blazer, the gesture too casual to be natural. "And after yesterday morning's practice..."

"Wait...it's not..." I pause, Penelope's lips puckering as if trying not to grin as wide as the Cheshire cat.

"He wants to make up for yesterday, and I think he could really help you," she says quickly, defending her case.

"With all due respect, Penelope," I start, because, well she is my boss after all, "yesterday's practice is exactly the reason he should be focusing on his game, not charity auctions."

I turn back to my computer screen, hoping she'll drop it. The image of JP missing that save because he was looking at me still makes my stomach twist. "Besides, I told him last week I didn't need his help."

"And yet," Penelope says, looking toward the door and then straightens with entirely too much enthusiasm, "here he comes."

My head snaps up. Sure enough, JP is walking toward my desk, his confidence radiating with every step. His hair is damp, as if he just finished a shower after practice, the smell of fresh body wash wafting through the air as he gets closer.

He's wearing dark jeans and a fitted black Henley that does nothing to hide the muscles underneath. Muscles I spent hours exploring one night in San Diego. A familiar warmth spreads through my chest before I can stop it.

"I'm headed out for lunch with Slade. I'll leave you to it," Penelope says, her voice dripping with amusement as she retreats.

"Traitor," I mutter, earning a laugh as she walks away.

"Bon aprem, mon petit oiseau," JP says, coming to a stop at my desk. The French rolls off his tongue as sweet as honey, and I hate that I still react to it.

I keep my eyes firmly on my screen. "Still with the French, Jon Paul?"

"Still with the full name, mon ange?" He leans against my desk; the last part he says in French again so that I can't understand him. Further annoying me... intentionally.

He leans in close enough that I catch the scent of his deodorant, an unfortunate familiar smell from all the encounters we've had over the years that I'd prefer not to remember.

"I thought we were past that."

"Nicknames are reserved for friends or lovers, and we're neither—we're work colleagues at best." I finally look up, meeting his gaze and immediately wishing I hadn't. His eyes are the same bright blue I remember. Like broken sea glass that I could drown in if I'm not careful. "What can I help you with today? In English this time, if you don't mind."

He licks his lips, a slow, amused smile tugging at the corner of his perfectly sculpted cupid's bow, hand crafted by the devil himself.

"I'm here to help with the auction. Use me however you want."

I laugh, but there's no humor in it. "I already told you that I don't need your help. Thanks anyway, goodbye," I say, turning back to my computer as if this conversation just ended.

"Yeah, I know but that was last week." He picks up the stress ball from my desk—the one I got at last year's white elephant Christmas party. I didn't realize how much I'd use it. Turns out that I use it...a lot, especially with Phil selling the team, the stress of getting the auction items done right, and the idea of JP being back in my world.

At least a lot of the changes Everett is making around here seem to be for the good of the team. With the new practice rink about ready to break ground next year and plans for a new parking garage for the administrative staff, as well as buying into the team family dynamic by keeping the team Christmas and donating even more than ever to all of the Hawkeyes causes, I see why Phil felt good about selling to Everett. Even if Everett is bringing on more controversial players to make a splash his first year as owner.

"And what's changed?" I ask, leaning back in my chair, crossing my arms over my chest while I watch JP's thick forearm bulge every time he squeezes the red squishy ball.

His expression softens. "Maybe I have."

The sincerity in his voice catches me off guard. For a moment, I'm back in that house, walking in the front door to find a large group swarming JP. The moment I walked in, his eyes locked on mine, surprise glimmering—he hadn't thought I'd show up.

I shake off the memory. "Focus on your game. That's what the team needs from you, and that's what Everett is paying you to do."

"And what do you need?"

The question hangs between us, loaded with everything we've left unsaid. I stand, needing distance. "What I need is to do my job and to make sure that these auction items are the best that the foundation has ever put out. Briggs, Autumn, Penelope, and Everett are counting on me to make this happen."

"Then let me help," he says, his voice dropping lower. "Please."

Something in his tone makes me pause. "Fine," I say finally, because this auction isn't about me. It's about these families and showing Penelope that she can count on me. And maybe someday, she'll move me up to the assistant GM position that was never filled after she became GM years ago. "Brynn and I are meeting up tonight to brainstorm. I'll text you if I need anything."

A slow grin spreads across his face. "You'll have to unblock my number first."

Heat rises to my cheeks. "Goodbye, Jon Paul."

He backs away, still grinning. "See you soon, Cammy."

I watch him leave, trying to ignore the way my heart races. This is exactly what I don't need—JP Dumont back in my life, speaking French and wearing that damn smile like he never broke my heart.

❧

Brynn's curled up on my couch, wine glass in hand, auction notes scattered across my coffee table when I tell her about the visitor I received earlier today and how Penelope couldn't get out of the office fast enough when he showed up.

"He's offered to help twice now?" Brynn's eyes widen, and a slow grin starts to stretch across her lips.

"Three times, actually," I admit, sinking deeper into my armchair. "Once when Penelope first mentioned the auction, again yesterday after practice with Penelope, and now earlier this afternoon with me."

She raises an eyebrow. "He's persistent isn't he?"

"You have no idea," I say, rolling my eyes at the thought of the years we spent flirting before I ever showed up at that house.

"And you're still saying no because...?"

I take a long sip of wine, letting the crisp white settle my nerves. "Because I don't need his help. And because the last time I trusted JP, I woke up alone in a guestroom of the Hawkeyes' mortal enemy while he was wrecking his car into a guardrail with another woman."

Brynn winces. "Okay, fair point. We don't like him—got it. I'm not on his side... just so we're clear." She nods in solidarity. "But that doesn't mean you can't use him for your benefit. You still have a lot to do to gather everything together, and you have only five weeks left to do it. Plus, Penelope said that he wants to show Coach Haynes that he's a team player... so let him."

She makes a good point. This isn't about him and me; it's about the charity, and we both want to prove something to our bosses. Having him wrangle some of the players wouldn't be the worst, considering I still have so many emails to get through, merch to get signed, and I need to create an itemized list in the software for the auction items.

"Some help would be great. I can't deny that. It's just that whenever I look at him, all I can think about is how easy it was for him to sell me complete and absolute lies. How can I ever trust anything he tells me again?"

"What did he tell you?" she asks.

"That once he was done with the Blue Devils, he'd find a way to get on the Hawkeyes so he could be close."

"Oh... whoa, okay, that's not what I expected you to say. So, you two were making plans for him to move here?"

I shake it off. It's not helpful to think in terms of the future he sold me. It's better not to relive any of that at all.

"I guess," I say, shaking my head. "I don't know anymore. And it doesn't matter. He left hours later with a woman who I overheard had been hanging around the team trying to get his attention. He never meant any of what he told me. He caught the mouse—he got what he was after. That's all."

"Did you confront him about it?"

"He left text messages and voicemails, but he never gave a reason—just apologized for not being there when I woke up, and that it's not what it looks like, but his teammates who know him better than me sure had an idea of what he was doing with her."

"Yes, but he never said why he left with her, right? So, you don't actually know."

"No," I say simply. "He asked to see me so he could explain, but the fact that it's too complicated to tell me with a quick text, means it's too complicated for me to be involved. At least I found out when I did."

"So, you still need closure," she says, matter-of-factly.

"What? No... no closure. We're past closure. In fact, that door is perfectly shut and sealed solid with gorilla glue—can't even see daylight through it."

"Are you sure? Maybe you should hear him out. Because if I'm being honest, you seemed a little shaken up when he missed that puck yesterday. You both did."

A knock at my door cuts her off. We exchange looks.

"It can't be..." Brynn trails off, but her eyes are sparkling with mischief.

Another knock echoes through the apartment, but neither of us make a move.

"Come on, Cammy." JP's voice carries through the door. "I know you're in there. I just heard Brynn."

"No one's home," I call back, earning a giggle from Brynn.

"I brought food," he counters.

Brynn practically bounces off the couch. "Let the man in! He has sustenance! All you have in your cabinets is boring healthy food. I've been trained to live off half-eaten soggy peanut butter and jelly sandwiches and goldfish. My body doesn't even recognize fruits and vegetables anymore. It'll revolt."

I shoot her a glare, but she just grins.

With a sigh, I head for the door, knowing I can't fight against snacks. Brynn's here helping me out of the goodness of her heart.

When I open it, JP is standing there with bags of Chinese takeout. He looks unfairly good in a navy-blue Hawkeyes hoodie and sweats, his hair feathering where he just ran his hands through it.

"What are you doing here?" I ask, though the familiar aroma of kung pao chicken is already weakening my resolve.

"Helping," he says simply, holding up the bags. Steam rises from the containers, carrying the scent of ginger and garlic. "You said that you would text if you needed anything, but I figured since I'm still blocked that the text you sent me didn't go through," he teases. "Lucky that your telepathy worked. I got the message loud and clear. You still like kung pao chicken, right? Extra spicy, no peanuts?"

The fact that he remembers my exact order from that night a year and a half ago has me wanting to ask him why he said all those things if he didn't mean them, and why he left me for her that night. I hate that Brynn might be right about all these unanswered questions leaving me without closure.

"I didn't send you any brain waves for food," I say.

"Must have been me," Brynn says, walking up beside me.

She offers up her hand, and JP gives her a high-five. I'm dramatically outnumbered here.

"Fine," I mutter, stepping aside and pulling the door open. My apartment suddenly feels smaller with him in it. At over six-foot-three, he's not a small man. He fits better in a large stadium than in my apartment, and yet... here he is. "Come in."

Brynn practically drags him into the kitchen with the food he brought to bribe his way past my front door, no doubt. JP moves through my space with an ease that unnerves me, unpacking containers of food like he belongs here. When he hands me a pair of chopsticks, his fingers brush mine for the briefest moment. The contact sends electricity shooting up my arm, but I don't let it show.

"Want some wine?" Brynn asks him.

"Water is fine, but I can get it," he says, moving to the cupboards.

I open up my food on the kitchen island, the steam billowing from the box making my mouth water instantly. "Left side cupboard above the sink," I call out.

I hear the cupboard door open, but it seems that JP has stopped whatever he was doing. I look up from my food to realize he's staring up at the top shelf of the cupboards—the pucks he tossed to me over the years all sitting there. I never expected JP to be playing on my team, much less in my kitchen. No one else has ever asked about them, so I sort of forgot they existed all the way up there.

"You kept the pucks I threw to you." He seems to almost gloat, his tone sliding between surprise and pleasure. There's more behind his gaze, something that tugs at my heart. "And on the top shelf no less," he teases.

I run over as JP reaches up and pulls one down, spinning the puck between his fingers to read the silver marker.

"You look cold," he reads, and then grins. "I remember this night. It was a home game for the Hawkeyes on Halloween. You were dressed as Tinker Bell in that tiny little dress."

Oh God... how did he remember that?

"I don't remember that night at all," I say, grabbing the puck out of his hand, setting it back on the top shelf while pushing on my tippy toes. I grab him a glass, and then slam the cabinet closed. "You weren't supposed to see those pucks anyway—"

"I don't see how you could have forgotten," he says, cutting me off. "Your lips were turning blue. You looked miserable but also the cutest fucking thing I'd ever seen. I almost missed the winning save that night because I kept checking to see if anyone had brought you a blanket yet. I asked a couple assistants on the Blue Devils side to at least take you my jacket."

I remember blushing at the puck he sent me over the plexiglass, but I was too damn cold to think straight.

"You did?" I ask, my treacherous heart warming at his concern for me.

"Yeah, but don't let it go to your head," he says with a warm smile.

"All the girls were supposed to dress in theme. Brynn was Captain Hook, Penelope was Wendy, Slade was Peter Pan, and somehow we convinced my dad to be the alligator." I giggle at the memory. That night turned out pretty good, actually, though it took hours after we got to Oakley's after the game, to feel my toes again. "Just for the record, I didn't keep them as a memento... It's just blasphemous to toss away a perfectly good puck."

We face each other, his eyes searching mine for sincerity as I challenge him with a raised brow to call me a liar.

"I'm glad you kept them. It tells me what I needed to know," he says.

I lean a hand against the counter and roll my eyes. "Really? And what does a random pile of hockey pucks forgotten in the back of my cupboards tell you?" I ask.

"That each puck I tossed to you meant as much to you as they did to me. Maybe there's more to us than you think there is," he says, his eyes soft as he searches mine for some kind of answer.

"There is no us," I mutter, hating the way it sounds off my lips and for some unknown reason, wishing I could take it back.

"Maybe not yet," he says, taking a small step closer, his eyes drifting down to my lips.

I force myself not to wet my lips with my tongue.

The sound of Brynn moving on the couch breaks me from the moment between us. "What's going on in there?" she asks.

"Nothing," I singsong and head back for my food, swiping it off the island and sending JP a warning glare.

Eventually, he joins us, digging into the food he brought for himself.

"So," he says, settling onto my charcoal gray couch like he's been here a hundred times before—a box of noodles in one hand, setting another box of pot stickers on the coffee table. "What are we working on?"

"We're brainstorming auction items," Brynn explains, already diving into her lo mein. "Beyond the usual signed jerseys

71

and sticks."

JP leans forward, his knee brushing mine. I pull back, pretending to adjust my notepad on the coffee table, but the faint smirk on his lips tells me he noticed.

"Remember when Briggs offered to hang Christmas lights in a Santa costume?" Brynn laughs, tucking her legs under her. "It went for five thousand dollars."

"We could do something similar," JP says, reaching for his fried rice. "Get the guys to offer experiences. Skating lessons, dinner dates, that kind of thing."

A spark of an idea comes to mind.

"Autumn would love that. And what about if we turned those items into a live event?" I suggest. "We could make the whole experience more interactive."

Brynn's eyes light up. "Oh! What a great idea. Though the Santa lights might be off the table. I doubt Coach Haynes wants his players on slippery ladders."

I turn to JP. "Do you think they'd do it?"

He thinks for a second as he finishes a bite of food. "Probably. It's for a good cause, and there are a lot of players on the team who'd eat up the attention of marching onto a stage while people bid on them."

Brynn does a fist bump into the air with her chopsticks. "Perfect. Oh, my God, Autumn is going to freak out when she hears about this. We'll have to ask Juliet to rent a bigger stage for the event. Would a catwalk be too much to ask?"

"Yes," JP and I say in unison, chuckling.

Juliet is Coach Haynes' wife and the official event planner for the Hawkeyes, along with many other sports teams around Seattle.

I clear my throat and look back over the list on my notepad. "What should we ask the players to donate?"

"I could donate dinner with a player," JP says.

My stomach drops at the thought of someone else getting a night with JP.

"No," I say instantly, without thinking. "What I meant to say was that I'm sure we can find something unique to you that you could offer instead. Leave the dates to some of the other guys."

JP's eyes stay on me as he finishes his bite. If he saw through that, he's not saying, but he certainly is thinking something.

"I bet Luka and Hunter would love the idea of walking on a stage and having women beating each other with bid paddles to get a date with one of them," Brynn adds.

"What about a slapshot challenge?" JP suggests. "During the event?"

I pause, chopsticks hovering over my food. "Go on."

"It's simple. Guests make a donation, and they get three shots to score past the goalie." His eyes light up as he explains. "Bozeman and I could trade off covering goalie as long as Dr. Hensen clears him in time. It'll be interactive, and anyone can do it."

Brynn claps her hands together, nearly spilling her wine. "I love it! People will eat that up."

"Not bad," I admit reluctantly, though my mind is already running with possibilities.

His grin widens. "Not bad? I think it's genius."

I roll my eyes, but I can't stop the corner of my mouth from twitching. We fall into an easy rhythm, bouncing more ideas back and forth. JP's actually helpful, suggesting things I wouldn't have thought of.

Before I know it, I find myself leaning closer to JP as we riff off of each other's ideas. Adding all our ideas onto a shared notes app that Brynn and I have been using.

When I look over to Brynn, I see a sparkle in her eye, as if she's been watching us.

"Oh, look at that. Seven just texted and needs me to come home and help with Milo," she says.

"Brynn, your phone's on the coffee table. And it hasn't gone off in over an hour," I remind her.

"Oh, right," she says, biting the inside of her lip. "It's more like momma telepathy. Turns out I'm good at that," she says, sending a wink in JP's direction. "I should go."

I know it's an excuse—Milo's fine with my dad—but before I can stop her, she's gathering her things.

She stands up, swiping her phone off the coffee table and taking her wine glass and empty food container to the kitchen.

"Do you need a ride home? I can take you if you want?" JP offers.

He's seen the empty bottle of wine that Brynn and I split, and the offer to make sure she gets home safe isn't lost on me.

"No need, and don't stop on my account. You two are on a roll," she says, sending off a text. "I live just across the street, and I sent a text to Seven. He'll be watching for me."

I get up to chase after her and see JP try to hide his grin. "Brynn, you don't have to leave. I can see across the street. The living room lights are already off. I bet Milo and Dad are passed out together on the couch watching a documentary on fly fishing."

Brynn ignores me, grabbing her purse off the kitchen island. "Don't have too much fun without me. And update the list on the notes app. I'll check it tomorrow if I come up with anything else."

"Brynn..." I warn again.

She turns to me, wraps an arm around my shoulders and pulls me in, whispering in my ear. "Here's your chance for closure. Be nice."

Be nice? Why does everyone always say that to me?

I am nice.

Besides, he's the one who left, not me.

After she leaves, an awkward silence settles over the room. JP moves to clean up the empty takeout containers, and I busy myself with cleaning the wine glasses.

After we've both finished, I look over to find JP pushing back the floor-to-ceiling curtains in my living room, glancing down at the street.

"What is it?" I ask, concerned he sees something happening with Brynn.

"Just making sure Brynn makes it across okay," he says, eyes fixed on the street below.

I join him at the window, drawn by the genuine concern in his voice. Our reflections overlap in the glass, and for a moment, I let myself remember how it felt—believing we could be something real.

That's when I see it—my father standing at the window across the street a few floors higher than mine, staring down at my apartment. Even from three stories up, his disapproval radiates clearly.

"He's protective. I think it's his way of coping from missing out on half of my life," I say softly, wrapping my arms around myself.

JP's reflection nods. "He has good reason to be."

The admission hangs between us, heavy with unspoken words. I turn to face him, and suddenly we're too close. I remember how those eyes looked at me the night he walked into Cooper's massive kitchen filled with people. He made me feel like I was the only other person in the world.

Then my dad turns around, as if Brynn just walked into the apartment. JP clears his throat and then turns around. "Here, let me help you clean up."

"You already did," I tell him, following him to the kitchen as I open the notes app back up and input JP's contact information into it. "I just sent you the document list that Brynn and I are sharing for ideas. It has our updated ideas from tonight."

A ding sounds on his phone, and he pulls it from his back pocket. "You unblocked me? Does this mean you're going to start speaking to me again in public?"

"I wouldn't go that far. Call it a professional courtesy. Abuse the right and I can just as quickly block you again."

He chuckles. "Got it. Consider me warned."

He reaches over the counter and takes two fortune cookies out of the white plastic to-go bag, offering me one. "Would dessert better my chances?"

I can't help the smile stretching across my lips. "Well, I can tell you one thing. It's not going to hurt your chances."

We both begin to unwrap the cellophane around the cookies.

"How did you remember what I ordered that night?" I ask, busying myself with cracking open my fortune cookie and pulling out the paper.

His response is immediate. "Because even though you probably won't believe me, I remember every single thing about that night... with you." He breaks his fortune cookie open, tossing a small piece of broken cookie into his mouth and then pulls out the fortune.

My heart flutters at the thought that our night together wasn't as easy for him to forget either.

When I don't reply, he reads his fortune. "The path you are on will bring you great success if you stay the course." He seems to ponder his fortune for a moment and then looks at me. "What does yours say?"

I stare back down at my fortune cookie before reading it out loud. "Always check the weather before you leave the house." I crumple it in my hand, feeling the sharp edges against my palm..

"That's a wise cookie. Do you think it's literal or figurative?" he asks.

"I suppose it could be either." I consider it from both meanings. "But either way, if you always bring an umbrella—you'll never get wet."

Maybe that's what makes me the most bitter about what happened between us. I've been so good at protecting my heart—keeping it out of the rain, out of the torrential downpour around me. JP was the first time I closed the umbrella to let the sun shine on me. I didn't see the raging storm cloud about to burst just behind him.

"But then no chance for singing in the rain," he says thoughtfully, watching me carefully.

My eyes drop to the neon green hairband on his wrist. Was he wearing it when he came in to get his key? I feel like I would have seen it. "Is that mine?"

He nods, and glances down at it. "It is."

"Why do you still have it?" I ask.

"I've kept it. I wear it when I need a little extra luck."

"Why did you need luck tonight?" My voice is careful but curious.

I want to know, but I'm scared of what his answer might reveal.

"Because I thought you'd slam the door in my face."

"Brynn saved you," I mutter.

Before I realize it, I step closer, sliding my fingers over the bright nylon material over his wrist. Something magnetic pulling us back together. His hand lifts slowly, tucking a strand of hair behind my ear. My breath catches, and I don't pull away.

"Thank you for dinner," I whisper, and then suck in my lower lip, his eyes locking on my mouth. And for a moment, the world narrows to just us—no one else in existence—just him and me. Then he speaks, his voice low and rough. "Dis-moi quoi faire pour regagner ton cœur," he says in French.

"I don't know what that means," I murmur, my pulse hammering.

With every second, he leans in closer. He's going to kiss me.

And I already know that I'm going to let him.

"It means..." He hesitates, his eyes pinging back and forth between mine. "You're welcome for dinner."

The moment shatters as his phone buzzes loudly on the counter, breaking the spell.

He glances at the screen, and his expression hardens, causing me to look at it too.

Angelica.

I pull back, my heart dropping, though I wish I felt nothing.

Of course. Of course, she's still in the picture.

"Look at that. She's right on time," I say, turning away toward the island before he can see the hurt in my eyes. "Thanks for the ideas."

He steps closer again. "Cammy, it's not what you think. She's been helping me get back to the NHL—that's it."

I busy myself with the left-over chopsticks and napkins that came with the to-go order, refusing to look back up at him.

But then I consider that this might be the time to get my answers. His texts were vague, and his voicemails didn't bother to explain what he was doing with her either. If I want answers, as hard as they'll be to hear, even years later, this might be my last chance to get them before I kick him out of my apartment and block his number again.

"Then who is she?" I ask.

"She's a good friend from high school who's trying to help me out. I promise, there's nothing going on between us."

A good friend from high school. I can guess what that means.

"Right, because we all have good friends from high school calling us late at night and getting us walk-on multimillion dollar contract deals with Texas and Florida, just for the hell of it. Sounds like she wants more than her *billable* hours," I say, hating the way my voice seethes with jealousy.

This isn't how this is supposed to go. I'm supposed to be over this.

I shouldn't be jealous of her.

I shouldn't be jealous of any woman getting his time.

It's her loss, not mine.

"Cammy—" He reaches for me, but I step away, knowing that JP's touch has a way of soothing me, like he did when I bared my soul to him in that guestroom over a year ago, and that's the last thing I need right now. Falling back into his arms will only make me relive my mistakes a second time—once is plenty.

"I hope she's at least smart enough not to get in a car with you again." I head for the door, gripping the handle. "Goodnight, Jon Paul," I say, twisting it, opening the door for him to exit.

He walks slowly to the exit, his shoulders tense. "I did everything wrong that night. Everything except for the time I spent with you. I'm sorry I hurt you."

I pause, my hand on the doorknob. "Maybe this time, take an Uber to her place instead of driving. The Hawkeyes would prefer you didn't wrap your car around a tree."

His face pales, and for a moment, I think he might argue. But he doesn't. He just nods, tucking his hands into his pockets.

The door closes behind him with a soft click that seems to echo in my empty apartment. My phone chimes immediately with a text.

> **Dad: Be careful with him, kiddo. He has a reputation that I've seen firsthand.**

As the silence settles around me, I glance at the crumpled fortune in my palm. *An old flame may reignite.*

Not if I can help it.

CHAPTER SEVEN

JP

My phone buzzes for the third time as I walk through the quiet corridors of the Hawkeyes' stadium. My hair's still damp from the post-practice shower, and the chill seeping through my skin makes me grateful for my thick team hoodie.

I pull my phone from my jacket. The screen lights up with Angelica's name.

> **Angelica:** You're trending again. Congrats, Dumont. #GoalieComeback is all over socials, and I woke up to several emails requesting one-on-one interviews and sponsorship offers. The Dumont gravy train is back on track.

> **JP: I only care about one thing. Getting off PTO and earning a permanent spot on the team. I need that contract, Ang.**

Her response is immediate.

> **Angelica: I know. And with Everett wanting to make waves in the sports world, this is improving your chances. So, don't screw it up. If anyone from the media asks about the DUI charges or anything from that night, you say "no comment."**

My jaw clenches as I type. Being in this situation and not being able to tell Cammy the truth is what bothers me the most.

> **JP: There has to be another way to get her to trust me without anyone knowing what happened that night.**

> **Angelica: You got her to trust you once. Just do it again.**

I exhale. It took me three years to get Cammy to show up, to break through her walls and show her that I was worth taking a chance on. And if it takes me another three years, I'd do it gladly. But now I'm fighting against more than just hearsay. She thinks she's experienced it firsthand. Angelica's right, of course. I can't afford any mistakes—on or off the ice.

I type a quick response before shoving the phone into my pocket.

> **JP: Got it. Stay focused. Don't talk to strangers.**

> **Angelica: Love you**

> **JP: Je t'aime aussi**

Angelica's words echoing in my head as I make it to the edge of the rink, my vision fixing on the figure moving across the ice with deadly determination.

Cammy.

She's been out there with Seven for the past hour, staying after morning practice wrapped up and the team cleared out. From my position near the tunnel, I can hear the rhythmic thwack of pucks finding their mark against the net.

It's been a few days since I left her apartment and Angelica's poorly timed phone call. I wish I'd known what to say that night to make her believe that nothing happened between Angelica and me, but telling her means exposing Angelica. And then all the work her team has been doing would be a waste.

Above me, Penelope and Everett lean against the railing near the players' tunnel, their heads bent in conversation as they watch Cammy's practice. They've been out here all morning, watching the team's practice first, but something about the way they're studying her now feels different. More focused.

My attention shifts back to Cammy as she lines up another shot. The way she squares her shoulders, the slight bend in her knees, the fluid motion of her follow-through—Seven's coaching shows in every movement, but there's something else there, too. Raw talent. Pure Wrenley DNA.

The puck flies, but Seven stops it with his glove.

"Getting better," Seven calls out, pride evident in his voice. "Go again."

That pride—it's something I've never heard in my own father's voice. Jon Paul Senior's idea of encouragement was always more like: "You can do better than that," or "A real champion wouldn't have missed that save." Watching Seven with Cammy, the way he builds her up instead of tearing her down, makes something twist in my chest.

From what Cammy told me that night in San Diego, she only started skating after finding out Seven was her dad. Though she was born with an athletic edge—an all-state volleyball champ with full rides to multiple colleges... just not the University of Washington. She wanted to take an internship with the Hawkeyes and be closer to Seven.

I can't tear my eyes away, seeing her out on the ice—my ice. The only thing that would make this better is being out there with her. She sets up another shot, and my goalie instincts kick in automatically. Her wrist shot is lethal—quick release, perfect placement—but her slapshot? That's where the real power lies.

She needs more work, but her skills are impressive for the limited years she's put in. Seven glances my way, his expression hardening when he catches me watching. The message is clear: *Stay away from my daughter.* But it's too late for that warning. It was too late the moment I saw her at that first game over four years ago, the first time I tossed her a puck to go out to dinner with me.

I'm not one for the chase—it's never been my thing. But the moment I saw the look of disgust on Cammy's face when she read *Dinner?* on the puck, she hooked me. That was the first time I had ever gotten a reaction like that from a woman, and it intrigued me. Now, I'm addicted to her snarky comments, the warning look in her eyes, that sharp brow that tells me she thinks I'm full of shit. I have to fucking know what she's thinking.

What I wouldn't give to have subtitles for Cammy's inner thoughts. Those pointed remarks that absolutely destroy me, and yet, I can never get enough.

It's a game I can't win but can't stop playing.

Because I want every part of Cammy. Her rose petals and her thorns.

"JP," Everett calls from above, snapping me out of my trance. "Just the man we wanted to see."

Cammy finishes her last shot—top shelf, right above Seven's shoulder. Seven's attention fixes on me fully now, his protective instincts visible.

"That slapshot challenge you and Cammy proposed," Everett continues, "it's a great idea. I think the live-action interaction could bring in some bigger donors."

"Thanks." I scratch the back of my neck, oddly pleased by the enthusiasm. "It was actually Cammy's idea, too. We worked on it together."

"Speaking of which"—Everett's eyes track to the ice where Cammy's just landed another impressive shot—"I've got an investor coming in tomorrow. Deep pockets, lots of connections—exactly the kind of person we need interested in this auction to ensure the foundation gets the funding they need for those family condos near the cancer center."

I see where this is going. "And you want a preview?"

"If you and Cammy wouldn't mind?" Penelope asks, her tone careful. "Just a little demonstration to show him what he could expect from the auction and maybe encourage him to bring some friends along."

"Cammy!" Everett calls out. "Got a minute?"

Her eyes narrow slightly when she spots me, but she manages a smile for the others. "Yes, of course."

On the ice, Seven tells her to go while he grabs the rest of the gear. She heads for us, tugging off her gloves. Her cheeks are flushed from practice, and her nose is red from the chill of the ice, a few strands of hair stuck to her temple. She's beautiful—just like this, raw and real, no walls up yet.

"You look solid out there. Giving your old man a run for his money," Everett says.

"Thanks. He's a great coach. I'm lucky to get to learn from the best." There's pride in her voice, something no one would ever hear in my voice for my own father. The closest I ever got to making Jon Paul Senior proud was the day I signed my first NHL contract—and even then, his first words were about living up to the family name.

As Everett explains the situation, Seven approaches. His eyes meet mine for a moment, his eyes still a warning sign that I'm standing too close to her.

"Sounds good to me," Cammy says, though I know her willingness to be a team player isn't for my benefit.

Seven's jaw tightens, but he turns to Everett. "When were you thinking?"

"Tomorrow. After morning skate," Everett replies. "Does that work for everyone?"

We all nod, and slowly the group disperses. Seven lingers for a moment, his gaze promising bodily harm if I step out of line, before following Everett and Penelope toward the locker room.

My phone buzzes again in my pocket—probably Angelica with more advice—but I ignore it. Instead, I catch up to Cammy before she can escape. "Hey, that was some slapshot out there."

She pauses, surprised by the genuine compliment. "Thanks."

"You've been practicing."

"Maybe." A hint of pride creeps into her voice, her hazel eyes sparking with that competitive edge I can never resist.

I hesitate, then grin. "Want to make this preview interesting?"

Her eyebrow arches, and her lips twitch like she's already calling my bluff. "Interesting how?"

"Simple. Three shots," I say, stepping closer. Her scent—something soft and faintly floral—makes my chest tighten. "If I block all three, you agree to a real date with me. Dinner, conversation, no running away afterward."

She scoffs, crossing her arms. "And if I score?"

I shrug, feigning casual. "Your call. What do you want?"

Cammy studies me for a long moment, her lips pressing into

a thoughtful line. Then a sly smile curls the edges of her mouth. "Fine. If I score, you tell Penelope you're stepping away from the auction to focus on your knee. No excuses. No interference."

Her words hit harder than a slapshot, but I keep my expression steady. Of course she'd use this to push me away—it's classic Cammy. Practical, guarded, and unwilling to risk opening the door to something she can't control.

"Deal," I say, extending my hand.

Her hand meets mine, her grip firm, her eyes locked on mine. "Deal."

As she pulls away, that fire in her gaze ignites, and I know I'm in trouble. But I've spent the last hour watching her practice, studying her tells. The way her weight shifts before a wrist shot. The way her shoulders tighten before a slapshot.

I'm not letting a single puck past me.

I watch her walk away, that competitive spark in her eyes lighting a fire under my skin. She thinks this is about the auction. About proving myself to the team. And yeah, maybe it started that way. But this isn't about charity events or career comebacks.

This is about her and what I'm willing to do to get her back, no matter the cost, no matter the stakes.

I can still feel the hockey callouses on her palm where it pressed against mine, the strength behind her handshake that said she has no intention of letting me win. And I'm fine with that— hell, I want the challenge.

Because this isn't just a game to me. This is my shot at proving I'm not the guy she thinks I am. At showing her that even after everything, I'm still here. And this time, I'm not walking away.

I pull out my phone, seeing Angelica's latest text.

Angelica: Booked a flight for the opener. Still have seats for me?

JP: Always.

I touch the green hairband on my wrist—her hair tie, the one I've worn ever since that night. Some guys have lucky socks or pre-game rituals. I have this small piece of her, reminding me of everything I'm fighting to get back.

Tomorrow, I'll need all the luck I can get.

CHAPTER EIGHT

Cammy

My phone buzzes as I head for the rink, heading for the preview, though my nerves feel like someone dropped them in a blender and hit the power button.

> **Brynn: Stop ignoring me. What happened with JP two nights ago? Spill!**

I bite back a smile, grateful for something else to occupy my thoughts instead of what's waiting for me out on the ice.

> **Cammy: Have you forgotten that I have a preview today? I'm a little busy at the moment.**

> **Brynn: I know. I'm in the stands. I can see you.**

I glance up to see Brynn across the stadium, sitting with Milo and Aria. She lifts his little mitten-covered hand to wave at me. I give him a little wave back. I shoot her a quick text back since I don't see Everett in the stands yet.

> **Cammy: He helped me clean up and then he left. That's it.**

I know she'll keep bugging me if I don't just answer her.

> **Brynn: You expect me to believe that nothing happened?**

> **Cammy: He got a call from his "agent" Angelica Ludwig and then went on his merry way.**

> **Brynn: Wait, Angelica Ludwig. Isn't that the girl he got in the accident with?**

I don't text back. She's smart enough to put the rest together, and honestly, this situation still stings.

> **Brynn: Cammy, I've seen the way he looks at you. Did you ask him about that night? Why he left?**

I skate out on the ice, seeing JP already on the ice in front of the net.

I wave my phone at her and set it on the sideboard along the home bench to show her I am no longer getting her messages. I notice JP's phone sitting there, too, along with his water bottle.

I need to focus if I want to win this thing. I can't keep checking her messages.

Her reasoning that the way he looks at me means something is completely wrong, because he looked at me a lot that night we spent in that guestroom and still left.

The Hawkeyes' arena isn't usually lively at this time in the morning, post-practice. Players who normally rush for the showers linger in the stands, their voices bouncing off empty seats and plexiglass. I pause at the tunnel entrance, taking in the scene.

My stomach twists as I catch snippets of whispered bets and predictions floating down from the stands. This wasn't supposed to be a team event. Just a quick preview for Everett's investor. But word spread fast when Everett asked for a preview between JP and me, and now it feels like the whole organization is here to witness whatever's about to happen.

I adjust my stick tape for the third time, the familiar ritual doing little to calm my nerves. The cold seeps through my dad's old practice jersey, but my palms are sweating inside my gloves.

"Ready for this?" Hunter calls from the bench, his grin visible even from here. "My money's on you, Wrenley."

"Betting against your own goalie?" Luka asks, clutching his chest in mock offense. "That's cold, man."

"What can I say? I like an underdog." Hunter winks at me, and I manage a small smile.

"Hey, Wrenley," Aleksi calls out, leaning over the boards. "Monty's got a weak spot, high glove side when he's tired. And he always leans left after a butterfly save."

"Mäkelin!" JP shouts from the net. "Whose team are you on?"

"I'm on Cammy's team... obviously." Aleksi grins.

Their banter helps settle my nerves, until I spot my dad standing near the tunnel. His arms are crossed, jaw set. He almost appears to be holding himself back from skating out here to take my spot, but he wouldn't embarrass me like that. He knows I've been training, and after all, no one else knows what's on the line besides JP and me.

JP's already going through his warm-up routine. Even from here, I can read the familiar patterns—the way he stretches each leg, adjusts his facemask. The same ritual I'd seen each time the Hawkeyes played against the Blue Devils, back when I knew better than to trust a hockey playboy. Back before I spent that night believing every promise he whispered against my skin.

The scrape of my skates against ice feels deafening as I make my way to center ice. Each stride brings me closer to him, and my heart pounds harder with every foot of distance I close. I catch Brynn's eye in the stands. She gives me an encouraging thumbs up. I didn't tell her about the bet, and I'm glad I didn't—the pressure of her watching, knowing what's on the line as well, would have my heart beating faster.

"Looks like we've drawn a crowd," he says as I glide closer, that hint of amusement in his voice. His eyes catch mine through his mask. "Still good with our bet? If you want to back out, now is the time."

"Worried you'll lose?" I shoot back, though my heart races, and my hands sweat at the memory of our deal. Three shots. If he blocks them all, I owe him a date. If I score, he backs off. The stakes feel impossibly high, especially with the weight of everyone's eyes on us.

"Never. I won't lose today. The incentive to win is too high." He grins, adjusting his mask. I stare at his Hawkeyes jersey. It's the first time I've seen him in an official game day jersey. Number 51. The same number he wore in San Diego. "Just making sure you're ready to follow through when I win."

A laugh bubbles up before I can stop it, though it holds more edge than humor. "Pretty confident for someone whose teammate just gave up his weak spot."

JP and I could go rounds back and forth. I know... because we have, on many occasions, but then Everett's voice booms across the ice. "There they are!" He strides toward us with a man in an expensive suit—presumably the investor. I straighten my shoulders, grateful for the interruption. "Mark, these are the two I was telling you about. Jon Paul Dumont, our goalie, and Cammy Wrenley—Seven Wrenley's daughter."

Mark shakes both our hands, his enthusiasm evident in his firm grip. His eyes linger on me a moment longer than necessary, clearly trying to reconcile my presence on the ice. I'm used to that look—the one that says "coach's daughter doesn't quite explain what I'm doing here with a stick in my hands." But his smile is warm nonetheless.

"Everett says you've got something special planned for the auction?" Mark's polished exterior barely contains his curiosity.

"A slapshot challenge," JP explains, his professional charm sliding into place—the same voice he used to use for post-game interviews. "Guests can donate for a chance to score on a pro goalie. Olsen Bozeman should be cleared by Dr. Hensen by then. He and I will take shifts, and donors can pay as many times as they want to take three shots against either one of us."

"And you're going to demonstrate out on the ice for us?" Mark asks me.

"That's the plan." I twirl my stick, a nervous habit. "Though, usually I'm the one organizing events, not participating in them."

"A Dumont and Wrenley showdown," Mark says, "I like it. Donors will like it, too. This could be a big pull to get more donors in the door."

I never thought of it that way, but of course that's how outsiders see it.

"Well then"—Everett claps his hands together—"let's see what you two have planned for the auction. Good luck."

Before Everett walks away, he leans in closer. "I've got a hundred bucks on you. Give him hell."

The vote of confidence from Everett is what I needed. The longer I see what he's doing with this team to build up community around the city and going big with his own money to help make sure that this charity is a huge success, the more I believe in Phil Carlton's decision.

They retreat to the bench, leaving JP and me alone on the ice. The arena feels smaller somehow, like the walls are closing in. Or maybe that's just the weight of everyone's eyes on us, the whispered conversations, the anticipation hanging thick in the air.

JP settles into position, and I take my place. Three shots. That's all I need. Just one has to get past him. I close my eyes for a moment, remembering countless hours practicing with my dad, his voice steady.

"Read the goalie, find the weakness, commit to your shot."

The first puck feels heavy in my hands as I set it down. JP's weight shifts slightly left—he's expecting me to go right. It's such a subtle tell that most people wouldn't notice it, but I've spent more time analyzing his every move—more than I thought I had—over the years. I adjust my angle at the last second, sending the puck high glove side.

He catches it cleanly, the smack of rubber against his glove echoing through the arena. Even through his mask, I can see the satisfaction in his eyes. That little head tilt he does when he's pleased with himself—some things never change.

There are a few light claps for Dumont and a few "boos" from Hunter and Aleksi, but I ignore it, setting up for my second attempt. My hands are shaking slightly as I position the puck. This time I go low, trying to sneak it between his pads. He drops into a butterfly, the puck bouncing harmlessly off his leg pad.

"Come on, Wrenley!" Hunter shouts. "Show him what you've got!"

"You got this, Cammy!" Brynn's voice carries from somewhere above, steady and encouraging.

One shot left. My palms sweat inside my gloves as I line up the final attempt.

I channel my shot, putting everything I have into it. The puck flies true, heading for the top corner. For a split second, I think I've got him. Hope surges through me—and then his glove flashes up, snagging it out of the air like it was meant for him all along. Like everything about me has always belonged to him, whether I wanted it to or not.

The team erupts, a few cheers but mostly playful booing at JP for shutting me out. I'd laugh at the antics if losing didn't mean something else—something I agreed to.

A date.

My chest heaves as I try to catch my breath, try to swallow down the disappointment and something else that feels dangerously like excitement... maybe even relief? Is that even possible? Like this bet is forcing us together without me having to fully drop my guard.

He skates toward me, his mask pushed up to reveal that infuriating smile that still keeps me up thinking about it. Sweat glistens on his forehead, a drop sliding down his temple. I remember how that skin felt under my fingers, how his smile felt against my lips.

"Looks like you owe me a date," he says quietly, close enough that only I can hear. His breath fogs in the cold air between us, mingling with mine.

"A bet is a bet," I say.

"Yeah, but I'm not going to force you into anything you don't want to do, Cammy. I'd rather you come because you want to. Not just because you lost our bet."

Suddenly, I feel a heavy presence near us by the home bench.

"Bet?" I hear my dad's voice. "What bet?"

"Just a friendly wager. Nothing big," I tell him, for some reason jumping in to protect JP.

There's no way my dad would stand for the terms of our arrangement.

I can tell he isn't buying it, but before he can ask follow-up questions, Everett and Mark make their way down to us.

"What if I take Cammy's place?" my dad says, his voice cutting through the air like a slapshot.

Every muscle in my body tenses as I turn to face him. He's already stepping onto the ice, his skates slicing into the surface with practiced ease.

"A battle between the old goalie and the new?" Mark says, his excitement bubbling over. "Now that's something no one will want to miss. I hope you ordered enough tickets, Everett, because this event is about to sell out fast."

"What do you say, Dumont?" my dad asks, his eyes never leaving JP.

JP doesn't flinch, his jaw tightening as he meets my dad's gaze. "I'm in."

"Perfect," Mark says, already turning to Everett and Penelope to hammer out details. But I can't focus on them. Not when my dad and JP are locked in a silent battle of wills.

"Since you seem to like bets," my dad says, his voice calm but sharp enough to cut glass, "how about we make one of our own?"

The air feels heavier, every sound in the arena fading into the background as his words sink in.

"If I get a puck past you, you agree to leave the Hawkeyes. No arguments, no explanations. You forfeit your PTO and you walk away."

"Dad—" I say, but JP cuts me off.

"And if I shut you out?" JP asks. His voice is steady, but there's an edge to it, a determination that makes my chest ache. "I want your approval. No more warnings, no more interference. You let me stay here."

There's no way that Penelope, Coach Haynes, or Everett would be happy to hear this bet.

JP's eyes flicker to me, and that's when I realize this doesn't have anything to do with hockey... This has everything to do with me.

"Fair enough," my dad says, offering out his hand.

"Wait—stop... This is ridiculous! Neither of you can make that call," I say, stepping forward, my voice echoing across the ice. "You can't just bet his career on one shot. What would Coach Haynes or Everett say about this?" I ask, trying to bring my voice down so that Everett doesn't hear us, and also to bring them both to their senses.

Neither of them look at me. They shake hands, the weight of

their agreement settling over the rink like a storm cloud.

Without another word, my dad turns and skates off, his shoulders rigid as he heads for the stands. Brynn's eyes meet mine, wide with disbelief as she mouths, *What just happened?*

I shake my head, my stomach churning as JP turns to face me. His expression is unreadable, but there's something in his eyes that makes my chest tighten.

This isn't just about a shot anymore. It's about hearts and careers and second chances—and I'm not sure any of us are ready for what happens next.

Especially me.

CHAPTER NINE

JP

"That's what we're playing on?" Luka asks, staring at my PS3 like it's a museum artifact. He sets down a large stack of pizzas on my kitchen counter and opens the fridge door, setting a case of beers on the bottom rack of my fridge. The smell of pepperoni, spicy sausage, and bell peppers fills my apartment. "You played for the Blue Devils for four years with a multimillion dollar contract and this is the best you can do?"

"It's not about the system," I say, grabbing another slice of pizza. "It's about the memories. NHL 25 got me through road trips, lonely summers, and way too many nights when I should've been studying game footage."

Hunter comes through the door just in time. "And to think— the media calls you a spoiled brat, born with a silver spoon in your mouth. If they could only see you now."

I laugh. The media has no idea what growing up as Jon Paul Dumont Senior's son meant. I stopped asking for things from my father at a young age—it was all conditional, including his love. "Mind telling them? You'd be doing me a favor. I'll even let you sell a picture of my PlayStation to the tabloids. They'll have a field day with this kind of breaking news," I say. "Want me to pose with it?"

Aleksi snipes two beers and a box of pizza and heads for the living room. "I offered to bring my newer system, but your boy Monty here is what's known as a traditionalist, enjoying relics from our past," Aleksi says, slapping the box on the coffee table before sprawling out onto the sofa. "I, for one, am open to all forms of gaming consoles. It brings me back to my childhood."

"Make yourself at home, Mäkelin," I mutter around a mouthful of pizza.

"I always do," Aleksi says quickly.

"Where I'm from, someone who holds on to junk is considered a hoarder," Luka says.

Luka has a similar background as I do—both of us coming from competitive sports families. He comes from a wealthy family in Russia, with rumors of ties to the mob, and his dad is a well-decorated Olympic gymnast who's worked in the family business since he retired from the sport thirty years ago. From the little we've talked, he's familiar with unattainable fatherly expectations.

Aleksi grabs a controller, already queuing up NHL 25. "Where's everyone else?"

"Bozeman's helping his old college roommate move," Hunter says, cracking open a beer and settling into my armchair. "And Hartley's at Adaline's piano recital."

I've only met Trey's niece once, but she seems to have a good head on her shoulders for someone who lost her family at a young age.

The door opens again, and Slade walks in, nodding at us. His presence still commands attention—maybe it's the captain thing or that he's the longest-running hockey player on this team and the only one with a Stanley Cup win under his belt. "Ziggy sends his regrets. He's in New England for a funeral."

Wolf Ziegler—the nicest guy you'll ever meet off the ice and one of the meanest defensive players I've ever played against. Needless to say, I'm happy we're on the same team.

"More pizza for us," Aleksi says, already starting up the game. "First round loser buys next time."

We settle in, chirping at each other over missed shots and arguing calls. It feels... normal. It's strange how quickly I went from the new guy to a part of this team. There's plenty of ego in this room—enough to fill that big-ass stadium only a couple of blocks away, but there's also a sense of brotherhood that took me two years to break through with the Blue Devils. Even Luka seems relaxed, trash-talking Aleksi in Finnish just to piss him off.

"Speaking of scoring," Aleksi says during a break between games, his tone too casual. "I'm surprised Coach Wrenley didn't bench you for the rest of the season."

"What? Why would he do that?" I ask.

"Goddamn it, Monty. You're really going to pretend that we didn't all witness you eye-fucking the coach's daughter right in front of him during the slapshot challenge?" Hunter says, balling up his paper napkin and tossing it at me.

"I was just watching my opponent shoot pucks at me. It's literally my job," I say.

Chuckles from the guys fill the room, and more balled-up napkins come flying at my head from different angles.

The first game ends, and Slade stands, grabbing empty bottles. "Dumont. Help me get more beer."

I follow him to the kitchen, grateful for the escape. I turn to the fridge, grabbing beers out of it.

"You're serious about her."

It's not a question.

"Doesn't matter. Seven will kill me." I run a hand through my hair. "You've seen what he does to guys who even look at her the wrong way. And things aren't exactly going great between us right now."

Slade leans against the counter. "You couldn't have fucked up as bad as I did starting out with Penelope. I promise you that."

"Want to bet?"

"Did you threaten every guy on campus to stay away from her

and ruin her Olympic skating dreams?" He takes a pull from his beer. "Because that's what I did."

I stare at him. "You ruined her chance at the Olympics?"

He shrugs, as if playing it off like it's not a big deal, but his expression gives him away, darkening at the memory as if he still has regrets. "More or less. She ended up going... just a lot later than she had planned." He clears his throat. "The point is, her dad was my coach, too, and then my GM. If I can make it out of the doghouse for my sins, you can, too. But be sure it's what you want. Sam stunted my career for four years, sending me to the farm team when I was expected to be a first-round pick in the NHL draft, to teach me a lesson—Seven will end your existence all together."

My jaw tightens as Slade talks about Seven's wrath, but it's not fear I feel—it's doubt. Doubt that Cammy would even want me to fight for her. Doubt that I'll ever win her over without telling her what happened that night with Angelica hitting that guardrail. Or maybe it's doubt that I'm good enough for her—that I'm the right choice. Seven's wrong to think that I just want a casual one night with Cammy, only to toss her out when I'm done. But that doesn't mean he's wrong about whether or not I'm the right choice for her.

I shake off the thought. I can't think that way. Whatever it takes, I need to be the man who deserves Cammy.

"I know... he already told me he would, in far fewer words. Your wife threatened me, too. But you're saying she got over it?"

Slade laughs. "She won't let me forget it. I'll put it that way. But every morning when I wake up to her and the life we're building... I know that it was worth the shit days when I thought I might have given up the NHL for nothing," he says. "From what I understand, you two have history."

"Penelope told you that?" I shouldn't be surprised that she told him.

He shakes his head and takes a pull from his beer. "Nope. Welcome to the Hawkeyes. The stadium's too small to hold big secrets." His gaze flashes to the TV when the guys all yell at a play that Luka made, and then he turns back to me. "I don't know the details between you and Cammy, and I don't need to. Just know that Cammy is the unofficial little sister of this team, just like Penelope was. There are a lot of people in this franchise that won't take kindly to seeing her get hurt, especially by a player with a reputation. Whatever you decide to do, be intentional about it. Don't fuck around," he says. "That's the best advice I received from a very wise player."

"Really? Who?"

"Seven Wrenley."

I nod. "Okay... I got it," I say. "What should I do about him?"

"About Wrenley?" he asks, his eyes back on the TV, watching Luka and Hunter play against each other.

"He told me to stay away from her if I want a spot on this team."

He thinks for a second. "Then my advice is: don't let him find out."

"Great, thank you for that. Really helpful," I deadpan and head for the living room. I'm up next.

"I'm kidding," he says, holding out an arm to stop me. "All I can tell you is that when it came time for me to step up or step out in Sam Roberts' eyes, I already knew what my end game was. And I'll tell you a little secret—it wasn't hockey. Penelope's always been the end game for me, and she always will be. I'm not going to lie to you—it wasn't easy. I didn't know if Penelope would forgive me. I didn't know if Sam would ever give me a shot. But I knew I couldn't live with myself if I didn't try. The question you need to ask yourself is: 'what's my end game?' And what are you willing to give up to get it?"

Remembering the look on Cammy's face the other night, I could see that something was changing between us. She almost let me kiss her, which tells me that I'm not as far off as I thought I was when I showed up here weeks ago. Without hurting Angelica's chances for her promotion by coming clean with Cammy, I have to find a way to prove to Cammy that there's only ever been her since we met.

We head back to the living room where Hunter and Aleksi are arguing about a penalty call.

"Finally," Aleksi says. "I was about to send a search party."

"Or call Cammy," Luka spits out.

"Shut up and play," I tell them, but there's no heat in it. These guys might give me shit, but they've got my back... and I'm going to need it.

As we settle back into the game, I catch Slade watching me. He gives me a slight nod—approval, maybe. Or warning. Probably both.

I might not have all the answers, but I know one thing for sure: Cammy is my end game. And no matter what it takes, I'm going to prove to her—and to Seven—that I'm worth the risk.

CHAPTER TEN

Cammy

"Catch!" Brynn calls out, tossing me a cucumber from across the kitchen of Brynn and my dad's house in a gated community just outside of Seattle. Coach Haynes, and several other retired Hawkeyes players have houses here.

They bought this house when my dad retired, keeping Brynn's apartment across from The Commons as Brynn's writing sanctuary. They alternate between the apartment and house, depending on the hockey schedule.

I snag the cucumber in both hands just in time before it tumbles to the floor, and then reach for the cutting board she's laid out.

"Your volleyball skills are still sharp," she notes, mixing something that smells like honey and oatmeal in a bowl. "Now slice that up for eye covers while I finish this base for our facemasks."

I settle onto my usual bar stool at her massive kitchen island, watching as she scoops different ingredients from several bowls of natural ingredients all laid out. The familiar routine of our once-a-month Saturday girls' night is already starting to ease some of the tension lingering after the slapshot preview a few days ago.

Soon, Juliet, Isla, and Penelope will be walking through that door, all wives of retired or current Hawkeyes players. Aria, Kendall, and I are the only three single ladies in the group, but Kendall is at some sports medicine conference this week, and Aria said she is putting in extra hours at the office this week in an attempt to dazzle Everett so he'll see the value in having two assistants.

"You know we could just buy masks from the store, right?" I tease, carefully slicing the cucumber.

"Where's the fun in that?" She tosses me a block of cheese next. "And have you ever read the ingredient list on the back of most of those? No thanks. These facemasks are so clean, we could eat them," she says, mixing up her green goop that smells surprisingly good. "While you're being helpful, can you start on the charcuterie board after you're done with the cucumber? The girls will be here soon."

I begin arranging meats and cheeses and pre-slicing fruit, falling into comfortable silence as Brynn works her magic with the face mask ingredients. The quiet lasts approximately thirty seconds.

"Are we going to talk about what happened at the preview two days ago? Or are we just going to pretend it didn't happen like your dad is doing?" Brynn asks.

"He hasn't talked to you about it yet?" I ask.

Brynn keeps stirring her goop, adding more ingredients to it. "Nope. He's just walking around here like he didn't just bet the new starting goalie to kick rocks if he loses. Do you realize how insane this is? And if JP wins this bet, he's got a clean slate with your dad. That's a big deal."

The sound of the knife hitting the cutting board keeps a rhythm as I attempt to slice even cucumber rounds. "I know... and if dad wins, Penelope will never forgive me."

And then JP will leave, and who knows if I'll ever see him again.

"So, what's the real problem here? The bet itself, or the fact that he's willing to risk everything for you?" she asks, catching me off guard.

My knife stills on the cutting board. "Risk everything for me...?" I ask, playing dumb.

"Come on, Cammy. It's pretty obvious what this is all about. That boy has it bad for you."

My eyes lift up to hers. "What do you mean?"

"Think about it, Cammy. Two other teams were offering him secure contracts. But he picked a PTO with the Hawkeyes—the hardest option. Why? Because this isn't about hockey. It's about proving himself to your dad. To you. Don't you see what JP wants?" she asks, looking up from her bowl of smashed avocado and whatever else she put in there.

I shake my head. "It's not his last chance. Two other teams were ready to sign him. I'm sure he could still get one of those contracts even if he walked away from the Hawkeyes."

"I don't think you get it. He gave up signing with those teams for a PTO with the Hawkeyes. Now why would someone pass up a five-year contract to try out for a team instead?" she asks. "Unless he has other motives that maybe aren't hockey related."

Before I can tell her that she's wrong, heavy footsteps sound on the stairs. My dad appears in the doorway, dressed casually in a pair of shorts, flip flops, and a Scallywag's T-shirt, like he should be in Mexico at his beach house and not in the drizzly weather of Seattle as we move into late September and the pre-season.

"Did I hear JP's name?" he asks, his expression darkening slightly.

"We were just discussing the auction preview," Brynn says smoothly.

My dad turns to me. "Listen, Cam, I did what I did to protect you. Dumont's skating on thin ice—literally. A guy like him doesn't risk his career without an angle. Don't let him drag you into his mess."

"He's not trying to drag me into anything. You bet him his

career. How does he back down from something like that? Everett is not going to be happy if he finds out about this bet you two made."

My dad's facial expression doesn't change. It's hard to threaten someone when they have nothing to lose. My dad is coaching the special teams because Coach Haynes begged him to.

"Are you sure about that? He's already made his move, Cam. Now it's your turn to think about what happens if he loses."

"Seven," Brynn warns.

He raises his hands in surrender, pulling Milo off the counter and back into his arms. "All right, all right. We'll be in the man cave downstairs if you need us. Come on, buddy, let's leave the ladies to their spa night. By the way, you looked good out there at that preview. You're improving, kiddo."

After a brief pause, he asks, "How's the rest of the auction-planning going?" His tone suggests he's really asking about JP.

"It's... going," I say carefully. "Lots of moving parts."

"Mm-hmm." He studies me for a moment. "Just remember what I taught you about taking shots under pressure. Keep your head up, follow through—"

"And don't let the goalie get in your head," I finish with him, earning a proud smile that doesn't quite reach his eyes.

"It works on the ice but also everywhere else. You're doing good. I'm proud of you for taking this on and helping Autumn and Briggs, and all the families that need these condos built," he says.

"Thanks, Dad," I say.

He nods and then walks past Brynn, sticking his finger on the edge of the facemask bowl, swiping some onto his finger, and then sucking it off.

"That's delicious, baby. You could eat that with chips."

Brynn beams back at his praise.

Just as he disappears down the basement stairs of the house to my dad's man cave, the front door bursts open with enough force to rattle the wine glasses. Aria storms in, mascara streaking down her cheeks, her usual sweet-as-a-peach, prim and proper, polished appearance completely undone. The bow in her low ponytail left askew. Something's not right.

Brynn and I share a concerned look. We weren't expecting her.

She's supposed to be at the stadium putting in extra time.

"What happened to you?" Brynn asks, jogging around the island toward her.

"He fired me," she announces, her voice cracking.

"What do you mean he fired you? Weren't you going into work today?" I ask, jumping out of my seat and pulling out the one next to me for her.

She takes my offer and sits down, slumping in the chair.

Aria is as graceful as a swan; she never slumps.

"I knew Everett didn't see my worth. But you know what? I don't regret putting myself out there. Better to take the risk than sit around wondering 'what if.'"

Her words hit me harder than I want to admit. What if I'm too afraid to take the shot with JP? What if I've already missed it?

"Oh, honey." Brynn rushes forward to the chair Aria is perched on, pulling her into a hug.

I point to the carrot in her hand. I know what she needs. "Do you want some wine to go with that?"

"Got anything stronger?" she asks.

"That's my girl. Coming up," I say and head for my dad's office, where he keeps the good stuff.

The thought of Everett firing her has me thinking about my own situation with the slapshot bet. What if Everett finds out that I knew about this bet and didn't prevent it from happening? I try to push off the thought for now. Maybe JP will win the slapshot, and my concern will be for nothing.

Soon, the kitchen fills with the rest of our usual crew—Penelope, Juliet, and Isla, all bearing wine and sympathy for Aria. Brynn starts applying face masks to everyone while I finish the snack spread.

"We should go to Ground Zero on Thursday. It's ladies'

night," Isla, the wife of retired player Kaenan Altman, declares as Brynn smooths green clay over her cheeks. "A girls' night out to help Aria forget about Everett, and we haven't had a girls' night out on the town in ages."

The conversation shifts to planning our night out at Ground Zero, but I can't shake Brynn's words from earlier. A hockey player willing to risk his career for a chance with me. It should mean something—everything, really.

But then I remember Angelica's name lighting up his phone after the slapshot, how quickly he left that night in San Diego, how he left my apartment after she called again last week, not giving me an explanation for what happened the night of the accident.

If JP wants to be with me so badly, why is she still in the picture? Why can't he just tell me the truth about what happened? Or is he really the player my dad says he is?

"Earth to Cammy." Penelope waves a hand in front of my face, snapping me from my thoughts. "You're thinking too hard. I can see it through the face mask."

I force a laugh, accepting the fresh glass of wine she offers. "Just planning my strategy for Monday and that long list of emails I need to get through."

The wine and laughter should be enough to drown out my doubts. A hockey player risking everything for me? Maybe it's not just a game to JP after all.

CHAPTER ELEVEN

Cammy

I've been staring at the same spreadsheet for twenty minutes, but my mind keeps drifting back to the slapshot bet that my dad and JP are now willing to risk their careers for.

My phone buzzes, Brynn's name lighting up the screen.

> **Brynn:** We didn't get to finish our conversation on Saturday night. What are you going to do about that bet between Seven and JP?

I read her comment, biting on my thumbnail, trying to determine how to respond. But how can I respond when I don't even know what I'm going to do about it myself? Or if there is anything I can do about it.

> **Cammy:** I'm at work. And I haven't decided.

> **Brynn: Haven't decided? You're just going to let them duke it out on the ice?**

> **Cammy: It's not my call. I tried to talk them out of it on the ice. Neither of them would listen to me, and they both agreed to the bet.**

> **Brynn: This is crazy. Does Penelope know about this yet?**

> **Cammy: Not that I know of.**

I shove the phone into my purse, ignoring the conversation entirely. I have no idea what will happen if Penelope or Everett find out about the slapshot bet, and I'm hoping they never do.

I focus my attention on the list of emails Everett's assistant gave me. That's the one thing in my life I can control.

Sure enough, the Kauffmans are as well connected as Phil Carlton assumed. The list is triple the number of contacts that the Hawkeyes and the foundation had combined. I'm going to need a hand massage after this.

I glance back at the list in front of me when a shadow falls across my desk. I look up to find JP standing there, hair still damp from a shower after the morning skate, I assume. He's holding a to-go coffee cup and a paper bag from Serendipity's and wearing that infuriating half-smile that makes my stomach flip.

"Hello, mon petit oiseau," he says.

"I still don't know what that means." I straighten in my chair, aiming for professional detachment. "What are you doing here?"

He holds up the coffee and bag. "Peace offering? I heard you have a big day of auction stuff to do. I thought this would help."

"How do you know my coffee order?"

"I have my sources." He grins, setting the items on my desk. The familiar scent of Serendipity's caramel latte and what could be a breakfast sandwich waft toward me, making my traitorous stomach growl. "Plus, you look like you're about to bite someone's head off, and I figured it's better safe than sorry."

"I'm sure you could find someone more willing to accept your thoughtful gift. Like, say, Angelica?" I start, but my stomach betrays me with another growl.

"That would be a waste—she'd never eat this. She's lactose intolerant, and there's dairy in all of this."

"Of course she is," I grumble under my breath.

JP ignores my comment. "Besides, she's in San Francisco working on a big case. And I got this for you, not for her. And I'm glad I did... When's the last time you ate?"

A part of me wants to push him for answers like Brynn told me to, but I still have hundreds of emails to get to, and my boss's office isn't the place I want to have this conversation.

I glance at my computer clock, wincing when I realize it's almost noon. "I've been busy."

"Perfect timing then," he says, picking up my latte and sandwich. "Grab your purse. You can eat on the way. Let's go."

I blink twice at him and then lean forward in my chair. "You can't just barge into my place of employment and sweep me out of here just because you're the talent. I have work to do, and you haven't even told me where we'd be going."

His crystal-blue eyes glitter back at me. "That's because it's a surprise, but I promise you, you'll like it."

I lean back, crossing my arms. "I can't. I have work to do."

He glances down at the pages of emails I received from Everett's assistant this morning. "That list of emails? It'll be here when you get back." He raises an eyebrow. "I'm here to help you with the auction, remember? Come on, Cammy. I know a place that will help us check off a few more items on the list."

"Does this count as our date from the bet?" I ask.

His lip curls just a little at the corner of his perfect mouth. "Is that what it will take to get you to come with me?"

The door to Penelope's office swings open, and she emerges with her purse hanging off her elbow as her face is still buried in her phone, feverishly typing up an email.

"Hey, Cammy, Slade and I are going to lunch. I should be back in a couple of hours."

"Okay, have a good lunch," I tell her, though she hasn't looked up yet.

Does she even know that JP is in her office, trying to take off with her assistant? The door to the GM's suite opens, and Slade walks through the door in a pair of dark jeans and a Hawkeyes T-shirt. His smile illuminates when he sees Penelope. Then his eyes flash over to JP standing in front of my desk.

"JP. Good practice today. That knee seems to be doing better," he says, heading for my desk, flashing me a smile as well.

"Yeah, thanks, the new PT downstairs has been helping a lot."

"Good, I'm glad to hear it. Our previous PT, Keely, was great, but when Aisa retired and they moved to Texas, she made sure to train up a great replacement. Use that resource as much as you need," he says. "So, what are you doing up here?" Slade asks as he stops at my desk while Penelope seems to still be finishing up an email.

"I'm helping Cammy with the auction. I have an idea I want to show her."

Penelope's ears must be trained to the word "auction" because she perks up from her phone. "Oh, an idea for the auction? Well your last one was a huge success. I approve." She beams at JP and then at me. "Have fun."

"Are you ready to go?" Slade asks, offering his arm for her to grab onto.

"Yep, all set." She beams back and then turns to me. "You two have fun. I'm excited to see what you come back with."

An ulcer most likely.

I watch helplessly as Penelope and Slade leave, noting the way Slade winks at JP before they disappear down the hall. When did they become so chummy? I guess that happens with teammates.

JP holds up my latte and sandwich. "Shall we?"

I take it reluctantly, knowing I've been outmaneuvered. "Fine. But this counts as our date."

I want to say no, to push him away again, but the look in his eyes stops me. He's trying. And for once, I don't want to be the one holding all the walls in place.

"Of course," he agrees, but his smile says otherwise. "That's what we agreed to."

The moment we get into the cab, JP gives the driver a destination. "Pike's Place, please."

It's been years since I've been there. My dad took me to all the tourists' sights when I first got here, and I loved it. But why is JP taking me there now... I have no clue.

JP chats easily with the driver the entire way over, a die-hard Hawkeyes fan who recognizes him immediately. I watch, surprised by how genuine JP is as he answers questions about the upcoming season and signs the driver's hat.

"My kid's gonna flip when he sees this," the driver says, grinning at the signature. "He's been playing goalie since he was five."

"What's his name?" JP asks.

"Connor."

JP pulls out his phone. "I'll make a note to send home opener tickets to the box office for you."

Seeing JP like this with fans, it reminds me of why I've always thought there was a deeper side to him, past the cocky smile and reputation.

"I got it," I jump in and offer, pushing JP's hand down with his phone in it. "When I get back to the office, I'll have two of JP's home tickets waiting at will-call for you for the first home game."

JP looks at me and smiles.

The cab pulls up to the market, and JP steps out first, turning to offer me his hand. I hesitate for a split second before taking it, trying to ignore the spark that shoots through me at his touch.

"Ready?" he asks, his voice soft.

I nod as he helps me out of the cab.

The market bustles around us, filled with the familiar sounds and smells that always make me feel at home. Vendors call out their wares, fish fly through the air at the famous fish market, and tourists snap photos of everything in sight.

"This way," JP says, his hand finding the small of my back as he guides me through the crowd. The touch is light, barely there, but it burns through my jacket.

We stop at a small booth tucked away from the main thoroughfare. An older man sits surrounded by intricately carved wooden figures with gorgeous detailing—everything from tiny animals to larger pieces that seem like they belong in an art gallery.

"Hey, Pete," JP calls out.

The man looks up, and then I realize exactly who it is. It's Pete, the head of maintenance and the Zamboni driver.

"JP! Didn't expect to see you today." Pete shifts his vision to see me. We've met several times whenever he has a meeting with Penelope. "Cammy, what a pleasant surprise. You're both here together?" he asks. "Is something wrong at the stadium?"

JP waves off Pete's concern. "No, no, nothing like that. Actually, Pete, we're here about the charity auction. We're looking for vendors who would be willing to donate something for the auction. Would you be interested in donating a piece?"

Pete's eyes sparkle. "For the Kids with Cancer Foundation? Absolutely, it's a great cause—I'd do anything to help Briggs and Autumn and all of those families," he says, then thinks for a second. "I've got something special in mind. Been working on a design—a phoenix rising. Seems fitting, don't you think?"

As they discuss details, I catch JP watching me from the corner of his eye as I find a small bird carving, an intricately hand-painted, little finch with warm-colored cheeks.

It fits so perfectly in my hands, and the warmth of the wood heating in my hands brings the bird practically to life.

"Thanks for your time, Pete. We're going to walk around for

a bit, and I need to get Cammy some lunch. But if you don't mind bringing the item up to Penelope's office when you have it ready, that would be great."

We say our goodbyes and start to casually walk around, both pointing out different vendors or things we notice that neither of us have seen before.

"Hungry?" JP asks.

"Starving," I admit. The latte and sandwich were a good start on the way over, but now I need lunch.

He grins. "Good thing I know just the place. But first—" He stops at a popcorn vendor and asks what flavor I want. I pick BBQ, while he picks dill pickle, ordering a bag for each of us.

I scratch my nose. "Dill pickle?

"You're going to wish you ordered it," he warns.

"I don't think so," I say quickly.

His laugh is rich and warm. The vendor hands JP the bags, and he passes me the BBQ, still hot and perfectly salted.

We walk through the market, and I find myself relaxing despite my best intentions. JP points out his favorite spots, tells stories about the vendors he's met, and somehow makes me laugh more than I have in weeks.

I reach over and steal a piece of his popcorn.

"Thought you didn't want to try mine," he teases but tilts the bag toward me so I'll take more.

"Yours is better," I say, grabbing another handful, ignoring the fact that he was right.

"Tu es impossible," he murmurs, smiling fondly.

"What does that mean?"

"That you're impossible," he translates. "But in a good way."

I roll my eyes, but I'm fighting back a smile. "So, is this your thing? Do you have a feeder kink that I should know about?"

JP's laugh rumbles through him, warm and unrestrained, before he shakes his head, still grinning. "A feeder kink?"

As if a jock who's spent his entire life in a locker room doesn't know what a feeder kink is, he just wants to hear me explain it.

I lift a shoulder, feigning innocence. "Yeah. You know... do you become aroused by feeding your dates?"

He lifts an eyebrow at me like I've lost my mind, but the slow spread of his grin says he's intrigued.

I sigh, giving in. "First, the Chinese takeout at Cooper's, then food at my apartment last week, then Serendipity's this morning... and now this?" I gesture toward the popcorn between us. "You're feeding me."

His smirk turns wicked, his voice dropping low. "No, I don't have a feeder kink, but I'll admit that I enjoy feeding *you*. You're nicer to me when you're not hangry," He leans in slightly, eyes locked on mine, amusement flickering beneath something darker. Deeper. "Besides, this is a date, Cammy. I said dinner, which implies food." His fingers graze mine as he takes a piece of popcorn and pops it into his mouth, chewing slowly, deliberately. "But if you must know..." His gaze dips, trailing over me in a way that sends heat straight to my core.

"Anything that has to do with you is a turn-on."

The words hit me like a physical force, and I have to avert my gaze. Because for a moment, I almost believe him.

He looks over at me as we walk. "Am I going to get in trouble for saying that?"

I think about it for a second, feeling the warmth in my cheeks. "No, you're not in trouble. Not yet, anyway," I say.

"Come on," he says, sensing my withdrawal. "There's a pizza place around the corner. All-you-can-eat lunch buffet. Aleksi found it, and now the guys are here every afternoon."

"How will they stay in business when the entire Hawkeyes team finds it?"

"Too late. Aleksi heard about this place from Talon Brecka, the wide receiver for the Seattle football team."

The pizza place is exactly the kind of hole-in-the-wall spot I love—warm, crowded, and smelling like heaven. As JP holds the door open for me, I hear familiar voices.

"Monty!" Aleksi calls out from a corner booth. He's sitting

with Hunter, Luka, and Wolf, all of them surrounded by empty plates. "And little Wrenley! Come join us."

JP glances at me, letting me make the call. I hesitate for a moment, but having the guys here might make this easier. A buffer between me and whatever this thing is with JP.

"Sure," I say, heading toward their table.

"What are you two out doing today?" Hunter says as we slide into the booth.

"We went to Pike's Place to ask Pete for a silent auction item for the foundation... and since we have you here..." he starts.

"What? You need signed gear or something?"

I pull out my phone, opening my notes. "Actually, we could use some player participation. The silent auction is coming together, but we need some live auction items."

"Like what?" Wolf asks in the next booth with a mouthful of pizza.

"Date with a player?" JP suggests. "Hockey lessons?"

Hunter perks up. "I'm in for the date thing. Could be fun."

"Same," Luka says, then grins. "Though, I'll probably bring in more than Reed."

"You wish," Hunter scoffs.

Just like that, we're planning. The guys start one-upping each other, promising bigger and better auction items. By the time they leave, we've secured dates, lessons, and even a Christmas light hanging service from Wolf, who apparently has experience as a holiday decorator.

"That was... surprisingly productive," I say once we're alone, finding our own booth.

JP stands, offering his hand. "Come on, let's get some food before you pass out."

At the counter, he hands me a plate. "So," he says as we wait in line. "How'd you end up working for the Hawkeyes?"

I tense slightly. "You mean, how'd I end up working for my dad's team?"

"I mean, did you ever think about doing something else? Or

was hockey always the plan?"

Something in his tone makes me look up. He's watching me with genuine interest, no judgment.

"I've always loved sports. My volleyball team took state my senior year, and I planned on going to college in Minnesota for Sports Management. Then I found out about Seven, and everything just... clicked. It finally made sense why I was more athletic than anyone else in my family. Why I never quite fit into my mom's world, or why Eli and I never really had anything in common. Suddenly, it all just lined up."

"So, then you gave up on going to a college close to home and came here?" he asks, piecing together the rest of my story.

"My mom fought me on it—wanted to keep me close. I think she wanted to control my relationship with Seven. But then he offered to pay for my tuition to any college I wanted, and Penelope offered me an internship under her in Seattle. It all fell into place."

JP's mouth quirks up, but there's something guarded in his expression. "Your mom sounds like she and my dad would get along."

"Yeah? The great Jon Paul Dumont Senior isn't father of the year?"

His laugh is hollow. "Let's just say being the son of a hockey legend comes with expectations. Especially when you're named after him."

"Is that why you go by JP?"

"Partly," he admits. "But mostly because Jon Paul Dumont Junior is a mouthful, and I wanted something that was just... mine."

We find a quiet table in the corner, our pizza steaming between us. The conversation flows easier now, stories of growing up in the shadow of famous parents, of finding our own way.

"Sometimes I wonder," I say, wiping sauce from my lip, "if we can ever really escape our parents' legacy."

JP reaches across the table, his thumb catching a spot of sauce I missed. "Maybe we're not supposed to escape it. Maybe we're supposed to redefine it."

His touch lingers, and suddenly I'm very aware of how close we are. Of how easy it would be to lean forward, to close the distance...

A burst of laughter from nearby breaks the moment. JP pulls back, and I clear my throat.

"I should probably get back to the office," I say, even though we both know Penelope gave me the afternoon off.

"Let me walk you," he offers. "It's on my way."

The walk is quiet, comfortable in a way that scares me. The Seattle afternoon has turned gray, a light drizzle falling around us. JP pulls me closer under his umbrella, and I let him.

At the door, JP turns to face me, his expression serious.

"Thank you for today," he says.

"For what?"

"For giving me a chance to show you who I am now."

I swallow hard. "Jon Paul..."

"I know," he says quickly. "I know I hurt you before. But, Cammy..." He steps closer, his hand coming up to cup my cheek. "If I could tell you why I left that night—why I had to leave—I would. But it's not just my secret to share." His thumb brushes my cheek, and the vulnerability in his eyes steals my breath. "All I can ask is that you give me a chance to make it right."

I should step back. I should go inside. I should do anything but stand here, letting him touch me like this.

I don't move.

"The bet with my dad. It's insane. Why did you agree to it?"

He stares back at me for a moment. "Because I'm here for redemption, Cammy. From him, from you, from the Hawkeyes."

I never thought about it like this. That JP feels he's here to prove himself.

"Bonne nuit, ma belle," he whispers, pressing a soft kiss to my forehead before stepping back.

I watch him walk away, my skin tingling where his lips touched. This day carries the weight of possibility.

And I realize something terrifying.
I'm starting to believe him.

CHAPTER TWELVE

JP

"So," Aleksi says, his beer bottle halfway to his mouth, sitting on the armchair to the left of me in my living room. Hunter and I are going head-to-head on an old-school fighting game that was popular in Finland years ago. "You coming out tonight to Ground Zero with us or what? It's the dance club the girls are going to tonight to cheer up Aria. Cammy's going," he says, waggling his eyebrows as if to encourage me.

Hearing her name spikes the dopamine receptors in my brain.

I take a long pull from my beer, buying time. The truth is, I can't stop thinking about yesterday—about how natural it felt walking through Pike's Place with her, sharing stories over pizza, seeing her smile. About how close I came to kissing her.

My pulse ticks up at the thought of her being there. Out of the office. Relaxed. Maybe even happy. I tell myself it's curiosity. Nothing more.

My imagination instantly conjures up a dozen mental images I have no business entertaining. Her in some kind of short dress. Her hair loose, her smile lighting up the room. Probably surrounded by guys who don't have to fight their past just to stand next to her.

He leans back in his chair and takes another long swig of beer. "But hey, don't come if you don't want to. More room for me to swoop in."

Hunter snorts from his spot at the bar. "He's baiting you to come," he tells me. "Nice try, Mäk. We all know you've got eyes for the good doctor."

Dr. Kendall Hensen—the new Hawkeyes in-house doctor after Dr. Omar retired at the end of last season.

Hunter leans in toward me, both of us still focused on the game in front of us. "Word is, Kendall is back from her conference, and she's going out with the girls. Mäk doesn't want to go alone—needs an entourage."

Aleksi shoots a glare in his direction and then tosses a mini basketball at his shoulder. It bounces off, and Hunter laughs.

"Tell me I didn't see you in Kendall's office using the full-length skeleton like a ventriloquist. Making jokes about the funny bone."

We all laugh, except for Aleksi, who's sort of sulking in his chair. "I get nervous, okay? She's beautiful, and every time I go to see her—"

Scottie Easton's voice breaks through from the kitchen, cutting him off. "He starts jabbering like a buffoon and won't shut the hell up."

"Shut up, East." Aleksi snarls.

"No, you shut up, Mäk. I had to wait for twenty minutes and listen to you go on and on about how scientists believe that Pluto is just one giant space ice fart, while you were taking up my weekly check-in appointment," Scottie says, a large bowl of cereal in his hands, as if he hadn't just demolished two burgers and a side of BBQ ribs thirty minutes ago at lunch. "I just about stabbed my eyes out with my own thumbs to numb the pain of extreme secondhand embarrassment. You make it a goddamn art form."

Aleksi scoffs at Scottie and then looks over at me. "Forget him. So, are you in?"

Who the hell am I kidding? I'm not going to say no to being in the same room as the woman I can't stop thinking about.

"Yeah," I say as the game ends, kicking Hunter's ass for the third time this week. He mutters "motherfucker" and tosses the controller on the couch.

The truth is, seeing Cammy in the middle of a dance floor and being the only guy in the room that she won't let touch her is going to be painful. God help me for what I'm capable of if some prick walks up and thinks he's going to grind up against her on the dance floor right in front of me.

On second thought... Maybe it's better that I don't go. The last thing I need is another mugshot and Angelica coming down to bail me out of jail for a second time, even if the first time wasn't my fault.

Aleksi claps his hands together like he's won something. "That's the spirit, Dumont. Ziegler's meeting us there, and Hartley doesn't have a sitter for Adeline, so he's out."

"Hunter... you in?" Mäkelin asks, pointing to him.

Hunter stands up off the couch. "I'll go. But no breakdancing this time, Mäkelin, or I swear I'm not taking you to the emergency room again."

Then Aleksi looks at Scottie. "What about you? You in, East?"

I glance over to see Scottie topping off his bowl of cereal for the second time. "Can I bring the bowl?"

Aleksi shrugs. "Yeah, sure. Why not?"

An hour later, the music at Ground Zero is deafening. Strobe lights flash across the packed dance floor, highlighting sweaty bodies and wild grins. There's only one thing I'm here for. When I spot her across the room, I forget all about the crowd.

A woman walks up and grabs my hand, gripping it with both of hers, attempting to pull me toward the dance floor. "You're cute. Dance with me!" she says, yelling over the music.

"Sorry, I'm with someone," I tell her, and then twist my hand out of her grip.

She looks disappointed for a second, and then her eyes slide to the guy behind me—Hunter—and her eyes light back up.

"No problem," she says. "I'll take him."

She pulls him toward the dance floor, and he goes willingly.

Aleksi wanders off, too, leaving Scottie and me to search for an open table.

I catch the sight of Wolf sitting at a large table already with beers ready to go. He waves us over.

In a matter of minutes, I glance out from my spot at the table, a cold beer in my hand. Wolf and Scottie are deep diving into puck theory, now with diagrams drawn on napkins.

Hunter's moved on from the blonde, already charming his way into dancing with three different women with that easy smile of his. He's in his element here.

Aleksi is attempting what he claims is dancing, but it looks more like he's having a seizure. I could care less about my teammates inability to dance because my attention keeps drifting to her.

Cammy's dancing with Aria and Kendall on the dance floor while Brynn, Penelope, and Isla are taking shots at the bar.

She's beautiful. No surprise there.

Anyone can see that, but seeing her like this—relaxed, happy, free—it hits differently. Makes me want to be a part of that somehow.

"You're staring," Aleksi says, sliding onto one of the barstools at the table.

"I'm not," I lie.

"Right." He follows my gaze. "You haven't taken your eyes off her since we got here."

I don't bother arguing. We both know he's right.

"I haven't seen you make a move with Dr. Hensen yet," I counter.

He looks over his shoulder. "Soon. I need to warm up."

I laugh, looking around to see the first round of beers are

gone. "Want a beer? I'm going up to the bar to get another round," I offer.

"Sure, thanks," he says, distracted by the diagram that Wolf has drawn as he gets sucked into their conversation.

I move through the crowd, but it's not easy. This place is packed for a Thursday night, but I guess Ladies' Night is a solid marketing gimmick.

When I finally make it through the crowd, I see the bar, at least three people deep around the entire perimeter. Six bartenders are working as fast as they can to fill drink orders. I see an opening as a small group moves away from the bar, and I slide in, beating out a few others. The crowd fills in quickly around me.

"Sorry... umm... excuse me," a familiar voice says, and my whole body tenses.

Cammy.

She's trying to squeeze in a few feet down the line from me without any success. Most everyone else is in the same position as she is, waiting for their drink order. She still hasn't seen me.

I can see the bartender on his way down the line—I'm up next.

I glance over to see Cammy moving down the line, trying to find another spot to get in, but she seems flustered. Just then, someone bumps into her, almost tripping her up in those four-inch heels of hers.

I whip an arm out and reach around her, my hand gripping her hip, yanking her to me. She crashes against my chest—the heat of her body radiating into my skin. She makes a cute squeaking noise, and I see the moment she notices her green hairband around my wrist, causing her eyes to shoot up finding mine—recognition flashing across her eyes.

"It's you?" she says as relief settles over her. "What are you doing?"

She doesn't pull away from me like I half expect her to.

"Helping," I say close to her ear, my cheek against her soft hair and my thumbs brushing against her hip bones, before I reach out for the bar. "This place is a zoo. Let me help."

Before she can argue, one of the people to our left loses their balance, causing me to cage her in with my arms as I press my palms to the bar, holding them off of bumping into her. The move has her flush against me, her back fitting perfectly against my chest. She freezes.

"Relax," I say. "Just keeping the animals at bay."

She hesitates, then relaxes slightly against me. "Thanks. I didn't think I was ever going to get through."

The bartender turns to us with a look that says he hates Ladies' Night. "What can I get for you?"

"Whatever she wants," I tell him.

"Are you sure?" she asks.

The guys can wait. I look over my shoulder, to find that everyone is preoccupied. No one is waiting on a beer.

"None of us are in a hurry. Ladies first."

A small smile pulls at her lips before she turns back to the bartender and bends forward to order, getting closer so the bartender can hear her.

Her ass presses against my crotch in our tight proximity.

I muffle out a groan at the feel of her ass pushing against me.

"Oh, I'm sorry. Are you okay?" she asks after she makes her order, seeing me grimace. She has no idea what she just did, and I won't tell her.

"I'm fine, don't worry about it. Did you get your order in?" I ask. Since I was preoccupied trying not to get hard and have Cammy running for the hills, I missed every word she told the bartender when she ordered.

I feel the heat of her through the thin material of her dress, the smell of her light floral perfume and sweat from her dancing. It would be so easy to pull her closer. To wrap my arms around her and lay a kiss on her bare shoulder, then imprint my lips on every inch of her beautiful neck. But I'm still on thin ice with her, and doing something like that will only push her further away.

"Thanks," she says when her drinks arrive.

He gives her the price, and I slap my card down before she can reach wherever she's keeping money in that tiny dress. If we were somewhere alone, I'd be happy to find out exactly where she puts it, myself.

"JP," she says, turning to argue, but the bartender takes the card and is already gone. "You don't have to do that. We can buy our own drinks."

The sound of her finally saying my nickname hits me—*JP*.

Off her lips, it sounds like an angel. My angel.

"You just called me JP."

She stalls for a second, her eyes searching mine. "I guess we're not at the office, so... I don't know, maybe it just slipped out."

"I like it when you call me that. It's worth every penny of the highway robbery prices here," I tell her with a grin.

She smiles back. "We can pay you back. None of the girls are going to expect you to pay for these."

I shake my head. "I've got it—I promise."

"Thank you... again."

"Anytime," I manage, fighting the urge to lean down and taste the words on her lips.

The bartender returns, and Cammy turns back.

She slips away before I can do something stupid, disappearing back into the crowd with her friends. I order a round of beers, but I know the bartender is going to make me wait longer this time, since I gave up my place in line.

It doesn't matter, as long as I can see her from where I'm standing.

Another ten minutes later, I get the beers and head back to the table, when I notice immediately that something has changed. She is over at her table, and all of the girls are standing with her. Her smile fades, and she presses a hand to her stomach. I'm moving before I can think better of it.

"Cammy?" I reach out for her. "What's wrong?"

"Nothing," she insists, laying her hand on my arm like she needs me for stability. Her face suddenly pales. The carefree glow from earlier is gone, replaced by a faint sheen of sweat on her forehead. She stumbles slightly, and my instincts kick in before she can hit the ground. "I just need some air."

"She mixed her drinks," Kendall explains. "Shots, a sugary martini, and then wine. She's not feeling well. I tried to see if she wants to go to the bathroom with me but—"

"I'll just get a cab and go home. You girls stay," she says.

"I've got her," I tell Kendall, Brynn, and Aria, who are all hovering. I wrap an arm around Cammy's waist. "I'll make sure she gets home safe."

Brynn eyes me carefully, then nods. "Text me when you get her settled?"

"I will."

I pull her with me, spotting Scottie getting up to head to the bathroom. He sees me and asks, "You two okay?"

I nod. "I'm taking her home. Can you and the guys make sure that all the Hawkeyes girls get home safe?"

He nods. "Of course. We'll make sure of it."

I help Cammy outside, grateful for the cool night air. She leans heavily against me as we wait for a cab, and I try not to think about how right she feels in my arms.

It's fucked up to be enjoying that, for once, she's not fighting me.

"I don't feel so good," she mumbles against my chest.

"I know," I say softly. "Let's get you home."

"And this is annoying." She pushes her hair out of her face a couple of times.

"Your hair?"

She nods, and then I remember that I have a way to fix that, though I've never done this before. I reach around her, pulling her green hair tie off my wrist, and then try to gather every strand together on the top of her head. It looks like a bird's nest with perfectly curled tendrils falling out of it, but it's the best I can do. I wrap the hair tie enough times that I know it will at least stay out of her face until she feels well enough to adjust it.

"My hair tie? But I thought it was your lucky charm?" she says. She's not fighting me, and I can already tell she's more comfortable with her hair out of her face and off of her neck.

"I'll get it back from you later. And anyway, I think it needed a recharge."

There is a small content sigh that comes out of her, against my chest as I wrap my arms back around her.

The cab arrives, and I give them the address to The Commons. As I get her into the elevator, she tells me she left her purse at Brynn's because she was going to crash there tonight. She only brought a credit card and her cell phone. She doesn't protest when I guide her up to my apartment or when I help her to my room.

"Here," I say, leading her into my walk-in closet. "You'll be more comfortable in one of my shirts. Pick out whatever you want to wear. I'm going to make you some chamomile tea. Maybe it will settle your stomach."

I leave her in my closet and head for the kitchen, giving her time to find what will be most comfortable for her.

By the time I heat the water, steam the tea bag, and put a little honey into it, she is asleep in my bed. She looks like she's always belonged there.

I set down the tea and some saltine crackers on the nightstand—just in case. And then I pull the comforter up over her shoulders and pull back the hair that's fallen into her face.

"Thank you," she murmurs, half-asleep. "You're not so bad sometimes."

I smile. "Get some rest. I'll be on the couch if you need anything."

"Why'd you have to go and screw it all up?" she murmurs, her words slurred but filled with raw emotion. "I thought... I thought you were different."

My heart clenches. This mess is of my own doing. I should be sliding into bed next to her. Holding her against me and kissing her goodnight.

"I'll earn it back. I promise," I say, pulling my comforter higher up over her shoulder. "However long it takes."

She's asleep before I finish speaking, but I mean every word. I'll spend the rest of my life making up for that night in San Diego if she'll let me.

Because Cammy Wrenley is my end game.

CHAPTER THIRTEEN

Cammy

I wake to the pattering of raindrops against the window and the darkness of the room. An alarm clock nearby reads that it's just before three in the morning. I stir against the pillow, trying to burrow deeper into the mattress, but it's no use—this isn't my bed.

The sheets are too smooth, the pillow too firm, and the room smells distinctly of JP. The smell of his cologne, the faint musk of sweat from long practices, and something I can only describe as... him.

This isn't my room, and I'm not in my apartment.

Flashes of last night flood back in, resolving my disorientation. I didn't get drunk last night, but I still remember the feeling of my stomach beginning to turn on me only halfway into our girls' night.

The club, the overly sweet cocktails that have my stomach churning just thinking about them, the overzealous DJ and his relentless bass amplifying it all. And then I remember JP steadying me, stepping in to help me at the bar, becoming a human shield to protect me, buying our drinks. Then I remember feeling sick, his arms anchoring me to him as he guided me through the chaos to take me home. His soft reassurances as he insisted on getting me there safely. Except... we didn't go to my place.

The memory of leaving my purse at Brynn's comes back to me.

I sit up carefully, my head feeling a little woozy with sleep and a slight headache, but so much better than when I left the club. There's a mug of chamomile tea gone cold, a plate of crackers I didn't touch, and water with a lemon slice sitting on the nightstand with two Tylenol. My phone's plugged into a charger I didn't bring, but clearly, JP thought of everything.

The blanket slides off my shoulders as I swing my legs over the edge of his bed. The plush carpeted bedroom floor touches my feet, as I look around. JP's packed Hawkeyes duffel bag with *Dumont* stitched on the side. The team leaves later this morning for their first out of town game.

Something else catches my eye—a figure stretched out on the floor beside the bed.

JP.

One arm is flung over his face, the other resting on his chest—he's asleep on the hard floor. It's not lost on me that he didn't try to sleep next to me on his memory foam mattress. A far better option for a professional athlete who's expected to play his first away game later tonight.

He could've taken the couch. It would have been far more comfortable.

Something warm stirs in my chest—he stayed. And also gave me space, not trying to use this moment as a time to get closer when I was too weak to care.

The dim glow creeping through the curtains from the city lights softens the sharp lines of his jaw and the strong column of his neck. I've never seen JP in an unflattering light—in fact, I don't think there is such a thing, but this right here—him asleep after taking care of me. This might be my favorite of all.

Without thinking, I crouch beside him, my hand lifting

slightly before hovering over his cheek. I don't touch him, but the thought lingers.

"JP," I whisper, my voice uncertain and quiet.

Should I be waking him up? Maybe it's better to let him sleep before he leaves town.

He stirs, his brow furrowing before his arm drops away. Slowly, his eyes flutter open, blinking a few times and then quickly sharpening with concern as they find mine.

"Cammy?" His voice is thick with sleep, but his worry slices through it. "What's wrong? Are you okay?"

I swallow against the lump in my throat. "Yeah. I'm sorry, did I wake you?"

"No, not exactly," he says.

"Couldn't sleep either?"

He chuckles softly. "It's hard to sleep when I know you're in my shirt, sleeping in my bed."

Heat climbs up my neck at his admission.

"I didn't mean to take your room. I didn't even realize—"

"It's okay," he cuts in, his tone gentle. "You didn't feel well, and I wanted you to be comfortable. Do you feel better?"

"Yeah... I do, thank you. But you're sleeping on the floor." My vision glides over him stretched out in a blanket that barely covers his feet.

"I wanted to be close in case you needed me. I was worried about you," he says, his voice soft. "I thought about lying next to you, but you'd been drinking, and with our history..." His words trail off, but I know where they're headed.

"And you didn't want me to think that you were taking advantage," I finish for him.

He just stares back, no point in confirming it—we both know.

"Your voice sounds better." The corners of his mouth lift slightly into a grin.

"After a long, hot shower, I'll be good as new," I admit, my voice quieter now. "Thank you for taking care of me last night. I feel bad that you had to leave your friends to take me home."

The corner of his mouth curves up. "Say that last part again," he interrupts, his tone teasing.

"What part? Take me home?"

I catch the glint of his smile in the low light. "Yeah." He lets out a gravely sigh. "I like the sound of that."

I bite my lip and glance down at my toes digging into the carpet, fighting back the smile threatening to take over. "You're ridiculous."

"I didn't mind leaving my friends or that club. Without you in it, it would have lost its appeal anyway," he says, his voice dipping low. "And I like taking care of you. I think that's becoming obvious."

His words hang between us, the weight of them sinking into my skin.

"Is that why you've been tossing pucks at me for years?" I ask, deflecting with humor to steady myself. "Or is that something you do for all the puck bunnies?"

JP's laugh is quiet but warm. "You think I toss pucks at everyone?"

I raise a brow, crossing my arms. "Don't you?"

He leans forward slightly, his eyes locking on mine. "Besides the kids in the stands who ask for them, I only toss pucks at one person."

The space between us shrinks, the air thickening as his words settle over me. "Why just me?"

He sits up, his movements slow, deliberate, until he's closer—so much taller than me even though I'm kneeling before him. His hand shifts, brushing against my knee in a touch so fleeting it could almost be accidental. But it's not.

The contact is electric, sparking something inside me that I know I should extinguish for the sake of my own heart. He hasn't told me the truth about that night, the one that left me doubting everything. But here, in the quiet darkness of this room, it's easier to push those fears aside. At least for just this moment.

"Because you're the only one I have a message for."

"And what's that?"

JP leans closer, his voice a rough whisper. "That I want a shot with you."

The world tilts. My throat tightens as I try to process his words, but there's no sarcasm to shield myself with, no witty comeback to deflect the truth I see in his eyes.

Before I can overthink it, I push up on my knees, my hand finding the back of his neck, pulling him toward me. My lips crash against his, desperate and searching. His arm wraps around my waist, and suddenly I'm in his lap, straddling him. His mouth claims mine, his hands skim up my sides. The heat of his touch sears through the thin fabric of his shirt I'm wearing, and his thumbs brush just beneath my breasts, sending a jolt of heat pooling low in my belly. I arch into him instinctively, a breathy moan escaping past my mouth as he deepens the kiss.

He groans against my lips at the friction. "You have no idea what you do to me, or what I would give to be close to you. Every time I see you, it's all I can do to not pull you into the nearest corner just to feel you close—to steal a minute with you. Just to get your beautiful hazel eyes on me for a second. My world calms when you're near."

His words hit me like a truth I've always known. He's always sought me out, always found a way to get time with me, no matter how crowded the room or how impossible the timing. Whether it was at games, charity events, or chance encounters, JP Dumont has been relentless in making me feel like I was worth the effort. The girl from his rival team.

I tilt my head back as his lips trail down my neck, grazing the sensitive curve where my pulse races. My fingers tangle into his hair, pulling him closer, needing more of him the way he needs me. The tension between us builds with every kiss, every touch.

"JP," I breathe, grinding down against him. The hard length of him pressing against my panties sends another jolt of heat spiraling through my core, dampening the thin fabric. His groan vibrates against my skin, low and guttural.

I feel so small in his arms—as if he could take me any second that he wants—but he doesn't. He's watching, waiting, letting me take control of where this leads.

"Say my name again. The way you know I like it," he demands, his voice rough.

I whisper it again, my voice trembling with the weight of how he's breaking down my walls I've built to keep him out.

"What do you need, Cammy? Whatever it is, it's yours. Just please... let it be me."

I pull him tighter, and his lips trail farther down, pushing the collar of the shirt I'm wearing to lay his lips against my chest. His hands shift to grip my ass cheeks, guiding me to grind on him even harder. If he keeps this up, I'll come just like this in his lap.

"I want to forget about San Diego, about you leaving. Just one night where none of that exists. No lies. No truth. Just us," I say, pulling his jaw up to kiss me.

"I want to tell you what happened. And I will someday," he says.

Someday. The word tastes like a promise I can't afford to believe in. I can't wait for someday. I'm barely holding on to today.

"And if someday never comes... then at least we'll have this."

His grip tightens like he feels the weight of my words. Then, suddenly, he shifts, rising to his feet with me in his arms, his voice rough and sure.

"Then I guess this is my last chance to make sure you never want to leave."

"Give it your best shot," I challenge.

JP lays me down on the bed and then pulls back slightly, his dark eyes locking with mine as if searching for any hesitation. "Tell me to stop, and I will."

My voice shakes as I cup his jaw, guiding him back to me. "Don't stop."

His groan rumbles through me, and in one swift motion, he pulls his shirt over his head, exposing the hard planes of his torso. My breath catches at the sight of him, but before I can say anything, his lips are on mine again, hungry and insistent.

His hands push up the hem of the shirt I borrowed, exposing my bare skin to the cool air. He follows the path of his hands with his lips, leaving a trail of heat as he goes. When he reaches my breast, his tongue swirls around the peak, drawing out a whimper from my lips. His hand mirrors the attention on the other side, kneading and teasing until I'm a trembling mess beneath him.

"JP," I beg, my voice breaking. "Please."

He lifts his head, his eyes dark with desire. "You're giving me one last time. You can't blame me for wanting to take my time, making sure that it's so good for you that you never forget me."

His hands slide down my sides, hooking into the waistband of my panties. Slowly, he peels them away, his lips following the movement until I'm bare beneath him. His vision glides over me, taking in every inch, as if this is the first time he's ever seen me naked.

"You're the vision of my fantasies. I'll never forget how perfect you look tonight," he murmurs, his voice deep yet gentle.

His knees hit the floor, his lips trailing heat down my stomach. His tongue swirls around my belly button and then kisses it gently before descending farther. And then he's there, lifting my legs over his shoulders, lowering his body until his head slides between my thighs. His tongue is hot and wet at my center, spreading me open with one long lick, pulling another whimper past my lips. Each graze of his teeth and flick of his tongue drawing me closer to the edge. My fingers thread through his hair, anchoring him to me, begging him to show me that he'll take care of me—that he won't let me fall again, like I did that night.

The physical act of the words I can't say out loud.

When his head dips even lower, abandoning my clit, his tongue presses into my center. A wave of pleasure shoots through me as I moan out a garbled version of "Oh, God." His thumb presses gently against my other entrance but doesn't penetrate. My breath catches, reminding me that he's the one in control. Every flick, every stroke of his fingers and tongue pushes me closer to the cliff, the tension building hotter and tighter until it's unbearable. His tongue traces a path that leaves me gasping, his name falling from my lips.

He tests me slowly, but then all at once, two soaked fingers slide gently but fully into me until I cry out his name as I come—my world shattering around me. My body trembles while wave after wave of pleasure crashes over me as he licks every drop of my arousal that he inspired. My hands fall away from his hair, my legs like Jell-O still wrapped around his shoulders.

"I'll never get tired of hearing you scream my name when you come," he says with a satisfied smirk.

"Then what are you waiting for?" I ask, challenging him to do it again.

He grins and then gently lets my legs down, wrapping them around his waist. He pulls my arms around his neck, lifting me up with him higher on the bed, laying my head on the pillow.

His lips find mine in a kiss that's equal parts passion and tenderness, and I lose myself in the sensation of his hands, his mouth, his body against mine. His hard cock, hot and heavy, cradles against my stomach, building heat low in my belly again for him—the promise that this moment between us isn't over.

He reaches for a condom in the top drawer of his nightstand, then rips the foil and slides it on.

He stares down at me, and I nod, letting him know that this is what I want, too.

He presses into me slowly, the stretch and fullness stealing my breath and leaving me gasping for air. We both groan in unison, as my fingers grip his shoulders, holding onto him as he fills me inch by inch. His every movement is deliberate and careful, like he's savoring this moment as much as I am.

A low groan rumbles from his chest when he finally seats himself fully, our bodies perfectly aligned. The sound vibrates through me, making every nerve in my body come alive. My head falls back against the pillow as I try to catch my breath, my heart pounding in my ears.

JP stills, his forehead pressing gently against mine. I can feel the slight tremble in his arms as he holds himself up, his jaw tight like he's fighting for control. His warm breath fans over my lips, mingling with mine in the shared space between us.

"Are you okay?" he murmurs, his voice thick and quiet, like he's afraid to break the fragile moment.

"Better than okay," I whisper, my arms wrapping around his neck as I pull him closer. My legs tighten around his waist, urging him on. "Move, JP. Please."

He does but slowly, his hips rolling in deliberate, unhurried strokes that send waves of pleasure rippling through me. His gaze locks on mine, intense and unyielding, and I feel completely exposed under the weight of it. I dig my nails into his back, dragging them lightly down his skin, and his response is instant—a guttural growl that has my name tangled in it.

"You feel incredible," he rasps, his voice rough with raw emotion. "You have no idea what you're doing to me. What it feels like to be inside you. Jesus Christ, Cammy, I never want to pull out."

I know how he feels. I don't want him to ever leave either, but my heart isn't built for another fall from him. My heart and my pride can't take it again. Tonight has to be the last time.

I tilt my hips, seeking more, desperate for the slow burn to ignite into something I can't control. "Don't stop," I beg, my voice barely above a whisper. "Please, don't stop."

"I won't," he promises, his lips brushing against the corner of my mouth before capturing mine in a kiss. "I've got you. And you'll always have me."

The rhythm shifts as he picks up the pace, his thrusts deeper, stronger, dragging me closer to the edge. His body feels like it was made for mine, the way every movement fits together perfectly. The tension coils tighter and tighter, a live wire sparking through me with every stroke.

His thick cock brushes against that devastatingly sensitive spot inside me, the one he's already worked into a needy bundle of nerves. Over and over, he finds it, relentless, precise. He knows exactly where to push, exactly how to drive me wild, and he's doing it on purpose.

I can feel my earlier release amplifying everything—every touch, every brush of his skin against mine. My body trembles beneath him, overwhelmed by the sheer intensity of it all.

I whimper his name, my nails digging into his back as my body tingles with pleasure.

JP groans, his voice dark with satisfaction. "That's it, mon ange... I can feel how close you are." His grip tightens on my thigh, lifting it higher, spreading me wider, and the change in angle makes me cry out. He drives in deep, his thick length stretching me so perfectly it borders on too much, but I don't want him to stop. I need more.

"Oh, God," I gasp, my breath coming in sharp, uneven bursts.

His lips find my jaw, trailing hot, open-mouthed kisses along my skin, his breath warm and frayed with restraint. "I know, baby," he murmurs, his voice rough with need. "Just let go. Let that sweet pink pussy grip me when you come all over my cock, pulsating around me. Soak me, Cammy."

His filthy words unravel something inside me as his lips close over my hardened nipple, sucking deep. A strangled moan slips from my lips as the pleasure crests, sharp and all-consuming. My body locks around him, spasming in tight, rhythmic pulses as the orgasm slams into me. I cry out, and he swallows it with a kiss, as a tidal wave of pleasure drags me underwater, leaving me gasping, shaking, and clinging to him.

JP groans, a raw, needy sound that vibrates against my skin. He thrusts deeper, chasing his own release, my walls clenching around him, milking him as he follows me over the edge. He buries himself to the hilt, his grip bruising on my hips as his cock pulses inside me, his rhythm faltering, giving into his own release, his cock twitching deep inside of me as his cum fills the condom. He groans out my name into the crook of my neck as the aftershocks ripple through his body.

We collapse together, tangled in each other, our breaths mingling in the quiet aftermath. JP presses soft kisses to my temple, my cheek, my lips, murmuring words of praise and affection in French. Words he refuses to translate because he claims that the English translation won't do them justice.

For a fleeting moment, I let myself believe this could be more than a night. That maybe, somehow, I can forget San Diego and forget that he's keeping a secret from me with a woman who is still in his life.

But the thought doesn't last, because I've been there. My mother lied to me for fourteen years of my life. My entire family kept the truth from me for their own selfish reasons.

My mother kept the secret to keep Eli.

Eli kept the secret to keep me from Seven.

My grandmother kept the secret so my mother wouldn't withhold me from her.

I can't help but wonder what JP's motives are for keeping what happened that night a secret.

After JP pulls out carefully, and we each take a moment to clean up in the bathroom, we end up back in bed together.

His hand lazily makes swirls around my back—over my shoulder and around my hip bone, as I lay my head against his chest.

"I know you said one last time, but I need to know something," he starts.

I peer up at him from my spot, tucked carefully against his side and under his arm. "What do you want to know?"

He stares up at the ceiling, gathering his thoughts.

"Hypothetically speaking, let's say I find a way to earn back your trust, to convince you to give me a second chance, to show you that you're all I've ever wanted and still are... Your father will never approve of me," he says, his eyes glancing back down at me. "Could you choose to be with me, even against his wishes?"

Surprise settles over me. This isn't what I thought he was going to ask, and the question lingers over us like a heavy cloud.

"How do you know that he doesn't approve of you?" It's a silly question—one that we both know the answer to. My dad has made it clear that he doesn't trust JP.

"He's told me—multiple times. And the glare he gives me when I'm anywhere near you reinforces it."

"Well, I don't know. That's a lot of hypotheticals," I say. "You want me to tell you if I can go against the one person who I trust most in the world, when you can't even be honest with me about what happened in San Diego? Do you see how that makes it difficult for me to give you an answer?"

He nods. "I'm sorry. I don't want to put you at odds with Seven, and I don't want to keep this secret from you, though I know that's hard to believe," he says, wrapping his arms around me and pulling me tight. "Will you stay until morning?"

"It is morning," I joke.

It's still dark out as his eyes glance over at the window.

"Just a few more hours then. I have to get on the bus in the morning to head for the jet, but I just want to lay here with you as long as possible."

"Yeah," I say. "I'll stay. Besides, I don't have my key."

"Just my luck," he says and then kisses the top of my forehead.

I pull the hair tie out of my hair and slip it back over his wrist.

"I think it's fully charged now and ready for your away game tomorrow."

"Thank you," he says.

We fall asleep, just like that—him holding onto me like I'm his lifeline. It feels good to be back in his arms, as much as I know I should fight it.

A few hours later, the muffled sound of Seattle's early morning traffic filters through the window, but it feels distant, like the world outside doesn't exist.

JP's arm is draped across my waist, his hand splayed warm

and solid against my stomach.

I lie still, staring at the faint patterns of light on the ceiling. My mind spins with memories of last night and this morning. A lot has happened, and I'm even less sure of what to do as my feelings for him continue to grow, and he shows me the person I thought I saw in him over the years, before his accident.

And yet, the reality is still the same. He's keeping something from me. I've lived a life like that before—I don't want to go back.

Carefully, I shift out from under his arm, biting my lip to keep from making a sound. JP stirs but doesn't wake, his face relaxed in sleep. He seems so different like this—vulnerable, almost boyish. Gone are the sharp edges of the goalie I see on the ice, replaced by the man I've been trying so hard not to want.

I grab my phone from the charger on the nightstand and tiptoe toward his closet. His smallest pair of sweats sits folded neatly on a shelf, and I roll the waistband as many times as it takes to get them to stay up. I pull on one of his shirts, its hem brushing my thighs, and take a deep breath.

This isn't San Diego. And yet, it feels so similar.

I grab the dress I wore at the club and my heels and head for his front door. My feet carry me to the door before I can change my mind, but a soft knock halts me mid-step.

I freeze, my hand hovering over the doorknob. Through the peephole, I see Brynn standing on the other side, her head tilted and something in her hands.

"Thank God," I mutter under my breath, twisting the knob.

"Cammy?" Brynn's voice is muffled through the wood, but she must have heard me.

I crack the door open just enough to meet her smirking gaze. I put a finger to my lips to mimic shushing her. "He's asleep," I say.

Her eyes immediately drop to the oversized shirt I'm wearing.

"Well, this is familiar," she says, holding out my purse. "Figured you might need this to get back into your place."

I scowl, stepping out of JP's apartment with my club dress draped over my arm and my heels in my hand. "Not a word."

"Wouldn't dream of it," she replies, though her expression tells me otherwise. "You okay?"

I glance back at the closed door behind me as we start walking toward the elevator. "I don't know."

Brynn presses the button for the elevator, her smirk softening into something more genuine. "Fair enough. Just so you know, your dad asked a million questions last night when I showed up without you."

My stomach drops. "Oh no... I didn't even think about how he'd see that I wasn't with you."

Brynn nods. "I told him as little as possible, but you know how he is. He was like a dog with a bone."

"What did you say?"

"I just told him you mixed your drinks and went home early," she says casually.

"Okay, that's not bad," I say, relief flooding through me.

"But then..." Brynn grimaces. "He started asking more questions. Like if I let you walk home alone or something."

"Brynn."

"I couldn't lie, Cammy. I told him a team member escorted you back to The Commons. When he figured out it was JP, he just about drove down here in the middle of the night to bring your purse and haul you out of there."

I groan, letting my head fall back as my eyes flutter closed. "He's going to kill me. Or JP. Or both of us."

She grins, unbothered. "Worried about JP? Sounds like someone still cares."

"I have no idea what I'm feeling right now," I admit, my voice quieter. "I need coffee, a shower, and about twelve hours of sleep. But it's Friday, and I have to go to work."

Brynn nods, her teasing softened by understanding. "Call me later?"

"Yeah."

I take an elevator up one level to my apartment as she takes an elevator down.

As I unlock the door to my apartment, a heavy weight settles in my chest. I glance at my phone, knowing JP will be gone for the next few days.

Maybe the distance will give me time to think. Because by the time he gets back, I'll need to figure out what I want.

And what I'm willing to risk to have it.

CHAPTER FOURTEEN

I step out of my car in the stadium parking lot, adjusting the strap of my duffel and game-day suit bag over my shoulder. The early morning air bites at my skin, crisp with the promise of winter. My phone buzzes in my pocket—probably another message from the media team, wanting quotes about my first away game with the Hawkeyes.

But when I check, it's not the media team.

> **Cammy: Good luck today. Show them what you've got.**

My thumb hovers over the screen, the memory of waking up alone this morning replaying in my mind. The sheets still held her warmth, the faint scent of her shampoo lingering on my pillowcase. But she was gone, and I guess I deserved that. After all, she had made her boundaries clear. Just one night.

And still, waking up to that empty space beside me felt like a blindside blow I hadn't prepared for.

"Monty!" Aleksi's voice pulls me out of my thoughts as he approaches, dragging his own bags along with him. "You coming or what?"

I pocket my phone, forcing myself to focus. "Yeah, yeah. I'm coming."

"You look like shit," he observes cheerfully, clearly enjoying himself. "Ground Zero hit you hard?"

If he only knew.

"Something like that," I mutter, following him toward the team bus.

The guys are already loading up their gear, their usual pregame energy buzzing despite the early hour. Hunter's got his headphones on, already in game mode, while Wolf talks strategy with Coach Haynes near the front of the bus.

"Heard you left early. At one point, you were standing at the bar waiting for beers, and then I turned around and Scottie said that you left," Aleksi continues, his grin turning mischievous as we stow our bags. "With a certain GM's assistant?"

I spot Seven standing near the bus driver and shoot Aleksi a warning glare. "Not today, Mäk."

He holds up his hands in surrender, but the smirk doesn't leave his face.

The bus ride to the private airport is mercifully quick. Once we're on the team jet, I find a window seat five rows back—close enough to hear strategy talk but far enough for some peace.

My phone buzzes again.

Cammy: Try not to let any pucks in. Dad says that L.A. has a solid right winger this year.

I can't help the smile that tugs at my lips as I type up my reply.

> **JP: Are you worried about me?**

I'm teasing, but the idea of her thinking of me after she claimed that last night was a one-off has me hoping this is a sign that I'm breaking through the wall she put up between us.

> **Cammy: No, I'm well aware that you can take care of yourself, Dumont.**

> **JP: Tell your dad I've got it covered.**

Before I can put my phone away, a shadow falls over me.

"Mind if I join you?"

I glance up to find Seven Wrenley standing in the aisle, his expression unreadable. My stomach drops, but I keep my face neutral. I start to panic about whether or not he'll be able to smell Cammy's coconut and vanilla shampoo on me.

"Of course not, Coach."

He settles into the seat beside me, and for a long moment, neither of us speaks. The rest of the team files past, finding their seats. I feel Aleksi's curious gaze from across the aisle, but I don't look his way.

"You know why I'm here," Seven says finally, his voice low enough that only I can hear.

"I can guess."

He turns slightly, fixing me with a stare that could freeze the balls off a polar bear. "I've known your father for a long time, JP. I played with him my first three years in the NHL, and I watched him burn through every good thing in his life because he couldn't keep his priorities straight... or his drinking."

My jaw tightens, but I say nothing. I don't need the reminder—I experienced it firsthand as a kid before my mom left him and moved us away.

"When I found out about Cammy, about everything she went through at home... I swore I'd protect her from anyone who could hurt her again. I wasn't there for the first part of her life, but I'm damn well going to make sure she's cared for now."

I meet his gaze head-on. "What if I want to be the one to protect her, too?"

Seven's laugh is humorless. "Protect her from what? Your DUI? The reputation you can't seem to shake? The string of mistakes that follow you like a bad smell?"

I've built a reputation for getting into fights over the years— both on and off the ice—but never once have I been the one to start them. Not that it matters. My name always ends up in the headlines.

The media didn't help either, painting me as the guy leaving bars and hotels with a different woman most weekends.

None of it is doing me any favors with Seven.

But the man I was then isn't the man I am now. All of that changed the first time I saw Cammy sitting in Seven's stadium seats years ago.

"With all due respect, you're making a lot of assumptions about some things you know nothing about."

Angelica's text comes to mind again. *Just another year and a half...*

"I don't need to assume. Your reputation precedes you, and most of it you've earned outright. Am I wrong?" he says, his voice low as he glances around to see if anyone is listening in on our conversation.

I don't respond back, because, yes, my college and rookie years in the NHL were wild at times. I'll admit that, but Cammy changed everything.

"What I care about is my daughter. And I'm telling you now, as her father first and your coach second: Stay. Away."

The finality in his tone lands like a slap.

I think of Cammy, the way she let herself soften around

me early this morning, the way she clung to me in the dark. I think about everything I want to tell her—the truth about what happened with Angelica, the truth about me.

"Shouldn't that be Cammy's choice?" I say.

Seven's jaw tightens, and for a second, I think he might lose it. Instead, he leans closer, his voice dropping to a near growl. "Do you really want to test me on this, Dumont?"

Before I can respond, the captain announces our departure. Seven straightens, adjusting his tie.

"Focus on the game," he says as he stands. "Don't force me to make sure your career with the Hawkeyes ends with PTO. Everett wants to sign you, but he wants my recommendation after the charity event."

I watch him walk away, his words settling like lead in my stomach.

He's right about one thing—I need to focus. This is my shot to prove I belong here. That my knee is healed. That I'm worth the risk the Hawkeyes took on me.

But as we take off, climbing above Seattle, all I can think about is Cammy. About the way she looked at me last night. About how it felt to wake up without her.

The flight passes in a blur of strategy meetings and pre-game prep. By the time we land in Los Angeles, my game face is on. Or at least, that's what I tell myself.

"You good?" Aleksi asks as we walk into our hotel room. He's my roommate for the trip, which means I'll be dealing with his snoring and obsession with the Food Network.

"Yeah, I'm good," I lie, tossing my bag onto one of the beds.

He doesn't buy it. "Seven looked ready to murder you on the plane. That 'coach stuff'?"

"It's nothing you need to worry about."

He flops onto his bed, still grinning. "You know you can't avoid this conversation forever, right?"

I grab my headphones and turn on my pre-game playlist. "Watch me."

As I head down to the gym, his laughter follows me.

Hours later, I'm on the ice for warm-up. The empty arena feels massive, and somehow, I don't remember it feeling this big. Maybe it's because my career is on the line. I focus on the drills, on the weight of my pads, on the sound of my skates cutting the ice.

But as I track shot after shot, stopping every one, I can't help but think about Seven's challenge. About the look in Cammy's eyes as Seven and I shook on it. About the bet that will send me packing or give me a clean slate with Coach Wrenley in two weeks.

About how much I want the chance to prove to both of them—and to myself—that I'm more than my reputation. But the conversation in the jet has me wondering again if Seven is right. Am I good enough for her? I'm sure my father would say that I'm not. Though, I can't imagine how he'd feel to know I'm after Wrenley's daughter. He's not exactly Seven's biggest fan either.

The guys file off the ice, but I linger, taking a few extra shots from the coaching staff. Seven watches from the bench, his expression as unreadable as ever.

I stop every shot.

It's not enough, I know. It'll never be enough for him. But maybe, it's enough for her. As I finally head to the locker room to gear up for the first preseason game, I know that there's a lot more than hockey on the line.

The question is—can I keep Cammy *and* my position on the team?

CHAPTER FIFTEEN

Cammy

"You're late," Brynn says as I walk through Penelope's front door, shrugging off my Seattle Hawkeyes zip-up jacket—the same one all the office staff got last season. "We were starting to think you weren't coming."

"Sorry, I got caught up with auction emails," I say, though the truth is, I've been sitting at my apartment thinking about what I'm going to do about these feelings for JP. "But I brought chips."

She takes the bag from my hands with a knowing look. "Or maybe you couldn't stop thinking about your Ground Zero *afterparty*?"

I follow her into Penelope's stunning kitchen, where the other girls are already gathering. The sprawling open-concept space, with its professional-grade appliances and massive island—perfect for entertaining an NHL team—is filled with the smell of pizza and the sound of laughter. Aria's meticulously arranging a veggie platter while Kendall and Juliet disagree about pizza toppings—specifically the use of pineapple. Isla's perched on one of the leather bar stools, typing rapidly on her phone.

"Look who finally showed up," Penelope calls out from where she's restocking bottled hard ciders in the fridge for tonight. "Just in time for pre-game analysis."

"Please, tell me we're not dissecting Ground Zero again," I say, accepting one of the hard ciders that Penelope hands me.

"Oh, we're definitely going there," Aria says, abandoning her perfectly arranged vegetables. "You left with our goalie and didn't come back."

I take a generous sip of cider, needing liquid courage for this conversation. "I was sick, remember? I went to lie down."

"You went to lie down... Is that what we're calling it now?" Brynn teases. "Is that why I had to bring you your purse in the morning, and you were sneaking out, dressed head to toe in JP's clothing while he was still asleep? You didn't even wake him up before you left."

"Oh, that's cold... even for me," Kendall says but then reaches over to high five me.

The room erupts in squeals and questions that echo off the high ceilings.

"Ladies"—I hold up my hands, fighting to keep my expression neutral—"can we focus on the game? It's their first away game of the season, and I don't want to miss any of it."

"The game doesn't start for twenty minutes," Aria points out, her eyes sparkling with mischief. It's good to see her smile after everything with Everett. "Plenty of time for details."

If I'm being honest, Aria's situation makes me even more nervous about the bet between my dad and JP. I still don't know Everett that well. Would he fire me if he found out that I knew my dad challenged Everett's new goalie into walking away from the Hawkeyes, and I did nothing to stop it?

I mean, technically I did try to get them to listen to me, but neither of them would. Will he still see this as my fault? Will Penelope? And if Kendall doesn't clear Olsen in time, the Hawkeyes could be without a goalie after the charity auction if my dad wins.

"There are no details," I insist, though the memory of waking up in his bed, his scent surrounding me, threatens to weaken my resolve. "He was just being a good teammate, making sure I got home safe."

"That's all?" Kendall presses, twirling a baby carrot between her fingers. "Because Aleksi said—"

"Since when are you talking to Aleksi?" I counter, grateful for the deflection. My phone buzzes in my pocket, and I resist the urge to check it immediately.

Kendall's cheeks flush pink. "We're not...he just comes by my office a lot. That's all. I don't date professional athletes anymore, remember?"

"What does Aleksi come by for so often then?" Isla asks, finally glancing up from her phone, probably texting Kaenan about the upcoming game.

"Usually something ridiculous," Kendall admits, her smile fond despite her eye roll. "Last week he came in claiming his funny bone wasn't funny anymore."

We all laugh, and I silently thank Aleksi's terrible flirting for the subject change. My phone buzzes again, and this time I can't help but check it.

> **JP: About to hit the ice for warmups.**

My heart stutters, but I slip the phone back into my pocket without responding. He'll be on the ice soon, and he'll be in the zone. I probably won't hear from him the rest of the night, but I have a feeling I'll be checking my phone all night anyway.

"Speaking of details," Penelope says, "we need to go dress shopping for the auction. I've got a reservation at that French boutique outside of town that we usually go to. They're holding a private showing for us with a brand new collection."

"I don't know if I should go," Aria says quietly, her earlier smile fading. "I'm not really part of the organization anymore."

The room falls silent, the weight of Everett's decision hanging heavy in the air.

"Don't be ridiculous," Penelope says firmly, her GM voice making an appearance. "You're still a part of the Hawkeyes family, even if you're not on the payroll. Besides, it's a charity event. Anyone can attend who has an invitation and luckily, I have an extra one."

"Pen's right," I add, wrapping an arm around Aria's shoulders. "We need you there. Who else is going to obsessively analyze the silent auction table to make sure everything lines up perfectly?"

That gets a laugh from everyone, breaking the tension.

We settle into Penelope's massive sectional, plates balanced on laps as the pre-game show begins. The cameras pan across LA's arena, finally settling on the ice where both teams are warming up.

My breath catches when they zoom in on JP. He's tracking shots with laser focus, his movements fluid and controlled. Even through the TV, his presence commands attention. There's no sign of the knee issues that sidelined him for the last two seasons as he moves post to post, shutting down shot after shot.

"He looks good out there," Brynn murmurs beside me. "Really good."

I nod, not trusting my voice. My phone buzzes again, but I force myself to focus on the screen where Hunter's taking shots on JP during warmups.

The first period is intense but scoreless. JP makes several key saves, including a spectacular glove save that has us all cheering. The girls start a running commentary on everything from player performance to who's likely to end up in the penalty box first.

"Twenty bucks says Hunter gets the first penalty," Juliet announces, reaching for another slice of pizza. "He's been *chippy* lately."

"Nah, my money's on Aleksi," Kendall counters, her cheeks pinking slightly when we all look at her. "What? He's been fired up all week. You should see him in the training room."

"Oh, we bet you see a lot of him in the training room," Isla teases.

The second period starts rough. L.A. scores early, a deflection off Wolf's stick that even JP couldn't track. The Hawkeyes struggle to generate offense, and despite JP's continued strong play, they're down 2-0 by the intermission.

"They're not clicking," Penelope observes, her GM voice fully present now. "The new line combinations need work. And our power play is too predictable."

"JP's keeping them in it, though," Isla notes. "Thirty saves already."

I stay quiet, watching as the cameras catch him heading down the tunnel. His jaw is set, but his shoulders are steady. He appears determined, focused. Like the player I used to watch from across the ice, before everything happened in San Diego.

The third period is all L.A. Despite a late push, the Hawkeyes couldn't solve their goalie. JP makes a hell of a save toward the end, but it's not enough. Final score: 3-0.

"Well, that sucked," Aria announces, reaching for more wine.

"First away game jitters," Penelope says, "but it's just pre-season, and we have a lot of new players this season that haven't played together. The chemistry will come."

"So, Saturday for dress shopping?" Juliet asks as we help clean up. "Ten o'clock?"

Everyone agrees, even Aria, though she still seems hesitant.

"I can't wait to see what everyone picks," Kendall says, boxing up leftover pizza. "We should all try on things that are completely out of our comfort zones."

Later, as I'm getting ready for bed, a text comes through. It's a picture of a puck with silver writing "*Dinner?*"

And then a text that follows.

JP: I know what was throwing me off. I didn't have you to toss a puck to. It threw my whole rhythm off.

I know he's teasing, but it has me chuckling—a flutter in my belly telling me that JP is starting to get under my skin. Or maybe he's always been there?

Cammy: Good game, despite the score. Your knee looked strong. Maybe I didn't wear the hairband long enough.

His reply is immediate.

JP: The hairband still did its job. No one got hurt on the ice. You'll always be my lucky charm, Cammy.

I stare at the message, my finger hovering over the reply button. Finally, I type:

Cammy: Have a safe flight home. See you soon.

It's not much, but it's something. A small crack in the wall I've built around my heart. Whether that's wise or not remains to be seen.

JP: See you soon

But as I drift off to sleep, I can't stop wondering what would happen if I ever said yes to dinner.

Maybe someday, I will.

CHAPTER SIXTEEN

JP

Practice finishes, and I have my bag slung over my shoulder, post shower. I head for the corporate offices, my body tingling with excitement as if I'm about to play a game. But instead, I'm actually going up to see Cammy for the first time since she was in my bed four days ago. Though compared to an NHL in-season game, the stakes feel just as high when it comes to her.

Every night away, I found myself checking my phone, hoping for another text from her. They were always professional, always about hockey: *Good luck tonight. Nice save in the third. Way to bounce back after that first loss.* But no text like, *I miss you. Dinner sounds great.*

Simple. Friendly yet distant. But it's something.

Each one felt like a small stepping stone to building a new foundation. And after having my number blocked for the last year and a half, this is the kind of progress I can get behind.

The elevator seems slower than usual as it climbs to the executive floor, my mind racing with memories of the last time I saw her—wrapped in my sheets, her hair spread across my pillow.

Then waking up alone, understanding why she left but hating it all the same.

When the doors open, I hear her before I see her.

"No, no, no," she mutters. "This is not happening."

I round the corner to find her standing in the middle of what looks like a merchandise explosion.

Boxes are stacked everywhere—on her desk, the floor, spilling into the hallway. She's got her hair pulled back in a messy bun, reading glasses perched on her nose as she studies a clipboard. The morning light streaming through the windows catches the gold in her hair, and for a moment, I forget how to breathe.

"Need a hand?"

She startles, looking up. For a moment, neither of us speaks. The air feels charged, heavy with everything unsaid between us since that morning I woke up to an empty bed.

"JP." She tucks a loose strand of hair behind her ear, and I fight the urge to do it for her. "I didn't know you were back."

"The team got back last night. We had practice this morning."

Her eyes clamp shut, and she shakes her head as if she should have remembered that. "Right, yeah, of course. I've been a little busy with everything going on. And the auction is coming up in a week and a half."

"What can I do to help?" I ask, stepping closer, picking up a jersey that's fallen from one of the boxes. My fingers trace the Hawkeyes logo, buying time. "Are these for the auction?" I ask.

"You don't need to help. You've been out of town, played several hard games. You should get a day off—I've got it."

"Do you have it? Because it looks like you're about to square off with those boxes. Should I grab you a hockey stick at least?"

She glances up at me and takes a deep breath, her hands gripping her waist. "What are you doing here anyway? You should be at home icing that knee."

"I asked first. But judging by the disaster zone in here, I'd say you're trying to turn yourself into a human pretzel over this auction."

Her eyes roam over the forty or fifty massive boxes that Merchandise must have delivered for her this morning.

She bites her lip, clearly torn between pride and practicality. "I knew that Merchandise was coming in today to do this for me, but I guess I thought they were going to take everything down to the locker room. I'm going to have to carry all of these down today to get the guys to sign them."

I step inside, shaking my head. "Cammy, this is insane. How are you planning to get all this stuff downstairs?"

Her lips tighten—"I'm not sure..."—and she waves me off. "But I've got it under control."

"No, you don't." I walk farther into the room, surveying the situation, careful to maintain professional distance, despite every instinct screaming to pull her into my arms. Our text messages over the last few days show her warming up to me—I can feel it—but it's still a delicate balance. "Let me help. Actually..." An idea forms. "Give me ten minutes."

She raises an eyebrow, and I catch a hint of the spark that first drew me to her. "What are you planning?"

"Trust me?"

The words hang between us, weighted with meaning beyond this moment. She studies me for a long beat before nodding slowly.

I'm already heading for the elevator. "Don't move anything. I'll be right back."

In the locker room, most of the guys are still hanging around after the morning skate. Perfect.

"Listen up," I call out. "I need volunteers for a special mission."

Hunter looks up from taping his stick. "What kind of mission?"

"The kind where we help Cammy with auction merchandise instead of making her haul forty boxes down here."

"I'm in," Aleksi says immediately, jumping up. "Anything to avoid Scottie's protein shake lecture."

"Hey!" Scottie protests. "The importance of proper post-workout nutrition—"

"Save it for the rookies," Wolf cuts in, standing. "She can't carry all of those down here. Let's go."

I see Seven head my way, too. "Coach, can you make a Serendipity's Coffee Shop run?" His eyebrow furrows until I tell him why, and then he heads in the opposite direction as the rest of us.

Within minutes, I've got ten guys following me to the elevators. When we arrive, Cammy's exactly where I left her, though she's managed to create some semblance of order among the chaos.

Her eyes widen when she sees us all file in, and something in my chest tightens at the way her eyes sparkle with surprise. "What is this?"

"Your cavalry," I announce, starting to direct traffic. "Hunter, Wolf—grab those boxes by the window. Aleksi, start setting up stations in the conference room. Scottie, don't even think about bringing that protein shake in here."

To my relief, all ten guys jump into action, organizing all of the boxes for signing. I head to Cammy's desk, finding a stack of markers in her top drawer. Our fingers brush as I hand her one, and the contact sends electricity shooting up my arm. Her breath catches, and I know she felt it too.

"You didn't have to do this," she says softly.

"I wanted to." I catch her gaze, willing her to understand everything I can't say. "Besides, it's the least I can do after—"

"Yo, JP!" Aleksi calls from the conference room. "Where do you want the jerseys?"

The moment breaks, but something in Cammy's expression has softened.

I spend the next hour coordinating the most efficient signing operation the Hawkeyes have ever seen. The guys set up an assembly line, passing items down the conference table while trading chirps and stories.

"Remember to make them legible," Cammy reminds everyone. "We need people to actually know whose signature they're bidding on."

"Unlike Ziggy's chicken scratch," Hunter teases.

"Hey, my signature is artistic," Wolf defends.

"Yeah, if by artistic you mean that it looks like a drunk spider fell in ink," Trey adds.

Cammy moves between stations, checking items off her list and occasionally catching my eye with a smile that makes my heart stutter. At one point, she reaches for a box on a high shelf, and I'm behind her before I can think better of it.

"Let me," I say, my chest brushing her back as I grab the box. She freezes, and for a moment, we're pressed together, her warmth seeping into me.

"Thanks," she whispers, turning slightly. We're so close, I can see the flutter of her pulse at her neck.

Seven appears in the doorway then, coffee in hand. He takes in the scene—his daughter's flushed cheeks, my proximity, the organized chaos of players signing merchandise.

But instead of the scowl I expect, he just walks over to Cammy.

"Here," he says, handing her the cup. "JP mentioned you could use this."

He hands it to her and then gives her a kiss on the head. "I have to go to a playdate with Milo, but I'm proud of you and everything you're doing to help these kids and the foundation. Don't work too hard today, okay?"

As soon as Seven leaves, her eyes shift between the coffee and me, surprise evident on her face. "You asked my dad to get me coffee?"

I shrug, trying to play it cool, despite the victory I feel at Seven's small gesture of... well, not approval exactly, but something. "We're best friends now. Didn't you see that smile he just gave me?"

"Looked more like he was hoping that if he stared long enough, that you'd combust into flames," she says, but she's fighting a grin.

"That's just how he shows affection." I pull out her chair. "Sit. Relax. We've got this under control."

She sits, taking a sip of coffee, and I can't help but lean over her shoulder to look at her checklist. The scent of her shampoo hits me, and suddenly I'm back in my bed, her skin against mine, her breath on my neck...

"Monty," Aleksi calls out. "Here's your box to sign," he says, slapping the top of one of the boxes.

Right. Professional. I straighten up, catching Cammy's warm honey eyes before heading back to the signing station.

Two hours later, we've got everything signed and organized. The guys file out, but not before Aleksi whispers, "You're welcome," as he passes me.

Then it's just Cammy and me in the conference room, the air thick with possibility.

"Thank you," she says, straightening a stack of signed photos. Her fingers trace the edge of one absently. "This would have taken me days on my own."

I step closer, unable to help myself. "Anytime."

She looks up, and suddenly the air feels charged. We're standing close enough that I can see the flecks of gold in her eyes, count her eyelashes if I wanted to. Her lips part slightly, and I'm halfway to throwing caution to the wind when Cammy's cell phone rings.

I glance at my watch, hating that I have to leave. "Are you going to be okay up here?"

"Yes." She nods with a warm smile. "With no one else left in the offices, I won't have anyone sidetracking me, so I can stay on task."

"What more do you need to do?"

She looks around at the neat stacks of merch inside the office. "I need to catalog each auction item and give it a bid number. This was going to take me days to complete, but since the guys put everything in piles, I think I might get this done tonight. What you and the team did is amazing. Thank you." Her smile is genuine, bright enough to light up the room. Before I can respond, she steps forward and hugs me.

The contact is brief but electric. When she pulls back, our faces are close—too close. Her eyes drop to my lips for a fraction of a second, and I almost forget about my other commitment to the physical therapist waiting downstairs.

"I'd stay and help," I say reluctantly, "but PT only came in for a half day, and I need—"

She waves me off quickly. "Yes...of course. You've done more than enough," she assures me, still beaming as she looks around at everything laid out in Penelope's office suite. "I'm grateful, really."

Cammy bends down to look through a box, and I quickly pull out the carved bird she was admiring that Pete had made at his Pike's Place booth. I went back and bought it the next day for her. I set it down on her desk and then pick up my bag, sliding the strap over my shoulder.

I back toward the door, not wanting to leave but knowing I have to. "I have my own to-do list anyway. PT and then I promised Pete I'd run the Zamboni tonight."

"Go," she says with a soft laugh. "Take care of that knee."

As I head for the elevator, I can't help but steal another glance at her. She's already immersed in her work, grabbing a clipboard and taking a sip of her coffee, and I have to force myself to keep walking.

Some promises are worth keeping, even if they mean walking away from moments like this.

As I head down to the locker room, my phone buzzes.

> **Cammy: I can't believe you remembered the bird. I love it. Thank you.**

I smile, typing back:

JP: De rien, mon petit oiseau.
Anytime. Really.

Somehow I know, tonight isn't over.

CHAPTER SEVENTEEN

Cammy

Tonight, the office is silent.

No chatting office staff, no players, no media. It's calming almost, no pressure for deadlines, no phones ringing, no fires to put out. Just me and my little carved finch that now lives next to my computer screen.

JP tried to be sneaky, dropping in on my desk before he left, but of course, I knew immediately who left it. My heart squeezes at the sentiment.

The silence in the hallways of the corporate offices is only broken by the distant sound of the cleaning crew's vacuums and the echo of my platform Keds against the polished floors as I head to the breakroom for yet another coffee.

I check my phone, and the time is just after 10:00 p.m. At this late hour, even most of the cleaning crew have gone home by now, and security has shifted over to the nightly skeleton crew.

I've been cataloging auction items for hours, surrounded by the organized chaos JP and the team created earlier. Every signed jersey, puck, and photo has to be logged, photographed, and entered into the auction database. It's a lot of work, but there's something peaceful about being here alone, about having this massive space to myself.

Well, almost to myself.

Walking back to Penelope's office with a freshly brewed coffee in my hand, I glance down at the rink from the floor-to-ceiling windows at the end of the hall, and movement catches my eye on the ice below.

JP is still here, driving the Zamboni in smooth, precise circles. The sight of him—knowing that we're the only two in the building outside of security and the remaining cleaning crew—sparks an unexpected sense of camaraderie.

I take a sip of my coffee, admiring his work from a distance and thinking about how kind it was of him to offer Pete the night off. And the way he brought the team up to help me, convincing my dad to bring me a coffee from my favorite coffee shop. He keeps finding ways to take care of the things I need, even before I know I need them. Things that are important to me.

My phone buzzes with a text. My heart jumps, thinking that it's him, though I can clearly see that both hands are on the steering wheel, a set of headphones over his ears.

Brynn: Still at work?

Cammy: Just finishing up. JP's still here, too.

Her response is immediate.

Brynn: 👀

Cammy: Not like that. He's doing Pete a favor, running the Zamboni.

Brynn: Running the Zamboni?
Sounds like he wants to polish
more than just the ice. 😏

I ignore her last message, but my eyes drift back to the rink. JP's making another pass, the Zamboni making polished lines on the ice. Even from up here, I can see how relaxed JP is, the easy way he handles the machine. He looks... at peace.

Before I can overthink it, I head for the elevator. I should thank him again for this morning. I mean, it's just professional courtesy.

The ride down to ice level feels both too long and too short. My platforms clap against the cement floors, the sound bouncing off the empty corridor walls as I approach the player tunnel, each step making me question whether or not I should turn back. I realize a little too late that I forgot my coat upstairs. I cross my arms, moving my hands up and down to warm them.

JP spots me, and his whole face lights up in a way that makes my heart stutter.

He guides the Zamboni toward the tunnel entrance, that familiar half-smile playing at his lips. "Hey."

"You call me your little bird," I say.

"You googled it, I assume. You just killed my mysterious edge." He smirks.

"Don't worry, you're still shrouded in mystery. I can assure you," I tease, trying to ignore how good he looks in his after-practice sweats, a large jacket over top while he drives. I had no idea that JP on a Zamboni would do it for me... and yet, here we are. "You're still here?"

"I saw the lights on upstairs—figured you were still working." He cuts the Zamboni's engine. "I decided to stay until you were done. I don't like the idea of you being here by yourself."

"Security's here..." I say.

He nods, glancing up at the windows to the corporate office

where he saw the lights on. "Yeah, I know."

Something warms in my chest. "So, you stayed here for me?"

"That, and I told Pete I'd run the Zamboni so he can finish his carving for the auction. Plus," he adds, shrugging one shoulder, "I like running this thing. Ol' Bessie here knows how to show a guy a good time."

I snicker. "I'm sure you're never short of options for a good time," I say, aiming for teasing but hearing the edge in my voice.

His expression turns serious. "The only good time I'm interested in is time spent with you, Cammy. I'm not interested in anyone else."

Heat floods my cheeks at his honesty. How does he do that? Just say exactly what he's feeling, no games, no pretense? His openness to my closed off walls.

"Want to take a ride with me?" he asks, breaking the moment. "I'll give you my coat. You look freezing."

A shiver breaks through as he reminds me that I'm not dressed warm enough for this.

"On that?" I point at the Zamboni.

"Yeah." He nods. "She's a lot more fun than she looks. You should give it a try."

"How do you know I haven't ridden a Zamboni before?"

He shakes his head, his grin soft and teasing. "If you've ridden another team's Zamboni, keep it to yourself. You'll ruin my new favorite fantasy of you."

He sends me an easy smile—making something so arbitrary like riding a Zamboni feel like a secret he's sharing with me.

I should say no. Should maintain professional boundaries. I should protect my heart from falling for him again, but he's making it so difficult.

"Okay," I hear myself say.

"I knew you couldn't resist ol' Bessie here." He unzips his coat and takes it off. "But unfortunately, there's only one seat. Guess we'll have to make do." He slaps his lap to let me know exactly where I'll be sitting.

I hesitate for half a second, but the way his eyes soften, waiting for my decision, has me stepping forward. He offers me his hand, and I take it. "Okay, just don't crash. I don't want to have to explain this one to HR when they're filling out a workers' comp claim," I tease, as I take the first step onto the Zamboni, and he guides me to settle onto his lap.

"Don't worry. I've got you." His voice is low against my ear as he settles me onto his lap and then drapes his jacket over us.

"Are you comfortable?" he asks, the heat under his jacket warming me.

"Yes. Similar to ol' Bessie here... you're a lot more comfortable than you look," I say.

"Good." There's a grin in his tone, and I can feel it radiating off him. "You trust me, right?"

I glance over my shoulder, his face inches from mine. "On the ice? Sure. Off the ice... still deciding."

He chuckles, the sound vibrating where our bodies connect. "That's fair."

The Zamboni lurches forward as he puts it back into gear, and we begin to move. I'm hyper-aware of the heat from JP's chest against my back, the steady pressure of his thighs beneath me. His arm wrapped around my middle protectively, holding me securely as the machine glides across the ice.

We start making slow circles around the rink. JP tells me stories about learning to drive one of these from his dad when he was younger, back when being on the ice meant pure joy to JP, before his father's expectations and pressure took over.

"He used to be my hero," JP admits quietly. "Before the divorce."

"How old were you when they separated?"

"Five," he says. "Looking back, he wasn't the best father he could have been. He was gone more than he had to be for work. But then he'd show up, and there would be these moments when he'd make up for it."

"Like teaching you how to drive a Zamboni in an empty

hockey stadium, just the two of you," I say, though I can't relate to those childhood memories.

At five years old, Eli, the man I grew up thinking was my father, was struggling with crippling PTSD after losing his best friend to an IED while they were both deployed overseas, and deep down, I think he always knew I wasn't his. Not to mention that my mother needed constant reassurance that he loved her. She took up what little energy he had for giving a shit.

Eli is so different from Seven, my real father and the man who brings me coffee on a Saturday morning, who kisses the top of my head before he leaves me, who will do anything and take on anyone to protect me. Now at twenty-four years old— and considered a grown woman in society—those moments are starting to heal the little girl in me who was robbed of him.

"The great Jon Paul Dumont Senior," JP says, pulling me out of my own memories. "...only to those who don't know him. But then something happened that made me step back and realize I was following too closely in his footsteps, and I decided to clean up my act to become a better man."

"What happened that made you want to be a better man?" I ask.

"Meeting you at that first game, tossing you a puck, and you not wanting anything to do with me." He chuckles.

I try to hide the blush blooming in my cheek, so I change the subject.

"You must have had someone in the hockey community that you looked up to growing up?" I ask, adjusting his jacket over my shoulders.

"Yeah, after we moved out, I found someone new."

"Who?"

He stalls for a second before answering. "Your dad."

His answer surprises me, but it shouldn't. My dad has been playing since before JP ever laced up a pair of skates. I listen quietly as he continues.

"Seven's everything I want to be as a goalie, as a franchise player, as a teammate. The man I wish my father had been. And now I see him with Milo and Brynn... and with you. Protective, supportive, puts family first. The man my father will never be. Even when Coach Wrenley puts me through it during drills, I respect him for it."

I chuckle at the thought of my dad's perpetual scowl, not that it's ever aimed at me... usually.

"And the bet? Do you respect him for that?"

He pauses for a moment, as if he's collecting his thoughts.

"Yes, I respect him for it. He's trying to protect you, and he's putting a lot on the line to do it. He'd do anything for you, Cammy—you know that right?"

"And you agreed to it because...?"

He looks at me over my shoulder, his gaze steady and unflinching. "Because I'd do anything for you, too."

The weight of his words lands squarely between us, heavy and undeniable. As everything feels heavy around us—emotions I'm not sure I'm ready to unpack.

I clear my throat, forcing a lighter tone as I lean back slightly. "So," I say, a small smirk tugging at my lips. "Do you do this often?"

He turns a dial on the machine, making a small adjustment to something. "Do what? Drive the Zamboni?"

"More like, is this how you get all the girls to ride *your* Zamboni?" I ask, looking over my shoulder.

His eyes shoot up from the dials, locking on mine.

"You're the only girl I've ever given a Zamboni ride to," he says, his eyes honest, "and you're the only girl I'll ever ask."

His hand at my waist shifts slightly, fingers brushing just beneath the hem of my shirt. It was an accident, but it still sends a shiver through me. I know he feels it by the way his grip tightens, anchoring me closer.

"Cammy," he murmurs, his voice low and gravelly.

"Yeah?" I manage. His fingers skim against my bare skin and then slide farther up, under my shirt, his touch burning a trail along my stomach, the delicious feeling of little scratches from a calloused hockey player's hand. "If you want me to stop..."

"I don't," I say quickly, cutting him off. My voice is barely above a whisper, but it's enough to make him pause, his forehead resting against the back of my head for a moment as if he's gathering himself.

"Good."

The Zamboni stops in one of the corners of the rink.

I lean back resting my head against his shoulder, giving him better access as his fingers dive under the lacy fabric of my bra. His thumb and index finger find my hardening nipple, pinching gently, pulling a soft whimper from my lips. I arch against him, pressing my ass harder into his lap. A guttural growl vibrates through his chest, and I feel it against my back.

I look up into the stands, remembering where we are. Though, no one would be able to see what we're doing under his jacket if they walked in, I'm sure they could guess.

"The security cameras..." I start.

"They can't see us," he finishes. "We're in their blind spot. And the guys on duty tonight play online poker in the breakroom, ignoring the cameras unless an alarm goes off."

Good to know we have the best of the best on the night crew.

"There's a blind spot?" I ask. "How do you know where it is?"

"Hunter knows about it. Don't ask why," he says, laying a soft kiss behind my ear. "Is this still okay?"

"Yes. It's still okay."

His other hand leaves the wheel, snaking around to rest just above the waistband of my jeans, his thumb brushing over the exposed skin of my hip. The sensation sends a wave of heat coursing through me.

JP's lips trail along the curve of my neck, leaving a slow burn in their wake that cools quickly from the chill of the rink. I tilt my head to the side, giving him better access as his hand moves back and forth, kneading each breast, giving attention to both. His other hand snakes down over my belly, sneaking down past the waistband of my jeans, his fingertips teasing against bare skin.

I reach up and cup the back of his neck, giving me somewhere to anchor myself to him. I rotate my hips, feeling his hard length under me, grinding slowly on top of him. He groans at the friction, his hand continuing its descent down my body until his middle finger slides through my slick folds, swirling over my clit and sparking a heat deep inside of me, his touch deliberate and maddeningly slow.

My nails dig deeper into the back of his neck as I struggle to stay grounded. He presses soft kisses along my neck, murmuring words of praise that I can't quite make out in broken French. But there are some I catch that have my body responding to him. "Such a good girl," "...soaking wet pussy just for me," "...I never thought I'd get you like this," and "...you're my fantasy, Cammy."

I breathe out his name, my voice trembling with need.

"I've got you," he says softly, his voice steady. "Just let me take care of you."

His words send another wave of liquid heat soaking through my panties and lubricating his fingers, and when his finger dips lower, sliding inside me, I gasp. The way he moves is unhurried, exploring, his thumb coming back up to rub slow, lazy circles over my clit as he pumps his finger in and out. My hips instinctively roll to meet his hand, chasing the pressure that's quickly building inside me.

"You feel like silk on my fingers," he whispers, his lips brushing against my ear. "The softest thing I've ever felt."

"I can't believe I'm letting you fuck me on a Zamboni," I say breathlessly.

"I haven't fucked you yet, mon ange. This is just foreplay."

I bite down on my bottom lip to keep from crying out, the overwhelming sensation of his fingers working me, driving me closer to the edge. His free hand cups my breast again, his thumb flicking over my nipple, adding to the chaos of sensations flooding my body.

I can't stop the soft whimper that escapes my lips as he curls his finger just right, hitting a spot that sends a bolt of pleasure shooting through me. My head falls back harder against his shoulder, and he presses a kiss to my temple, his movements relentless, his fingers stroking just right, drawing me closer and closer to the brink.

The tension coils tighter in my stomach, a pressure so intense I feel like I might burst into flames. And then, with one final stroke, I do. My body pulsates around his fingers as the pleasure crashes over me, wave after wave pulling me under. I cry out softly, his name a breathless whisper on my lips, knowing that someone other than JP in this stadium might hear me, as he holds me through it.

As the aftershocks ripple through me, his hand slows, his touch gentle now. He kisses the side of my neck again, his lips lingering as I come down, my body still trembling from the release.

"You're incredible," he says, his voice thick with awe. "Watching you fall apart in my lap..." He trails off, his lips brushing against my skin. "I'll never forget it."

I turn my head to meet his gaze, his eyes dark and intense, his expression raw. My chest tightens at the sight, my heart hammering for an entirely different reason now. Without thinking, I lean in and kiss him, pouring every emotion I can't say into it. He kisses me back as if he knows what I'm trying to tell him, his hand still resting on my waist, holding me close like he never wants to let go. But slipping away is the last thing on my mind.

The rumble of the Zamboni fades into the background as JP moves us across the ice, his grip firm on my waist.

As we near the Zamboni bay, the massive garage doors open, revealing the dimly lit, heated space beyond. The warmth hits my skin, a stark contrast to the cool bite of the ice, and I shiver—not from the temperature, but from the anticipation curling in my stomach.

JP reaches past me, his fingers grazing my hip as he presses the button to seal us inside. The mechanical whir of the doors closing is the last sound of the outside world before we're completely alone, tucked away from prying eyes.

I twist, turning in his lap to face him, my legs sliding to either side of his hips—straddling him. JP's hands immediately settle on my thighs, his fingers digging in just enough to send another shiver through me. His eyes meet mine, dark and filled with raw, unfiltered desire.

"You're playing a dangerous game, Cammy," he murmurs, his pupils dilated, his cock hard underneath me.

"Am I?" I ask, a teasing edge to my tone as I press myself closer, feeling the length of him beneath me. His sharp intake of breath fuels my boldness.

He doesn't answer with words—he doesn't need to. His hands move to my hips, guiding me to grind against him, and the friction is enough to pull a soft moan from my lips.

"You've been driving me crazy all night," he murmurs, his lips brushing against mine. "I can't hold back."

"Then don't hold back," I whisper, my voice unsteady as I press my hands to his chest, feeling the rapid thrum of his heartbeat beneath my palms.

That's all it takes.

JP surges forward, his mouth claiming mine in a kiss so fierce it leaves me gasping. His hands slide under my shirt, gripping my waist, then gliding up the smooth expanse of my back before yanking the fabric over my head. My skin prickles with heat, and the coolness of the rink as I push his jacket from my shoulders, letting it pool at our feet, lost to the urgency consuming us.

We move frantically, shedding layers in a fevered blur of motion. The quiet thumps of our clothes hitting the Zamboni, the floor, the tool bench—it all melts together, background noise to the rush of need pounding through my veins.

His lips never leave mine, his kisses deep and consuming, his hands mapping every inch of bare skin as he backs me toward the side of the Zamboni. I gasp as the cool metal presses against my back, the contrast against my heated flesh sending a delicious shiver down my spine.

"Fuck, Cammy," he groans, his lips tracing a slow, agonizing path down my neck, his stubble scraping just enough to make my breath hitch. "You have no idea what you do to me."

I do. Because he does the same to me.

His hands slide lower, gripping my thighs before lifting me onto the edge of the Zamboni. I brace myself against the machine as he steps between my legs, his body flush against mine, nothing between us now.

"JP," I breathe, my fingers threading into his hair, tugging just enough to make him groan.

His mouth claims mine again, slower this time, deeper—like he's savoring the moment, like he's trying to memorize every inch of me. His hands explore the curve of my waist, the dip of my spine, the heat between my thighs.

Then he stills, his forehead pressed against mine, his breath ragged. "I don't have a condom." His voice is rough, like it pains him to admit it. "Tell me this is okay. Tell me you want this."

I don't hesitate. "I do. I'm on birth control," I whisper, my nails digging into his shoulders as I pull him impossibly closer. "I want you, JP. I've always wanted you."

Something shifts in his expression, something desperate and reverent, like the weight of my words hit deeper than I expected.

Then he's there, aligning himself with me, the thick head of his cock pressing against my entrance. His breath shudders as he pushes forward, the slow, torturous slide of him stretching me inch by inch stealing the air from my lungs.

A strangled moan escapes me, my head tipping back as my body adjusts to the sheer fullness of him.

"Cammy," he groans, his hands gripping my hips, holding me steady as he bottoms out, completely buried inside me. "Jesus, you feel—" He cuts himself off with a curse, his forehead dropping to my shoulder as he exhales heavily.

We stay like that for a moment, our bodies locked together, our breaths mingling in the heated air of the garage. The scent of ice and machinery lingers faintly, but all I can focus on is him— his warmth, his scent, the way his fingers tighten just enough to let me know he's barely holding on.

Then he moves.

Slow at first, his hips rolling against mine, dragging out the sensation until I'm trembling beneath him. His hands slide up my ribs, his thumbs grazing the sensitive undersides of my breasts before his mouth follows, lips closing around my hardening nipple, sucking just enough to make my back arch pressing me farther into him.

I whimper, my nails raking down his back as I rock against him, meeting each thrust with a desperation that makes my head spin.

"Fuck," he groans against my skin. "You're perfect. This—" He thrusts deeper, hitting just the right spot to make my vision blur. "This is fucking perfect."

He speeds up, our bodies moving together in a rhythm that's both frantic and unhurried, like we're both desperate and unwilling for it to end too soon. Each roll of his hips sends pleasure rippling through me, my body tightening, coiling, ready to snap.

I gasp, my legs tightening around his waist, pulling him impossibly deeper.

His hand slips between us, his fingers finding the swollen bundle of nerves between my thighs, as if he knows my body better than I do. The moment he presses down, my body shatters around his cock. Pulsating over and over, squeezing him tightly inside of me, milking him as I come.

I cry out his name, clinging to him as I free fall from the cliff, diving into an ocean of white-hot bliss, my vision almost blacking out as I come harder than I thought was physically possible.

JP curses, his grip on my hips tightening as he thrusts once, twice more before he stills, his entire body tensing as he finds his own release, spilling into me with a guttural groan. Filling me completely, without a condom.

For a long moment, neither of us moves. The only sound in the garage is our ragged breathing.

Then, with a satisfied sigh, JP pulls me against him, cradling me in his arms. He kisses the top of my head, his lips lingering as he murmurs, "I think I'm going to need to drive the Zamboni more often."

I let out a breathless laugh, my body still humming from the aftershocks. "As long as I'm your passenger."

His arms tighten around me, his voice filled with certainty. "You're the only one. I promise."

JP's lips brush against my temple, his arms still wrapped around me as we catch our breath. The heat between us lingers, but now it feels so much more than just sex... everything feels so different.

"I walked here from the apartment, but I saw your car in the players parking lot. Can I drive you home? I'm not ready to let you out of my sight yet."

I should say no. Should maintain some distance. But... I don't want to anymore. He told me that he'll tell me what happened in San Diego, as soon as he can. Maybe I need to trust him—but can I?

God, I want to.

"Okay," I hear myself say.

As we leave the stadium hand in hand toward the parking lot. I can only think of one thing.

Maybe some chances are worth risking. Even if they might break your heart.

CHAPTER EIGHTEEN

Cammy

Heading toward the rink this afternoon after work, I adjust the strap of my duffel bag over my shoulder. Dad texted me late last night about fitting in another practice this week. With the auction only a week away, I've been busy getting things ready, and he's been busy with the team's hectic schedule.

I told him to give me a head start after work. I need to warm up first and honestly, I'm still processing everything that happened with JP two nights ago on the Zamboni, even though I already know that I've decided to give us a chance, even if the idea still scares the hell out of me.

The ice has always been the place I do my best thinking.

As I lace up my skates, my mind wanders to him and the night he and I were out here together as he drove me around on the Zamboni, telling me about his dad and how meeting me for the first time made him want to give everything else up. I feel like I finally understand him better than I ever have.

It's no wonder that JP has been in my head nonstop. God, I can't stop replaying every moment we've had together over the last five weeks since he walked back into my life.

I'm halfway to the ice when I hear laughter—high-pitched and bright, the kind of sound that doesn't belong to the usual chorus of hockey players or staff. I pause, confused, and glance toward the rink. A cluster of kids and parents are out on the ice, some stumbling awkwardly in rental skates while others laugh and cheer.

And there, in the center of it all, is JP.

He's crouched low, helping a little girl steady herself as she clings to his hands. He grins at her, saying something that makes her giggle, her confidence growing as she takes a wobbly step forward. JP doesn't let go, his patience unshakable as he coaxes her into gliding.

"What's going on?" I ask, turning as Everett approaches, hands tucked casually into his suit pockets.

He smiles, nodding toward the ice. "Some of the families we're working with for the auction. They agreed to come out to the event and give their testimonials of how much the Kids with Cancer foundation has stepped in to help them. I think it will help donors give more if they can put a face to the cause. And I thought it might be good for them to see the space beforehand."

My gaze shifts back to the ice, where JP has moved on to another kid, tossing a puck back and forth with a boy who can't be older than six. "And JP?" I ask, unable to keep the curiosity from my voice.

"We ran into him when I was giving a tour of the stadium. When he saw the kids he ran down to the local rink to borrow skates for everyone," he says, his voice tinged with admiration. "Then he jumped right in, started giving the kids lessons on ice skating. The guy's a natural with kids."

My heart stutters. The sight of JP laughing and encouraging the kids tugs at something deep inside me. Everett's next words only make it worse.

"You've got a good guy there."

I flinch. "He's not mine," I say quickly, the words sour in my mouth.

Everett raises a brow, studying me with an expression that's far too knowing. "Are you sure? You could've fooled me," he says lightly before turning and heading back down the tunnel.

I stay rooted to the spot, my eyes fixed on JP as he kneels to tie a little boy's skate. He glances up then, catching me watching, and his face lights up with that infuriating, heart-stopping smile of his. He waves me over, but I shake my head, gesturing that I'll stay where I am.

JP huddles down with the kids, whispering something that has them all giggling. Then, in unison, they turn to me and say, "Please, come skate with us, Miss Wrenley!"

My heart squeezes. The way their voices echo through the arena, the way JP's eyes are practically daring me to say no—I don't stand a chance. With a resigned sigh, I step onto the ice.

The next twenty minutes are pure chaos—and pure joy. The kids swarm around me, giggling as they show off their moves or grab onto my arms for balance. JP watches from the edge, leaning against his stick with an easy grin, chiming in with encouragement or teasing when a kid does something silly.

At one point, he skates over to help me with a particularly bold six-year-old who's decided he's going to "race" me. JP crouches beside him, giving him tips on his form, his voice low and gentle. The boy nods and then takes off in a flurry of wobbly strides.

"You're good with them," I say as JP straightens, his eyes meeting mine.

"They make it easy." He shrugs, but there's lightness in his voice.

Before I can say more, the parents start rounding up the kids, herding them toward the tunnel with promises of lunch and naps. The arena grows quieter as they trickle out, leaving just JP and me on the ice.

"Want me to stick around for a bit?" he asks, tilting his head toward the goal. "I can help you with your slapshot."

I hesitate, the rational part of me screaming that this is a bad idea. But the way he's looking at me, with that mix of challenge and flirtation, is impossible to resist.

"Fine," I say, grabbing a puck and skating toward the blue line. "But only because I need to practice. Not because I need your help."

He smirks, following me. "Whatever you say, Wrenley."

We fall into an easy rhythm. JP feeds me pucks, offering tips on my stance and follow-through. Every now and then, he skates up behind me to adjust my grip or reposition my shoulders, his hands warm and steady on my arms.

Our bodies melding together like we belong connected. There's no awkward touch—no second-guessing.

Each connection has me looking forward to the next.

"You're gripping too tight," he murmurs, his breath brushing against my ear as he stands close behind me. "Relax your hands. Let the stick do the work."

I try to focus, but his proximity is distracting, his voice low and intimate. When he steps back, I release the shot, the puck soaring into the corner of the net with thud.

"Better," he says, grinning. "You're looking solid."

"Don't get cocky," I shoot back, though I can't help the small smile that tugs at my lips.

We keep practicing, each minute building on something that feels impossible to ignore. By the time I take my final shot, my legs are trembling—not from exertion, but from the way JP is looking at me, his gaze heavy like he's about to pick me up and carry me back off to the Zamboni garage again. It has me wondering.

What happens if my dad beats JP at the slapshot?

As crazy as it seems to leave everyone and everything I love here... do I go with him?

"Thank you for helping me today," I say.

He steps closer, his eyes searching mine. "Anytime. This is my favorite place on earth, and I get to be here, with you... well, there's nowhere I'd rather be than on home ice with you."

For a moment, I forget how to think, how to breathe. All I

can do is stare at him, my heart pounding so loud I'm sure he can hear it.

He leans in, his eyes dropping to my lips, and the world tilts on its axis. My pulse races, my body swaying toward him like a magnet.

He's going to kiss me. In the middle of the rink.

"Cammy!"

The sound of my name shatters the moment, and I jerk back, my head whipping toward the tunnel. My dad skates out, his expression hard and unyielding as his eyes lock onto JP.

JP steps back, his jaw tightening as he nods toward Seven. "I'll see you later," he says quietly before skating off, leaving me to face my dad.

"What's going on?" Seven asks, his voice clipped.

"Nothing," I say quickly, my cheeks burning. "JP was just helping me with my positioning."

Seven doesn't respond, his eyes narrowing as he watches JP disappear into the tunnel. When he finally turns back to me, his expression softens, but the tension lingers.

"Let's get to work," he says, motioning for me to line up at center ice.

As I skate to my spot, I can't shake the feeling of JP's hands on my arms, his voice in my ear, his eyes on mine. And as much as I try to focus, my heart refuses to listen, beating a frantic rhythm that has nothing to do with the game.

CHAPTER NINETEEN

JP

I check my watch as I head down the service corridor toward the locker room. Two hours until puck drop. Plenty of time for pre-game routine, but Coach Haynes likes us suited up early for home games. Something about team unity, but then I hear her.

The sound of Cammy's laugh stops me in my tracks.

She's in the main concourse, leading a group of suit-wearing investors on what appears to be a stadium tour. Her voice carries as she explains the arena's recent renovations, professional and poised. But what catches my attention is the jersey she's wearing.

Seven's number. Her father's legacy stretched across her shoulders like a shield, reminding me what's at stake.

The sight stirs something possessive in my chest. Before I can think better of it, I'm moving toward the group. Cammy's back is to me as she points out the new digital displays, giving me the perfect opportunity.

"Excuse me, Ms. Wrenley," I say, keeping my tone professional. "Could I borrow you for a moment? Equipment issue."

Her eyes gleam back at me the moment they meet, causing

my cock to stir. Now my equipment issue is a real problem. But as much as I'd like to do something about it, I doubt Cammy would agree to a quickie in the broom closet before the puck drop. Shaking the thought away, I focus on keeping my expression normal as she tilts her head curiously and then answers.

"Of course." She turns to her tour group next. "If you'll excuse me, gentlemen?"

The moment we're around the corner, I pull her into the equipment closet. The space is tight, filled with the scent of rubber, cleaning supplies, and her perfume.

"JP, what are you doing?"

"You're wearing the wrong number," I say softly, fingers finding the hem of Seven's jersey.

She's taken by surprise but lifts her arms to let me finish as I slowly lift it over her head, leaving her in a thin camisole that has me rethinking our time constraint. I was supposed to be in the locker room five minutes ago, and Cammy has a hallway full of Everett's inventors waiting for her.

Before she can protest, I'm pulling my own practice jersey from my bag.

"What are you doing?" she whispers, but she's not stopping me as I help her into it.

The sight of my number stretched across her back unlocks something primal in me. I turn her gently, adjusting the fabric until it sits just right.

"You look good in my number," I say, "*Dumont*" written over her shoulders, making me wonder what it would be like to make that permanent.

She looks up at me through her lashes, a slight flush coloring her cheeks. "This is a pretty big statement you're asking me to wear..."

"It's more than a statement," I say back.

Voices pass by the door, and reality crashes back in. She steps back quickly, gathering Seven's jersey.

"I have a tour to finish," she says, but there's a smile playing on her lips that's brighter than it was before.

"Wear it tonight?" I ask before she can leave. "For the game?"

She hesitates for a moment before nodding. My first victory of the night.

But I have one more play to make tonight, and it won't be in front of the net.

❧

Back in the locker room, Slade's words from weeks ago echo in my head again as I tape up my stick in the locker room.

You want it all? Then prove it. Prove you're not just another player passing through. Prove your end game material.

End game. The word sits heavy in my chest as I suit up. Because that's what Cammy is—what she's always been, if I'm honest with myself. Not just another conquest, not just another chance at redemption.

She's everything.

The energy in the stadium is insane tonight. Fans are on their feet before the puck even drops, the sound of their cheers vibrating through the walls of the arena. It's my first home game, and I'm locked in, focused on stopping every shot. Everything but this game fades away. Cammy, Coach Wrenley, my father's expectations. Out here on the ice, I have no questions of what I should be doing; this is all muscle memory, split-second decisions that have to be made before I even have time to think.

But knowing Cammy's here—in the stands—wearing my jersey, brings an unfamiliar calm I've never felt before. As if no matter what happens out here, I might finally have a shot with her. Or at least, I'm about to find out if I do.

The first period starts strong. My saves are clean, reflexes sharp. Save after save, the crowd chants my name, and I can feel the momentum shifting in our favor.

During a timeout, I spot her in Seven's season ticket seats beside Brynn, my number clearly visible even from the ice. The sight sends a surge of energy through my blood.

Seven's at the bench, arms crossed as he watches me. His expression is unreadable, but I know he's seen the jersey switch. He's watching everything I do out here, judging whether I'm worthy of wearing his team's colors.

Of loving his daughter.

The game is a battle from the start. The Wolverines aren't pulling any punches, but neither are we. Every shot they take is faster than the last, they want this win just as bad as we do, but my reflexes are on point tonight. After a big glove save midway through the second period, I glance toward the stands where I know she's sitting.

Sure enough, I find her. Cammy's leaning forward, her elbows on her thighs, her knee bouncing, completely focused on the game. Her hands clench into fists whenever the puck comes too close to the net. Brynn is next to her, equally engaged but focused on Milo, too, who's screaming and shouting, cheering on his team.

When the buzzer sounds signaling the end of the period, we're up 2-1. As I skate toward the tunnel, I sneak another glance in her direction. Our eyes meet, and for a brief second, the chaos of the arena around me fades. Her lips curve into the smallest smile, and my pulse ticks up a notch... as if it wasn't already beating fast enough.

I force myself to look away before I trip over my own skates. She'll never let me live that down.

Passing through the players tunnel and the home bench, I glance over to see Seven's stance, arms still crossed, staring directly at me. The message is clear: prove it. But I know tonight isn't just about Cammy. This is about me proving that I've earned my spot here.

So, I will.

Right before third period starts, I have a puck in my hand, the one I pulled from my bag before we headed out for the last period—the one I marked earlier with a silver sharpie.

The toss is perfect, sailing over the glass. Cammy reaches up for it, letting it fall right into her hands. She looks at the puck and then reads the simple message: *Dinner?*

This time, her smile is different from all the times before. My heart nearly stops when she nods yes.

Suddenly, this isn't just another home game anymore. This is the best night of my career.

I play the final period like I'm invincible, stopping everything that comes my way. Each save feels easier than the last, powered by the knowledge that she's watching, wearing my number, and finally—finally—said yes.

After the final horn and the celebration on the ice, I catch Cammy and Milo at the plexiglass, pounding on it as I skate by. When they both blow me a kiss, I nearly lose my balance and wipe out right there in front of everyone.

After a quick congratulations in the locker room, I'm heading to media in my game-day suit when I spot her waiting near the press room. She's still in my jersey. My chest fills with pride.

"Nice game," she says with a soft smile.

"Nice jersey," I counter, stepping closer.

She glances down at herself. "I'm a little underdressed for dinner now, aren't I?"

I bend down, my lips close to her ear. "Not even close. Seeing you in my jersey is better than lingerie." I lower my voice even more. "I can't decide if I like it better on you... or laying on my bedroom floor."

She bites down on her bottom lip, her eyes dilating at my admission. It's worth every second I've waited for this moment, and it takes everything in me not to kiss her right here as all my teammates walk by.

"Come on, lover boy," Hunter says, stopping behind me and squeezing my shoulders. "Kiss your girl later. You still have work to do."

Aleksi gives Hunter a shove to keep him moving down the hallway. "Your public awaits on bated breath to see the beauty," Aleksi says.

"More like they want their pound of flesh," I hear Trey say weaving around us.

I wave them off as if it's not important, but we all know that the press is part of our job, as much as we all hate it. "Yeah, yeah... I'm coming."

I brace a hand against the cement wall, leaning in closer so no one can hear us, but really it's just because I want her all to myself. "Team's heading to Oakley's to celebrate," I say, Cammy's eyes twinkling back at me. "We'll make an appearance, then slip out for dinner? Just us?"

She nods, and then licks her lips. "Just us."

My eyes drop to her mouth. "Perfect." I resist the urge to touch her, knowing the media's watching. "Give me fifteen minutes with the press?"

Her breath catches, and I'm not ashamed of the satisfaction that curls in my chest at the sound. I brush my lips against the side of her neck, a barely-there kiss, and feel the shiver that runs through her.

She inhales sharply, her scent—something warm and sweet— filling my lungs. When I pull back, her eyes are wide, the warm honey of her irises darkened and dilated.

"Do you think we have time before your interview?" she asks, her voice soft but edged with something unmistakable.

I don't even hesitate. "Fuck yeah."

Without another word, I grab her hand, weaving us through the crowd of players and staff. No one pays us much attention, too focused on post-game routines and celebrations. My grip tightens as I lead her toward the back hallway, adrenaline pounding in my veins.

I lead her to the same broom closet we were in earlier, tucked away and forgotten. I pull her inside, closing the door behind us, and in the dim light, all the tension that's been building between us snaps like a rubber band.

She barely has time to catch her breath before my hands are on her, sliding over the fabric of the jersey, up her sides, until they settle on her hips. Her back presses against the wall, and I lean in, my forehead resting against hers.

"You're dangerous, you know that?" I murmur, my voice rough. "Walking around in my number like this. Like you own me."

Her hands find the lapels of my suit jacket, tugging me closer. "And you're too cocky for your own good."

"Am I?" I ask, my lips brushing hers in a teasing, featherlight touch.

She doesn't answer—not with words, anyway. Instead, she tilts her head, closing the gap between us. The kiss is everything I've been holding back, weeks of frustration and yearning pouring out as I press her against the wall, my hands roaming under the jersey to find bare skin.

She breathes against my mouth, her fingers tangling in my hair. "You know how you had a fantasy of us on the Zamboni?"

"Yeah," I say, pulling back just enough to look at her. Her cheeks are flushed, her lips parted, and I swear I've never seen anything so beautiful.

"Well mine's always been to fuck you in your game day suit," she says with a smirk, and pulls me back in.

Her hands reach down, finding the zipper of my slacks, and within seconds, her warm dilated hand reaches past my briefs, wrapping around my hard cock.

She begins a tortuous rhythm, one that will have me coming before I even touch her if I'm not careful. I growl against her throat, my teeth nipping against her neck.

"As much as I love this, I need you to come with me, and we don't have time for both. The new media guru is probably looking for me," I say, closing my eyes to enjoy her last few strokes. We'll be exploring more later tonight—after Oakley's, after dinner—when I take her home with me because I can't spend another night without her in my bed.

"Afraid we'll get caught?" she asks with a glint in her eye.

"No, I'm not worried about that. I just want to see your eyes roll back when you take my cock before I have to face the tyranny of the press. Is that okay with you?"

"Sounds like we're on the same page," she says, reaching for the bottom of my jersey she's wearing, attempting to pull it off.

"No," I say, stopping her hands. "Keep that on. I want to see my name on your back when I fuck you."

She sucks her lower lip into her mouth, her breath hitching as I twist her around, reaching for the button of her jeans. With deliberate slowness, I unfasten them, my fingers brushing against the soft skin of her lower belly. Her body shudders under my touch, and I feel the sharp inhale she takes as I slide the denim and her black cotton panties down her legs, leaving her bare for me.

I take a step back for just a second, my gaze drinking her in—the soft curves of her hips, the delicate dip of her lower back, the way my jersey hangs off her shoulders, oversized and perfect. The sight of my name stretched across her back sends a fresh surge of possessiveness through me. After all these years, this woman is finally mine.

"Fucking perfect," I murmur, my hands skimming up her thighs before I guide her forward, bending her over against the wall.

She arches for me so beautifully, her palms braced against the surface, her breath already coming fast. My fingers slide between her legs, teasing through her folds, finding her soaked and ready. A low growl rumbles in my chest as I drag my cock through her arousal, coating myself with her wetness.

"You're dripping for me, mon ange," I say, my voice rough with need. "You want me to take you like this? Bent over and bare? Tell me."

"Yes," she whispers, her voice trembling. "Take me, JP."

That's all it takes.

I line myself up, pressing the thick head of my cock against her tight opening, watching her pink pussy stretch to fit me, inch by inch, her center squeezing around me. We both groan as I sink deeper, stretching her, filling her until I'm seated all the way inside her, buried in the tightest heat I've ever known.

"Fuck," I bite out, gripping her hips as I hold still for a moment, letting her adjust, letting me breathe through the overwhelming sensation of being completely sheathed inside her.

She lets out a soft, whimpering moan, shifting back against me, urging me to move.

That's all the invitation I need.

I pull back and thrust forward, slow at first, savoring the friction of her slick walls around me. But I don't stay slow for long. My control is slipping, unraveling with every deep thrust, every desperate sound she makes. My grip tightens on her hips as I drive into her, the force of it making her gasp and brace herself harder against the wall.

"Cammy," I groan, watching between us as I disappear inside her again and again.

She's clenching around me, her body gripping me so tightly the friction almost unbearable.

"Look at you," I whisper, my voice thick with admiration. "Taking me so perfectly. Nothing's ever felt this good. I swear, Cammy, my cock belongs inside you—and it never wants to leave."

"Then don't leave. Keep me," she moans, pushing back against me, meeting every thrust with the same desperate urgency I feel burning in my veins.

"I plan to," I grit out, thrusting into her with a punishing rhythm, each snap of my hips sending a sharp, sweet slap of skin against skin. The sight of her—bent over for me, her ass shaking with every stroke, her body taking everything I give—nearly undoes me.

"You're mine, Cammy," I growl, my fingers digging into her hips, anchoring her to me. "And I'm yours. Nothing is going to change that after tonight."

The words feel too small for what she means to me. For what this means to me.

One of my hands slides down between her legs, finding that sensitive bundle of nerves, rubbing in slow, torturous circles before speeding up when she gasps my name.

"This is where you like it, isn't it, mon ange?" I rasp against her ear, my fingers teasing her clit. "Right here, Cammy. This is where you come for me. And then I'll fill you so full, coating every inch inside you that your body will only ever want me."

Her body tightens, her breath coming in sharp gasps. She's right there, teetering on the edge, and I feel it—her walls fluttering around me, her muscles clenching like she's trying to hold me inside her forever.

She cries out a muffled "Oh, my God, JP," her body locking up as she shatters around me, her orgasm ripping through her, drawing me in with her.

I curse as the pleasure grips me, white-hot and relentless. My hips slam forward one last time as I come deep inside her, my cock pulsing as I spill every drop into her, exactly where it belongs.

I don't let her go. I wrap my arms around her, pulling her up against me, her back flush against my chest, my lips pressing to her bare shoulder as we both come down, our bodies trembling from the aftershocks.

"Tu détiens les clés de mon âme. Je suis à toi," I whisper against her ear, my hands smoothing over her skin, grounding us in the aftermath.

She sighs, her body softening against mine.

For a long moment, there's nothing but the sound of our ragged breathing, the heat of our bodies tangled together, and the faint hum of the arena's cooling system beyond the closet door.

Finally, I press one more kiss to her shoulder and smirk. "I think I need to fuck you in a jersey more often."

She laughs breathlessly, tilting her head back against my shoulder. "Only if it's yours."

The possessiveness inside me flares. "Always."

I run my hands up her thighs, still not ready to let her go.

And based on the way she presses herself closer, neither is she.

"You okay?" I ask softly, pressing a kiss to the back of her neck.

She nods, turning her head to glance at me over her shoulder. Her cheeks are flushed, her lips parted, and she looks completely wrecked—in the best way possible.

"I'm more than okay," she says, with a blissful smile stretched across her lips. "But now you're really going to be late for that interview. Will they fine you?"

I laugh softly, pressing another kiss to her shoulder before carefully easing out of her. I look around and find a box of tissues for us to clean up. It's not the best option, but it's the best we can do at the moment. I hand it to her first so she can clean as I help her straighten up. I pull her jeans back into place, my hands lingering on her hips longer than necessary.

Then I take care of myself and pull up my slacks, my cock unhappy about only going one round with her, but we have later tonight. Maybe, if I do everything right tonight, she'll agree to come home with me again and sleep in my bed.

"I'll take whatever punishment they throw at me," I say, brushing a strand of hair out of her face. "You are worth every penny."

"You make me sound like a sex worker," she teases.

"No, never, because you fuck so good... I'd never be able to afford you."

"You have such a way with words. Isn't the French side of you supposed to be the romantic side?"

"I'll show you the romantic side... tonight. Then I'll show you the "French" side in bed later... if you're a good girl."

She shakes her head. "I should go before someone starts looking for me."

"Not without this," I say, leaning in for one last kiss. It's slower this time, less urgent but no less intense. When I finally pull back, her eyes are shining.

A sharp knock on the door jerks us both out of the moment, and I swear under my breath. Cammy stifles a laugh, her face buried in my neck as I steady her back on her feet.

"Dumont, you've got media waiting!" a muffled voice calls from the hallway.

"Be right there!" I shout back, my voice rougher than I'd like. Turning to Cammy, I brush a thumb over her flushed cheek. "Give me fifteen minutes to answer questions?"

She nods, her eyes still dazed. "I'll hold you to it."

As we step out of the closet, back into the chaos of the arena, I feel her hand slip into mine for the briefest second before she lets go. It's enough to keep me grounded, to remind me that this isn't just a fleeting moment.

It's the start of something bigger. And I'm not letting it slip away again.

The post-game media session is a whirlwind, as always. Cameras flash, reporters fire off questions, and I give the same canned answers I've rehearsed a hundred times.

"How does it feel to get your first win as a Hawkeyes, JP?"

"Great. The team played hard, and it's a privilege to be here."

"What does this win mean for your comeback?"

"Every game is important. I'm just taking it one at a time."

When it's finally over, I bolt for the locker room to change into jeans, desperate to get out of here and start the next phase of my plan. Dinner with Cammy.

Because tonight, Cammy said yes.

And that's better than any shutout.

CHAPTER TWENTY

This win feels different than any post-game I ever experienced before the Hawkeyes, mostly because I'm strolling into a team celebration with Cammy's hand in mine, her smile brighter than I've ever seen it. The team's already here—Hunter, Trey, Wolf, and Olsen are setting up a game of pool, Aleksi is trying to impress Kendall at the dartboard, Slade's holding court with Coach Haynes at one of the largest tables that Oakley reserves for the team on home game nights, while Scottie and Luka carry back another round for the guys.

My hand rests low on Cammy's back as I guide her to the table, and then pull out a chair for her beside Aria. She sits, shooting me an appreciative smile, and I press a quick kiss to the top of her head before straightening up.

"What do you want to drink?" I ask her, leaning in close to hear her over the crowd.

"White wine, please," she says, her eyes sparkling.

"Coming right up." I give her a wink before heading to the bar

I walk up to an open spot, bellying up to the bar next to Aleksi. I feel Aleksi's hand slap my back when he sees me.

"You finally got the girl, huh?" Aleksi teases, his grin wide. "About time."

"Let's just hope I can keep her," I reply, half-joking but feeling the weight of those words as I glance back at her. She's laughing at something Aria said, her whole face lit up. She's happy, and I hope that I'm a part of that.

The moment shifts as I turn back to the bar and catch Seven's eyes from across the room. He's leaning against the wall, arms crossed, his expression unreadable but far from happy, a pool cue in his hand. I've gotten used to his quiet disapproval, but tonight it feels sharper, like a threat.

He saw us come in—of course he did, but I won't hide it. If he wants to bench me, then he'll bench me.

At the bar, Oakley greets me with a nod. "Nice game, JP."

"Thanks," I say, sliding my card across the counter. "A beer for me, white wine for her. Merci."

As Oakley grabs the glasses, I feel a hand clap my shoulder. Turning, I'm met with a wide grin. "JP Dumont, you magnificent bastard!"

"Oliver?" I say, startled. "What are you doing here?"

Oliver Garcia, my former teammate from San Diego, the same one who got kicked off the team last year for getting into a fight with our mascot, sending him to the ER. Needless to say, he doesn't play for the Blue Devils anymore. He and I never had a problem, but I stayed out of the way of his fists when he'd get blackout drunk, which helped. He pulls me into a back-slapping hug. "Had a meeting in Seattle for a sportscaster job, saw you were playing, and I had to see it for myself. Good game out there— classic Dumont."

The easy camaraderie between us feels good, but as Oakley hands me the drinks, I feel the tension in the room shift. The air grows heavier, and when I glance around, I catch a few Hawkeyes regulars straightening in their seats, their eyes narrowing.

"You've got some nerve showing up here," someone calls out.

Oliver turns, his smile faltering. "Excuse me?"

"That hit on Slade," another voice adds. "Championship game against the Hawkeyes. Ring any bells?"

Shit. I hadn't been playing for the Blue Devils that year. They signed me the following year, but the memory flashes through my mind. I watched it all play out on TV—Slade going down hard, Oliver's stick coming up, the aftermath that nearly ended both careers. And the Hawkeyes fans who watched as Slade was carried off the ice, headed for the ER. They missed their chance at the Stanley Cup—none of them have forgotten.

I step in quickly, hoping to defuse the situation. "Guys, come on. It's ancient history."

"Easy for you to say," one of the regulars snaps. "You weren't here."

They aren't wrong, but my focus is on keeping things from escalating. I catch Cammy watching from the table, her brow furrowed with concern. She stands, moving toward me, and the protective instinct kicks in. I always want her close but not in the middle of this.

"Maybe we should all take a breath," Cammy says, her tone calm.

But then someone shoves Oliver. He stumbles back into a table, and chaos erupts.

I push Cammy behind me as Mike, one of the regulars, takes a swing at Oliver. I block it, trying to keep things from spiraling further. "Mike, stop—"

A fist connects with my jaw from somewhere I didn't see coming. I'm not even sure who threw the punch before the metallic taste of blood fills my mouth. I'm barely able to register it because I hear Cammy cry out.

"Cammy!" Seven's voice cuts through the noise as he races behind me helping her up. Blood trickles from a small cut on her forehead where she hit the corner of a table.

"Brynn," Seven calls sharply.

Brynn is there before I can get through the people squabbling, creating a wall between Cammy and me.

"I'm right here," Brynn says, kneeling next to Cammy.

"You two get out of here. Take her to our place. I'll meet you there after I help Oakley," I hear him say, and I push my way through players and regulars trying to calm down the small fight going on.

I leave Oliver to defend himself... He had this coming anyway. He's lucky Slade is still playing to this day and didn't press charges against him.

I try to reach for her, but Seven's glare stops me cold.

Oakley's whistle pierces the air. "Everybody out! Now!"

The bar clears quickly, Brynn pulling Cammy with her, leaving just me, Slade, and Seven behind. Oakley's employees are quickly running around, cleaning up broken beer bottles and turned over chairs.

"This is what I was talking about," Seven says quietly, his voice harder than I've ever heard it. "The chaos that follows your family name."

Slade steps up. "Seven, give him a break. He didn't cause this."

Seven turns to him. "Is she your daughter? The one you're responsible for protecting against anything that threatens her safety?"

Slade's jaw tightens for a second, and we both know that he can't help me. I've never seen Seven use that tone with Slade before, and I have a feeling that neither has he. "No," he says flatly, knowing that it's time to back off.

I appreciate him anyway. But Seven's right. This is my fight.

Slade heads to the back of the bar, looking for Oakley to see what he can do to help clean up.

"I didn't start this—"

"Doesn't matter." He steps closer, his hands on his hips as he lets out a deep sigh. "Your father was the same way. And innocent people always got caught in the crossfire. He never thought it was his fault either. I was at the bar the night your mom stepped in to stop a fight when your father got too drunk and started a fight with a group that he shouldn't have. She paid for that with a night in the hospital, and your dad woke up in some alley, claiming he doesn't remember her getting hit when she stepped in at the wrong time. She filed for divorce the next day and took you away, didn't she?"

The words hit like body shots, each one finding its mark. He's trying to prove a parallel between how my father treated my mother and how I will treat Cammy, and though I can deny it all I want, Cammy's in a cab right now after getting hurt during a bar fight that somehow I got pulled into.

"I'm not my father," I say instead.

"No?" Seven says, his tone calmer than before. "Then prove it. I've tried to warn you off of her. I've tried threatening your career. None of it worked, and I should have known that you're determined enough to think you could have both. But now I'm going to test just how much you care about my daughter." His eyes narrow on mine as if he'll find something he's looking for. "Walk away now. Before she gets hurt worse than a bump on the head, and then I might just believe that you're not your old man. He would have never done right by your mom, but at least she was smart enough to leave and take you as far away from him as possible."

I think about the cut on Cammy's head, about how my attempt to protect her ended with her getting hurt anyway. About how many times I've watched history repeat itself with my father.

"She deserves better," Seven continues softly. "And you already know that, don't you?"

I thought I could be good enough for her by simply trying. But maybe I'll never escape who I am, and I refuse to let Cammy live the life my mother did before she got a divorce.

"What do you expect me to do? I just got her back," I say, though I know what I have to do.

"Give her up. And make it believable," he says.

My phone feels heavy in my hand as I type out the message:

> **JP: I'm sorry about what happened tonight. You were right from the beginning. This isn't going to work.**

Seven watches me hit *send*, approval finally softening his features. "Thank you."

I nod once, unable to speak past the tightness in my throat.

Maybe some things really are genetic.

Maybe some people really aren't meant for happy endings.

And maybe, just maybe... protecting Cammy means letting her go.

CHAPTER TWENTY-ONE

Cammy

I stare at JP's text message for what feels like the hundredth time, my thumb hovering over the screen. It's been two days since the incident at Oakley's.

I'm sorry about what happened tonight. You were right from the beginning. This isn't going to work.

The words blur together as I read them again, trying to make sense of them. My head throbs where the small cut sits near my hairline, but it's nothing compared to the ache in my chest.

After everything that happened between us two nights ago—the jersey, the closet, him making me feel like I was his entire world—how could he possibly think we're not going to work?

I type out another message, adding to the string of unanswered texts I've sent over the last two days.

> **Cammy: What do you mean?**

> **Cammy: This is ridiculous. At least talk to me.**

I call JP. No answer.

> **Cammy: Are you honestly not going to pick up?**

The message shows as delivered, but like all the others, there's no response. No typing indicator. No sign that he's even reading them.

My phone records mock me: six calls, all sent straight to voicemail. Fifteen texts, all unanswered. Two days of silence that feel like an eternity.

The bruise near my temple has faded to a dull yellow, barely visible unless you know where to look. It's nothing—a scratch, really—but somehow it's become everything. The reason JP pulled away, the excuse he needed to run.

Again.

This all feels like Déjà vu.

I push away from my desk, unable to focus on the auction paperwork spread out in front of me. The arena feels different today, colder somehow. Through my office window, I can see the team practicing on the ice below. JP's guarding the net, his movements smooth yet mechanical as he blocks shot after shot.

He's playing better than ever. And somehow, that makes it worse.

Because while I'm up here falling apart, he seems completely fine. More than fine—he's excelling.

My phone buzzes, and my heart leaps. But it's just Brynn.

> **Brynn: You okay? Haven't heard from you since that night.**

> **Cammy:** I'm fine. JP's not talking to me.

> **Brynn:** What do you mean not talking to you?

> **Cammy:** Radio silence since Oakley's. Won't answer calls or texts.

> **Brynn:** Want me to talk to Seven?

> **Cammy:** No. I need to handle this myself.

It was his day off yesterday, and when I went to his apartment door to see if he was home so he could offer me an explanation in person, no one answered. His car wasn't in the parking garage either.

I watch as JP makes another impossible save, the small crowd of practice observers cheering—mostly Hawkeyes staff and coaches and family members. Even from here, I can see the tension in his shoulders, the way he's holding himself too rigid, too controlled.

Something's wrong. I know it in my bones.

The problem is, he won't let me close enough to figure out what it is.

I grab my jacket. If he won't answer my calls, I'll make him face me in person. I've done the waiting game before—back when he first left, when I spent months wondering what I did wrong, why I wasn't enough.

I'm not doing it again.

I spend the time during the walk down to the ice level preparing myself for the physical version of our digital interaction—which is a cold shoulder. How did we get here when only a couple of days ago, he pulled his jersey over my head like a claim and took me against the broom closet wall without a condom? Now, I doubt he'd even respond via carrier pigeon.

Practice is wrapping up; I can hear Coach Haynes giving final instructions, the sound of skates scraping ice as players head toward the tunnel.

I position myself near the locker room entrance, heart pounding. JP will have to pass by here. He'll have to acknowledge my existence.

The players start filing past, some nodding in greeting, others too focused on their post-practice routines to notice me. And then I see him, bringing up the rear, his mask pushed up on top of his head.

"JP!"

He freezes, his eyes meeting mine for a split second before darting away. The look in them is a mixture of pain and distance, as if he's shut down. There's no sparkle in them anymore—no fire. I take in a deep inhale.

"Cammy, can I grab you for a second?"

Matt's voice cuts through the moment, and I want to scream in frustration. The equipment manager is standing just a few feet away, holding a stack of jerseys and wearing an apologetic expression.

"You can see me?" I ask Matt as JP walks past us.

"Uh, yes, Cammy, I can see you," he says with confusion as if he's not sure if he answered the question correctly.

"Good, I thought maybe I died and returned as a ghost, and now I'm invisible."

I turn to see JP's shoulders tense. He's taking large steps away from us, but at least he heard me.

"No... not at all. I can see you just fine," Matt says while scratching his neck, not knowing where I'm going with my questioning.

I really shouldn't let JP turn me into Penelope's crazy assistant that no one wants to be around. I should be more professional than this. As Penelope's right hand, the crew have high expectations for me, and it's my job to deliver.

"Sorry, Matt. What can I help you with?" I try to steady my voice, putting my "assistant to the GM" face back in place.

"It's about the auction items—there's a mix-up with the jerseys, and I need your input before I take them to be signed."

I glance back toward JP, but he's already walked away, his broad shoulders disappearing around the corner. My chest tightens, anger and hurt warring for dominance.

"Fine," I say to Matt, following him into the equipment room even as my heart screams at me to go after JP.

By the time I finish sorting out the jersey issue, JP is long gone. Again.

I lean against the wall outside the equipment room, letting out a shaky breath. This can't keep happening. I won't let it keep happening.

My phone feels heavy in my hand as I pull it out one more time.

> **Cammy: You can't avoid me forever. We work in the same building.**

The message shows as delivered, and for a moment, I see the typing indicator appear. My heart leaps—

And then it disappears.

Just like him.

౿

The next two days pass in a blur of auction preparations and failed attempts to corner JP. He's become a ghost in his own arena, appearing only for practice and games, vanishing the moment the final whistle blows.

I catch glimpses of him—in the hallway, on the ice, leaving the parking lot—but he's always just out of reach. Always one step ahead of me, as if he's memorized my schedule just to avoid it.

"It just doesn't make any sense," Aria tells me over coffee at Serendipity's. "You two looked... I don't know, settled at Oakley's. Does that even make sense?"

I know what she means. It seemed like finally, we were on the same page. That we had made the conscious decision to be a couple, even though we were technically only going on our second date. That is if you call the Pike's Place outing a date.

I stir my coffee more aggressively than necessary. "I thought we were settled, too. Oakley's was supposed to be the start. I don't know how it could have changed so quickly."

"And he's seriously dodging you after practice?"

I nod and then pull my cup up to my lips to take a sip.

"What are you going to do?" she asks.

"I can't let him disappear without explanation. Not a second time."

She reaches across the table, squeezing my hand. "Then don't let him."

I glance back at my friend, knowing she's going through it, too.

"How's the job search?" I ask.

She rolls her eyes, taking a sip of her own coffee. "Not great. Phil was incredibly considerate with my salary. He knew what I had going on at home and was generous to help my sister and me."

"Why didn't you tell Everett any of this?" I ask, knowing that her sister's cancer treatment is expensive, and she's now draining her hard-earned savings.

"Because I don't want to be anyone's charity case. Not even the billionaire whose monthly budget on suit ties would probably wipe out my sister's medical bills in one go."

I know she needs this job, and I hate that she hasn't found anything yet. "Speaking of charity, you're still coming out with us to try on dresses, right?" I ask.

"I wouldn't miss it. Penelope is demanding to buy my dress. I feel like she's up to something," Aria says with a raised brow.

"Oh... Penelope Matthews is always up to something," I wink.

❧

The opportunity comes later that afternoon. I'm heading to the media room with some paperwork when I spot JP coming out of the training room. He's alone—no teammates, no staff, no convenient interruptions.

This time, he doesn't see me coming.

"We need to talk," I say, stepping directly into his path.

He stops short, his eyes widening slightly before his expression smooths into something carefully neutral. "Cammy—"

"Don't 'Cammy' me," I snap. "Four days of silence? Really? After everything that happened at Oakley's?"

His jaw tightens. "I sent you a text."

"A text?" I laugh, but there's no humor in it. "You mean your cryptic 'this isn't going to work' message? That's not an explanation, JP. That's not even close to good enough. The last time you did this, I got over two dozen text messages and a handful of rambling voicemails. So, don't tell me your one text was good enough."

He shifts his weight, his eyes darting past me like he's searching for an escape route. "I can't do this right now."

"Can't or won't?"

"Both." His voice is rough, strained. "We're at work, Cammy."

"At work?" The words taste bitter on my tongue. "The same place where you fucked me on top of the Zamboni and almost missed media because you had me bent over in the broom closet? Is that the work you're referring to?"

Something flashes in his eyes—pain, maybe, or regret—but it's gone before I can be sure. "It's better this way—for you."

"Oh... how sweet, you're doing this for me?" I step closer, close enough to catch the familiar scent of his cologne. "Because from where I'm standing, it looks like you're running away. Again."

He flinches at that, and for a moment, I think I've broken through whatever wall he's built between us. But then his expression hardens.

"I'm not running," he says quietly. "I'm protecting you."

"From what?" I demand. "From Oliver Garcia? From a bar fight that wasn't even your fault. Or from yourself?"

He doesn't answer, but his silence says enough.

"You don't get to make that decision for me," I tell him, my voice shaking with anger and something else—something that feels dangerously close to heartbreak. "You don't get to decide what's best for me without even talking to me about it."

"Cammy—"

"No." I cut him off, stepping back. "You want to protect me? Fine. But don't pretend this is about anything other than you being too scared to face whatever this is between us. You sabotaged this as soon as it got real. Just like San Diego. I guess your text wasn't full of shit after all... I was right not to trust you."

I turn to leave, then pause, looking back at him one last time. "You know what the worst part is? I actually thought this time would be different."

The walk back to my office is a blur, my vision clouded by tears I refuse to let fall. I've barely made it through the door when my phone buzzes.

> **Brynn: Just a reminder to meet for dress shopping tomorrow.**

I stare at the message, thinking about the auction, about JP, about everything that's led us here.

I need a night with the girls outside of the walls of this stadium, dress shopping and forgetting everything between him and me.

Cammy: I'll be there.

Because if JP wants to push me away, fine. I'll give him exactly what he wants.

And I'll look damn good doing it.

CHAPTER TWENTY-TWO

Cammy

Picking out dresses with the girls today is exactly what I need after seeing JP yesterday. The French-style decor of the boutique pulls me out of the hockey world I've felt like I've been drowning in for days, waiting impatiently for JP to explain what the hell happened at Oakley's that night. But now I know that he's not going to give me one.

"At least try the black one, too," Penelope insists, passing me another dress through the fitting room curtain.

I catch my reflection in the mirror, fingers tracing the small bruise near my hairline; the cut is already smaller. The mark has faded to a yellowish green, barely visible unless you know where to look, but the memory of that night at Oakley's plays in my mind like a movie I can't stop watching.

One moment, I was on top of the world. JP's jersey hung perfectly across my shoulders, his number on my back feeling like a claim–a promise. His hand rested warm and sure against my lower back as he guided me to the table. The kiss he dropped on my head in front of everyone made my heart soar, the sensation between my thighs of where he took me in the broom closet less than an hour earlier still deliciously tingling from the friction.

After all these years between us, of fighting the pull, the attraction neither of us could deny—and then the night when it all went wrong a year and a half ago—it all was leading up to that night at Oakley's, and no one was more ready for it than me.

Our plan was simple: make an appearance, celebrate with the team, and then we'd leave. The dinner date he'd been asking me out on for years was finally going to happen, and I couldn't have been more ready.

Then Oliver Garcia walked in, and I should have known the minute I saw him that it was a bad omen for our future plans. Only minutes later, everything blew up—everything happened so fast.

The memory floods back, sharp and clear.

I reached them just as the first shove happened. JP immediately pushed me behind him, protective instinct taking over. But there were too many people, too much movement. Someone's elbow caught my temple as they lunged past, sending me stumbling into a table corner.

The pain was sharp but brief—more surprising than anything. But my dad's voice cut through the chaos like a blade: "Cammy!"

Before I could process what was happening, Brynn was pulling me toward the door, Seven's orders ringing in my ears: "Get her home. Now."

I tried to look back, to catch JP's eye, but the last thing I saw was his face—blood on his lip, expression torn between reaching for me and calming down the crowd—trying to regain order with Oakley and the other Hawkeyes players.

"You okay in there?" Brynn calls out, pulling me from the memory.

"Yeah," I manage, though I'm anything but okay. The black dress slides on easier than the red one from earlier, but it feels wrong. Everything feels wrong. That dinner we never got to have hanging over me like a ghost of what could have been. His lack of reasoning for why we're better apart is the most painful of all.

What happened to the JP who sent me countless texts and voicemails after he got bailed out of the jail after the accident? The one who did everything to get my attention—to win me back—only to fold so quickly just because of a little fight at the bar? He's a hockey player for Christ's sake. Of course, there are going to be occasional fights—mostly on the ice, but still.

Something just doesn't add up.

Nothing makes sense.

When I step out, Aria whistles low. "Damn, girl."

"The bruise is barely visible now," Penelope notes, studying my reflection.

"Unlike JP's absence," Aria mutters, earning an elbow from Brynn. "Has he texted you back yet to give you a reason for what happened at Oakley's?'"

I blow out a breath as I stand in front of the floor-to-ceiling three-way mirrors in front of the girls, most of whom have already chosen their dresses. I got here late, trying to get the last people on the donor list confirmed for tickets. With the auction coming up, it's crunch time. Thankfully, at least at work, I've been so busy that it's kept my mind mostly off of JP and our fall out. At least, until our conversation today.

"Not exactly," I say, adjusting the black dress against my hips. "I've texted, called—no response. I knocked on his door the night Brynn dropped me back off at my place after my dad cleared me. And then, I saw him today at the stadium and I took my shot to get some answers."

One of the other doors to the dressing room opens, and Kendall walks out fully dressed with the gown she picked out slung over her arm. It's perfect for her, and it was a unanimous vote from all of us when we saw it on her. "What explanation did he have for ghosting you since Oakley's?" Kendall asks.

"Barely. He just told me that I'm better off without him.'" I tell her.

The memory of him looking straight at me when he uttered

those words, still stings.

She hands her dress to the saleswoman to hold for her while she waits for Aria and me to pick out our dresses, and then takes a seat next to Penelope. "So what are you going to do?" she asks.

I pause for a second, staring back at myself, unable to think of anything else besides if this dress is enough to bring JP to his knees and realize he made a mistake. "Nothing. " I say.

"You're not going to do anything?" Brynn asks softly.

"He won't even look at me. He's been avoiding me for days and he wont return a text or phone call. I had to ambush him in the halls of our workplace to get him to talk to me." I admit, the words burning my throat. "As if I need more ways to be rejected."

"Men are idiots," Aria declares on the other side of her changing room door, but Penelope shakes her head.

"I don't disagree with that statement, but I think there's more to this. We've all seen the way that JP looks at you. And he's been relentless with his efforts to get you to see him differently after the whole fiasco in San Diego. Slade's mentioned some things too..." she says with hesitation as if maybe she shouldn't be saying anything.

"What do you mean Slade mentioned some things to you? Like what?"

"Nothing specific, unfortunately... and trust me, I shook that man like a fruit tree in the bedroom, trying to get it out of him, but he wouldn't give much up this time. He said that the conversations that he's had with JP would suggest that not even hockey would stand in the way of him winning you back," Penelope says.

"Aww," Aria fawns, the sound of a taffeta fabric rustling around as she pulls on another dress of her own.

Penelope's intel from Slade only serves to further increase my frustration over all of this.

"If that's true, then why did he fold so easily? Why did he send the text about ending things between us after only a small scuffle with an old Hawkeyes rival at a bar? This is the second time he's left me with no explanation for his actions."

"Yes, the hit you took didn't send you to the ER, but it was bad enough to scare the hell out of JP," Aria comes out with a dress slung over her arm. The first dress she tried on that everyone loved. "I don't know what he's thinking but you should have seen his face when he saw Seven at your side."

Brynn lips crinkle at one corner as she thinks hard about it. "We're missing something here. There's some kind of influence causing him to make this decision, and if he's already told Slade that hockey won't keep him from you, what other options do we have?"

We all fall silent for a moment, but no one comes up with an idea. Or at least not one they are willing to offer up for conversation.

Finally, Penelope clears her throat. "Well, all I know is that he needs to man. You deserve a full explanation."

As if getting dumped before our relationship ever started, for yet a second time, and having the entire Hawkeyes team witness it, isn't bad enough, he's treating me like a pariah–ignoring me every chance he gets.

I turn back to the mirror, sliding my hands down the black silk gown. It's gorgeous, but it's not the one. I need a dress that makes JP swallow his damn tongue..and then choke on it. "Yeah, well, he made his feelings clear enough yesterday in the hallway," I say. I glance over at the dress that Brynn pulled for me earlier. An emerald green dress that Jessica Rabbit would surely approve of. Everything about it screams revenge dress—it's plunging neckline, corseted, mostly sheer bodice with perfectly placed nipple coverage, and just the right amount of delicate beading to make it shimmer under these lights.

"At least the auction is coming up. He'll have a hard time ignoring you then," Kendall says.

I stare at the dress, and make the decision to go all out. "I'm going to try on one last dress."

Brynn jumps up immediately with a smile. "Here, you're going to need help with that zipper." She follows me to the changing room and then turns to the rest of the group before closing the door behind us. "Our appointment time is almost up. Why don't you girls go ahead and check out with your dresses. We'll show you this one once it's on."

They all agree and stand, Aria with a revenge dress of her own that had Penelope's smile turning wicked. I've seen her working up some kind of match-making scheme. But who does she have in mind for Aria?

I don't get a chance to think too long on it before Brynn shuts the door behind us. I can tell she's listening for all the girls to walk away.

We both know she has something she wants to discuss with me in private because I can do just fine with the zipper on my own.

Once she seems satisfied that no one else is in ear shot, she keeps her voice low enough that it doesn't echo.

"The auction's in one more week," she says, making a circle with her finger to tell me to turn around. "Are you ready for the slapshot challenge?"

I spin around, giving her my back. "You mean am I ready to watch JP let my father ruin his career, by causing JP to drop his PTO contract?" I ask.

Now I know why she wanted alone time. Penelope still doesn't know that my dad's bet might single-handedly cause the Hawkeyes to lose their new goalie before their other goalie is even cleared to come back.

"Yes, the bet. How are you going to feel if your dad wins, and JP leaves?" she asks, unzipping me out of the black dress and carefully letting me step out before turning to set it back on its hanger.

I let the thought of that sit for a moment as I pull the other dress from its hanger, and I step into it.

"I'm not sure. I'm tired of all his secrets. I need to know the truth... about everything. But if he's going to make a habit of letting my father make his decisions for him, then maybe he should go."

"Your dad means well," Brynn says softly, helping me lift the dress into place. "Even when he's wrong about how to show it."

"I know he does. But this isn't about Dad. It's about JP choosing to walk away. Again."

Brynn zips the dress up, and she lets out a small gasp the second we both stare into the mirror.

"Oh, my God, Cammy. If I didn't know better, I'd say they made this dress for you. JP is going to eat his heart out when he sees you in this."

"I don't want him to eat his heart out. I want the truth about San Diego–about Oakley's–about everything...and this dress is going to get it for me."

Three years of saying no to him, and the one time I say yes, it leads us here... again. One almost-perfect night, and he's gone.

"The auction isn't just about fundraising anymore, is it?" she asks, but she knows the answer.

"No," I whisper. "It's about making him choose. Stay and fight for this—for us—or leave. No more letting my dad or his past or anything else decide for him."

"And if he chooses wrong?" Brynn's question hangs in the air.

I lift my chin, meeting my own eyes in the mirror. "Then at least I'll know."

As we head to the register, my phone finally buzzes. For a moment, my heart leaps, but it's just Everett confirming auction details. I try not to feel disappointed, but Penelope catches my expression.

"You know," she says softly, "sometimes the biggest goals come from the shots we're most afraid to take."

I think about JP, about the bet, about everything that's led us here. "Yeah," I reply, "but sometimes I wish the net wasn't so well defended."

The emerald dress feels heavy in my arms, like the weight of decisions yet to be made. It's seven days until the auction. Seven days to figure out if I'm really ready to face what happens next.

And seven days to decide if I want him to save it or let the puck slide in.

Because the truth is, I'm not sure which would hurt more—

my dad scoring and watching JP leave, or JP saving it and knowing he stayed because of a bet, not because he chose to fight for us.

CHAPTER TWENTY-THREE

JP

The sound of blades scratching against the ice drowns out any other thoughts I have besides watching Luka, Trey, and Slade heading straight for me. Slade shoots the puck to Trey as they haul ass toward me. I keep my vision on the puck, my breathing synchronizing, my mind quieting. Out here there's only one thing on my mind—blocking that puck.

I focus on the familiar weight of my gear, the way my pads settle against my legs as I drop into position. Practice has become my sanctuary lately—the one place where muscle memory can override everything else.

Trey shoots the puck to Luka at the last second.

"Heads up, beauty!" Luka calls out, winding up for a shot.

I track the puck's trajectory, my movements automatic. High glove side, trying to catch me cheating left. The save is clean, maybe too clean. Everything feels mechanical lately, precise in a way that has my save percentage climbing but my chest feeling hollow.

"Getting cocky there, Dumont," Aleksi chirps, skating past

with a grin. "You know what they say about goalies who peak during practice."

"Better than peaking after two pumps like you, Mäkelin," I shoot back, earning a chorus of "oohs" from the team.

The banter feels good, normal even. But there's a distance to it now, like I'm watching from behind glass. Just like I'm watching her.

I catch a flash of movement in the corporate offices above— Cammy's silhouette against the window. My chest tightens as she pauses, papers in hand, clearly visible even from here. Three stories of space between us, and she still feels within reach.

"Again!" Coach Wrenley's voice snaps me back to the ice. "Two-on-one drill. Slade, Hunter—show our goalie what a real shot looks like."

I force my eyes away from the window, settling into position. Slade and Hunter weave down the ice, their passes quick and spot on. The shot comes fast—Hunter to Slade then back to Hunter— but I'm already moving, stretching out to make the save.

"Nice work, Dumont," Seven calls out, the words clipped but genuine.

The praise should feel good. After all, Seven Wrenley, who I grew up emulating, is telling me that I had a good practice. Instead, it all falls flat. Because I know the cost of earning it—my relationship with Cammy. I've thrown myself into hockey because it's all I have left.

There is still an edge to the glances between Seven and me. The bet we agreed to still lingers between us, and with only two more days until the auction, it's evident that it's on both of our minds.

"Looking sharp out there," Trey says as we break for water. "Though you might want to ease up before you break something. Your intensity's been through the roof lately."

If only he knew. The intensity isn't about hockey—it's about not looking up, not letting myself think about her, about that night at Oakley's, about the way her blood looked dripping down her face.

"Just focused," I say, taking a long drink.

"Yeah?" Slade skates up, his expression knowing. "On the game or on avoiding a certain someone?"

I ignore him, skating back to the crease. The ice welcomes me back, cold and unforgiving, just like I need to be.

Because every save, every blocked shot, every moment of perfect positioning is one more reminder that I'm doing the right thing. That keeping her safe means keeping my distance. That some goals aren't worth the risk of scoring.

Even if it kills me to walk away.

The locker room used to feel like home. Now, it's just another place where I'm going through the motions, peeling off my pads while the guys' voices bounce off the walls around me.

"Food?" Hunter calls out, already halfway out of his gear. "I'm thinking about that diner off Fifth. The one with the waitress Bozeman's afraid to talk to."

"I'm not afraid," Olsen protests, throwing a roll of tape that misses Hunter by inches. "I don't date during the season."

"Bullshit. You dated that cheerleader from the Seattle football team for three months last year. And you've been on the Long Term Injury list for months, so being on the team isn't an excuse." Slade laughs. "The last time we went there for dinner, you physically hid behind your menu when Bristol came by to take your order."

The familiar rhythm of their chirping washes over me as I focus on my routine. Pads off, hung properly. Skates untied with careful attention. Each motion is deliberate, a distraction from the thoughts I can't quite shake.

"Dumont?" Luka calls out. "You in or what?"

It's been well over a week since the incident at Oakley's, and I've kept mostly to myself, I'll admit that.

I glance up, finding several pairs of eyes on me. "Yeah, I'll meet you there."

"That's what you said last time," Wolf points out from across the room, slinging a towel around his waist and heading for the showers, "and then you bailed."

"And the time before that," Hunter adds.

"I'll be there," I cut in, sharper than intended. The locker room falls quiet for a beat too long.

Slade breaks the silence, his voice casual but his eyes knowing. "Better be. You owe me for the NHL 25 match I beat you in two weeks ago."

I manage a grin that doesn't quite reach my eyes. "Pretty sure you still owe me from the match before that."

"Details, details." He waves it off, but I catch the way he studies me, like he's trying to read between the lines of my carefully constructed expressions.

The guys return to their usual chatter—upcoming game strategies, weekend plans, the latest drama with Cammy trying to get Hunter to do a podcast with a woman from Bleacher Report—but I feel disconnected from it all, like I'm watching a TV show about someone else's life.

"Hey." Slade's voice is low as he drops onto the bench beside me. "You know you don't have to do this, right?"

"Do what?" I ask, though we both know what he means.

"This whole lone wolf thing. The team's got your back. And I don't know what's going on with you and Cammy, but you've been off this last week—"

"Don't," I cut him off, the word coming out rougher than intended. "Just... don't."

I haven't told him about Cammy. About the text I sent, ending it to protect her from me at Seven's request. But I don't have to. Slade is intuitive enough to know that something is going on.

He holds up his hands in surrender, but his expression says this conversation isn't over. "All I'm saying is, sometimes the best defense is a good offense."

"Save the hockey metaphors for the ice," I mutter, standing to grab my bag.

"Fine," he calls after me. "But you better actually show up to the diner this time. I wasn't kidding about you owing me, and I plan on kicking your ass next week, too. Wouldn't want those bets stacking up too tall, wouldn't want to bleed you dry."

Normally, I'd laugh at him thinking that he has any chance of beating me in the next game, but I don't have it in me this time.

I wave in acknowledgment, heading for the showers. The hot water beats against my shoulders, but it does nothing to wash away the memory of that night at Oakley's. The sound of breaking glass. The chaos. The sound of Seven's voice cutting through the crowd. The sight of Cammy's blood.

By the time I'm dressed, most of the guys have cleared out. The locker room feels bigger somehow, emptier. Or maybe that's just me, echoing in all the spaces I've carved out between myself and everyone else for the last week.

I check my phone—no messages, because of course, there aren't. I made sure of that.

"Hey, JP." Hunter pokes his head back in. "You coming or what?"

"Yeah," I say, shouldering my bag. "I'm coming."

Because what else is there to do? Hockey is all I have left. Might as well lean into it for as long as I still have this team.

In two more days, I have to make a decision to fight to keep it, or do myself the favor of letting go and keeping distance from the woman I want more than any of this. Maybe the best thing I can do is leave and try to forget the moment when I almost had it all—twice.

The diner off Fifth is exactly what you'd expect from a hockey hangout—worn leather booths, memorabilia covering the walls, and enough carbs on the menu to fuel three teams. The familiar bell chimes as we push through the door, and the waitress—the one Olsen's been avoiding—gives us a knowing smile.

"The usual table?" she asks, already grabbing menus.

"Thanks, Bristol." Hunter grins, then stage-whispers, "Olsen says hi."

Olsen's face goes red as she laughs, and I almost smile. Almost.

We slide into our usual booth, the vinyl seats creaking under our weight. I end up wedged between Slade and the wall, trapped in more ways than one.

"So," Hunter starts, studying his menu like he doesn't order the same thing every time, "anyone want to talk about how Dumont's trying to break every save record we have?"

"Trying?" I arch an eyebrow. "Pretty sure I already broke three."

"There he is." Slade elbows me. "I was starting to think we lost you to the robot apocalypse."

The guys laugh. I have been different lately—more focused, more exact, more... empty.

Bristol appears with waters, and Olsen suddenly becomes very interested in his phone. "Ready to order?"

"Give us a minute, will you?" Slade asks with a patient smile, then turns to me once she's gone. "Seriously, though, what's going on with you? You're playing better than ever, but..."

"But what?" I challenge, even though I know exactly what he means.

"But you're not you," he finishes. "It's like watching a highlight reel on repeat. Perfect form, zero joy."

I stare at my menu, the words blurring together. "Maybe I'm just focused on the game."

"Bullshit," Hunter cuts in. "This is about Cammy."

The name hits like an ice bath, knocking the air from my lungs. "We're not talking about this."

"Fine," Slade says easily. "Then we'll talk about how you haven't been to team breakfast in the last week. Or how you skip out on every post-practice hangout. Or how—"

"I get it," I snap, then immediately regret it when several heads turn our way, "I'm here now, aren't I?"

"Yeah, but are you really?" Olsen asks, finally looking up from his phone. "Because it seems like you're just going through the motions."

Before I can respond, Bristol returns with two extra-large

orders of fries—on the house—while we wait for our meals. Most of us ordered more than one. We're here often, always leaving a generous tip, and she knows we're starving after practice.

Once she walks away, the table falls into an uncomfortable silence.

"She got hurt on my watch, okay? Maybe the Dumont genes run a little deeper than I thought. She's better off without me."

Slade's eyebrows furrow. "That's what this is about? Are you serious?" Slade says finally. "You think you and Cammy are going to end up like your parents? Oliver fucking Garcia is the only motherfucker responsible for what happened to Cammy that night. And I get it—you're protecting her. Noble, self-sacrificing, very on-brand for you," he says sarcastically, "but have you considered that maybe she doesn't want to be protected? If you haven't noticed, Cammy isn't exactly a wilting wallflower. She can hold her own. You're not giving her a chance."

I think about the cut on her forehead, the way my heart stopped when I saw Seven lifting her off Oakley's wood floors and Brynn wrapping her arm around her, pulling Cammy out of the bar. "It's not that simple."

"It never is," Hunter agrees. "But, man, you're playing like you've got nothing left to lose. And that's not okay."

"Maybe I don't," I admit quietly, the words slipping out before I can stop them.

The table falls silent again, but this time it's heavy with understanding. These guys know loss—we all do. It comes with the sport, and every one of us has had losses in other parts of our lives. But this is different. This is about choosing to lose something before it can be taken away.

"You know what your problem is?" Slade says suddenly, stealing a fry from Hunter's plate. "You're thinking like a goalie. You're on the defense."

"That's literally my job," I point out.

"On the ice, sure. But off it?" He shakes his head. "Sometimes you have to take the shot, even if you might miss."

I think about the upcoming charity auction, about Seven's challenge. About how easy it would be to just... let the puck go in. To walk away from everything—the team, the city, her.

Watch my entire life go up in flames, and watch it happen from between the pipes.

"Or sometimes you come to terms with the fact that you can't win every game," I say back.

This isn't about a game, or a shot... this is about doing what's right for Cammy, no matter what it costs me.

Soon, the baskets of fries are gone, and Bristol shows up with our food. The guys carry on about our next game and the team we're up against as I quietly eat, thinking about everything Slade and Hunter said.

The walk back to my apartment feels longer than usual. The guys offered to share an Uber, but I needed the air. Needed the space to think.

My phone vibrates, Angelica's name lighting up the screen. For a moment, I considered letting it go to voicemail, but I've been avoiding her calls and texts since the fight at the bar.

"Hey," I answer, my breath fogging in the cold November air.

"Hey..." she starts. "Are we finally going to talk about what happened at Oakley's? You know I saw the news. Did you think I'd forget?"

I close my eyes, remembering the way Cammy looked in my jersey that night. The way she fit against me. The way everything felt right until it all went wrong.

"Of course, I didn't think you'd forget—you never forget my shortcomings. Like I said before, it's your worst quality."

She chuckles. "Yes, well, you weren't blessed with an obnoxious little sister, so God gave you me."

"So, he's the one I have to blame for this phone call? Got it," I say. "Is that all you had to call about?" I ask, hopeful but knowing it never goes this easy.

"Not a chance. Sounds like Garcia strikes again, huh? Ballsy for him to think he could walk into the Hawkeyes lair without getting served up. That idiot always did have bigger balls than brains."

That earns her a chuckle from me. It feels foreign almost, as if it's not coming from me.

"I think he forgot that he's no longer traveling with a group of hockey players willing to fight his battles for him."

"And Cammy? I think I heard something about that," she says.

"She got hurt because of me," I say quietly.

"No, she got hurt because some drunk idiot punched a wasp's nest and got stung. That's not on you."

"You didn't see her face after it happened."

"I didn't have to see her face to know what this is about. You think this is history repeating. That your mom stepping in for your dad is going to happen to Cammy—"

"Ang—"

"No... you've silenced me long enough over the last week, and now you've answered my call because deep down, you want to hear what I have to say."

She got that wrong. I don't want to hear what she has to say, but I know well enough that if I didn't answer the phone, she'd fly her happy ass down here to tell it to my face.

"Okay then, say your peace," I sigh, stuffing one hand into my jacket pocket.

"You need to fix this with her. You're not your father's son—"

"Ang—" I try again.

"JP, you're not him. And Cammy's not your mom. There's no way that your dad would do what you've done for me—what you've done for her. You're protective and caring. You want to shield those you love, even when it means taking the hit yourself."

I get to the end of the cross walk. I pull my hand out of my jacket and slam it against the crosswalk button as I wait for it to signal WALK, frustration building. I can do everything right, but I still don't get Cammy. "What do you want from me, Angelica?"

"I want you to fight," she says simply. "For once in your life,

I want you to fight for what you want instead of accepting what other people think you deserve."

The words echo in the empty street, cutting through my carefully constructed defenses.

"That's why I'm coming to town," she continues, softer now. "My flight lands tomorrow morning."

"Angelica, you don't have to—"

"Yes, I do. Because someone needs to knock some sense into you before this charity game. And since Cammy can't do it herself—because you won't let her—it might as well be me. You won her over without even telling her about San Diego. You kept our secret intact, and she still fell in love with you a second time. Don't you get it? Cammy sees the real you through it all."

I think about the upcoming game, about Seven's challenge. About how easy it would be to just let the puck slip past, to give everyone what they think they want.

"The couch pulls out into a bed. I'll have it made up for you," I say finally, because there's no point in arguing with Angelica when she gets like this.

"Thanks. And JP?"

"Yeah?"

"Stop practicing so hard. Your save percentage is already ridiculous, and we both know you're not doing it for the team."

I hang up, her words following me the rest of the way home. She's right—I have been pushing harder, playing better. But not because I want to win.

Because when I'm focused on stopping pucks, I don't have to think about everything else I've lost. About how empty my apartment feels without Cammy's laughter filling it. About how the arena feels colder now that I can't look up and meet her eyes.

Tomorrow, Angelica arrives. Maybe she can help me figure out where I'll end up if I leave the Hawkeyes. I need to learn to accept that walking away might be the right thing to do.

⤝

The elevator doors open to my level after a run with Hartley this evening, and I notice that I missed a text from Angelica—her flight landed early. I pocket my phone as I step out, seeing Angelica standing at my apartment door, her rolling bag in hand and her laptop bag over her shoulder.

"You look like shit," she announces as I walk up.

"Missed you too," I mutter, pushing the door open and holding it for her as she walks in first in her high-powered lawyer suit and heels. "Make yourself at home. I just got back from a run with Hartley. I'm going to jump into the shower first," I say, dropping my apartment key and phone on the kitchen island.

"Oh, I plan to," she says, already laying out on the couch, stretching out her legs, and kicking off her heels as she grabs the remote control to the TV. "And when you're done, we're having a real conversation about Cammy."

I'm under the hot spray, trying to wash away the weight of the last week and a half, when I hear my phone ringing in the other room. Angelica's voice carries through the bathroom door.

"Hello? Yes, this is Angelica. JP's in the shower right now..."

My stomach drops as I realize who must be calling. I shut off the water, but by the time I get to the door, wrapped in a towel, the call has ended.

"Was that..." I ask, pointing to the phone in her hand. I can't bring myself to say her name, hoping my instincts are wrong.

"That was Cammy," Angelica says quietly, holding my phone. "And based on how quickly she hung up, I'm guessing she doesn't know I'm in town."

"Fuck." The word echoes in the quiet apartment. Because, of course, this would happen now. Of course, Cammy would call at the worst possible moment.

"You need to call her back," Angelica says. "Explain—"

"Explain what?" I cut her off. "That the woman she thinks

I left her for in San Diego is the same woman currently in my apartment tonight, after I ended things with the woman I'm in love with for the second time? Yeah, that'll go over well."

"Better than letting her think history is repeating itself." Angelica's voice is sharp.

The memory of that night still haunts me. Cammy's hair spread across the sheets, smiling over at me before she fell asleep, and then that late-night phone call, the wreck, the ambulance lights, the mug shot.

"To do that, I have to tell her the truth. Something that puts too much in danger. And what does it matter anymore anyway? Being with me means I'll keep letting her down."

Angelica's expression changes. His eyebrow lifts as if she figured it out. "So, that's really what this is about. Isn't it? Falling short. You're scared that you're going to fall short in Cammy's eyes, like you think you did in your father's, and in Seven's, and in the Blue Devils who dropped you. But she's the one you're the most scared to let down, so you're ending it before it breaks your heart."

"I don't need you to psychoanalyze me, Ang. You're a lawyer not a shrink."

"You know I'm right," she says, but I turn to walk down the hall. "Come on, JP, tell me, what part did I get wrong?" She asks, a challenge in her tone.

I know she's baiting me. No matter how I answer, she's got me, so I'll give her the truth. "I'm not ending it before it breaks my heart. You can't break something that's already broken," I admit. Her eyes soften toward me, but I'm done with conversations tonight. "I'm going to bed." I head toward my room down the hall, then pause. "Thanks for coming, Ang. Even if your timing is terrible."

"Someone has to save you from yourself," she calls after me. "Might as well be me."

"Yeah... we'll see."

CHAPTER TWENTY-FOUR

Cammy

The arena feels emptier at night without a home game going on, like all the energy and life have been sucked out, leaving nothing but echoes and shadows. I sit at my desk, staring at the dark ice below, remembering how just ten days ago, JP was down there celebrating his win, looking at me like I was his entire world.

What a difference almost two weeks can make.

My phone sits face-down beside my laptop, silent but somehow still screaming at me to pick it up and make another call to the man, who I know, won't answer. I've been trying to focus on auction details all evening, but my mind keeps drifting to JP, to our confrontation in the hallway a week ago, to the way he's been avoiding me at practice.

A knock on my door startles me from my thoughts.

"You're still here?" Brynn asks, leaning against the doorframe. She's got Milo on her hip, his little head resting against her shoulder. "Seven sent me to grab his playbook before Milo and I head home from mommy and me class. He forgot it after practice, and then I saw the lights on up here."

"Yeah, just…" I gesture vaguely at my laptop. "Work."

She studies me for a moment, then sets Milo down. He immediately toddles over to my desk, reaching for the stress ball I keep there. I grab it and hand it to him. He squeals with delight and tosses it across the room and then chases after it.

"Have you heard from him?" she asks softly.

I shake my head. "Radio silence since our confrontation. I thought maybe…" I trail off, not wanting to admit how many times I've checked my phone.

"Maybe it's time to try again," she suggests. "One last time, and then…"

"And then what?" I laugh, but there's no humor in it. "Accept that I fell for Jon Paul Dumont's charm a second time, and as soon as he got what he wanted, he bailed? Same player—same playbook."

Milo runs to me and throws the stress ball, and it bounces off my computer screen. The gentle thud feels like punctuation to my words. I grab the ball as it settles into place and hand it back to him, and then off he goes again.

"And then closure," Brynn says, her arms cradling my dad's binder between her arms. "Dumont is a good player, but your father is better, and he only has to make one goal. The odds aren't in JP's favor. You know that, right?"

I think about the auction, about the bet, about everything hanging in the balance, including my job when Everett and Coach Haynes realize that my dad sent away the only healthy goalie that the Hawkeyes have. "Yeah, I do."

"If there's anything left that you need to air out with JP before he inevitably leaves, you should do it. And you should do it now."

I think about it for a moment, and then I realize that there is a question I want to know. "I just want to know what I ever did to him to deserve this."

"Then ask him, Cammy. Because by next week, who knows where he'll land? You may never see him again."

"Promise?" I say bitterly. The truth is that the NHL is too

small to hope that I'll never see him again.

Brynn lifts an eyebrow as if she's not buying it, and then we say our goodbyes before she leaves with Seven's playbook and a sleeping Milo against her shoulder.

I find myself staring at my phone again. The office feels too quiet, too still, like the whole world is holding its breath.

Before I can talk myself out of it, I pick up the phone and dial JP's number. My heart pounds as it rings once, twice...

"Hello?"

I still. The voice that answers isn't JP's. It's a woman, causing my stomach to drop instantly. I pull the phone away from my ear quickly to make sure I didn't hit send to the wrong contact, but the name Jon Paul is listed as the caller on the other side.

"Um, hi," I manage, my throat tight. "Is this... JP's phone?" I ask, just for good measure. Maybe the phone lines got crossed.

"Yes, this is Angelica." Her tone is pleasant, but there's almost a knowing tone to it. "JP's in the shower right now. This is Cammy, right?"

The world tilts sideways. Blood rushes in my ears, drowning out everything except those words: *JP's in the shower.*

"I'm sorry to have interrupted, I didn't know—"

"Wait, don't hang up," Angelica says quickly. "I think we should talk—"

I hang up before she can finish, the phone slipping from my fingers onto the desk. The sound it makes seems too loud in the sudden silence of my office.

Angelica.

She's there. With him. While he's in the shower.

Did he break things off with me to get back with her?

The signs were there, and I ignored them. I let him charm his way back in just like he had done the first time.

And now, here I am again, cutting myself on the same sharp edges.

I grab my keys and bag, needing to get out of this office, away from the memories, away from the evidence of how stupid I've been. The drive to Brynn's is a blur, streetlights smearing together through tears I refuse to let fall.

She opens the door before I can knock, one look at my face telling her everything she needs to know.

"What happened?" she asks, pulling me inside.

"Angelica answered his phone," I say, my voice cracking as I try to hold back tears. The words taste like ash. "He's with her. Again."

Brynn leads me to the couch, her hand warm against my arm. "Maybe it's not what you think—"

"What else could it be?" I cut her off. I shouldn't snap at her; she's done nothing wrong. "She said he was in the shower, Brynn. In the shower. Just like..." I can't finish the sentence.

"Okay," she says softly. "But—"

"No." I stand up, unable to sit still. "No buts. No maybes. No more excuses for him. I'm done."

"Cammy—"

"He made his choice," I say, pacing the length of her living room. "Again. And you know what? Fine. Let him have her. Let him have whatever he wants. But if he stays, I go. I can't be in the stadium with him."

The thought of leaving the only real home I've ever known is painful, but staying and being in the same building with him— knowing that he could throw me away a second time so easily and seeing her in his seats, wearing his jersey—is the kind of chronic ache I just can't live with. My heart will die a slow and torturous death.

Understanding dawns on Brynn's face. "The auction bet."

"No matter the outcome, one of us leaves." My voice sounds foreign to my own ears, cold and hard. "Three shots and then it's over."

"Are you sure about this?" Brynn asks carefully. "Once you make this decision—"

"I've never been more sure of anything." I stop pacing, meeting her eyes. "He made the rules. I'm just finally playing the same game."

The short drive home feels different somehow, like I've crossed a line I can't uncross. But as I park in the underground parking garage of The Commons, I feel something settle in my chest. Not peace, exactly, but certainty.

JP Dumont has broken my heart for the last time.

CHAPTER TWENTY-FIVE

JP

I've been in and out of this stadium a hundred times or more since I signed my PTO with the team, but today it feels different. Heavier. Like the walls themselves know what I'm about to do and are trying to hold me back.

Coach Haynes' office door is slightly ajar. I knock twice and push it open, my heart pounding like I'm heading into sudden death overtime.

"JP," Coach says, looking up from his laptop. "You're early. Is everything all right?"

I step inside, closing the door behind me. It feels final, like sealing my fate. "Got a minute?"

"Always," he says, leaning back in his chair, arms crossed over his chest. "What's on your mind?"

I sit down, trying to find the right words. How do you tell someone you're walking away from everything you've worked for without sounding like a complete idiot?

"I need to talk to you about a transfer," I say finally.

Coach's eyebrows shoot up. "A transfer? What the hell are

you talking about?"

"To the farm team," I clarify, leaning forward, my elbows resting on my knees. "I've been thinking about it for a while now. I think it's the best move for the team—and for me."

He stares at me like I've just sprouted a second head. "You've got to be kidding me. You're the starting goalie for one of the top teams in the league, and you want to go to the farm team?"

I nod, trying to keep my voice steady. "It's not about my performance. It's about focus. I'm a distraction, Coach. You know it, I know it, and the guys know it. This team deserves someone who's all in."

"And you're not?" he challenges.

I hesitate, my throat tightening. "I can't be. Not right now."

Coach leans forward, his hands clasped on the desk. "This about Cammy?"

The question catches me off guard, and I glance away. "It's about a lot of things."

"Bullshit," he says, his voice sharp. "You think leaving is going to fix whatever's going on with her?"

"It's not just about her," I say, trying to convince myself even more than him. "It's about doing what's right for everyone. For the team, for her, for—"

"For you," he finishes, his tone dripping with sarcasm. "Right. Because running away is the right move."

"It's not running away," I argue, but even I don't believe it. "It's stepping back to give everyone space."

Coach shakes his head, his disappointment clear. "You're making a mistake, Dumont. Everyone on that team, from the people who run the day-to-day, to the players out on that ice, are all here for the same goal—to win another championship. It would be disrespectful to the people who give it their all for me to attempt to talk you into staying on if you're not fully invested."

"I understand, Coach," I say with a nod. "I appreciate the opportunity that you've given me. And I appreciate you doing this last thing for me."

He stares back at me for a beat, as if thinking I might feel the weight—the call back—to stay with the team, and though my hands are sweating and my blood pressure must be through the roof, I know that I can't give my all to this team. Not when I already gave it all to Cammy, though she'll never know it.

"You have talent. I hate to see you throw it away. But at the end of the day, it's your choice."

"Thank you," I say, standing up. The words feel hollow.

I'm halfway through my second set of bench presses when the gym door slams open. I don't have to look up to know who it is.

"What the fuck are you doing, Dumont?" Slade's voice booms across the empty space.

I rack the barbell and sit up, wiping sweat off my face. "Morning, Matthews."

"Don't 'morning' me," he snaps, marching over. "Haynes just told me you're asking for a transfer. Care to explain why you're suddenly out of your goddamn mind? Please, tell me you're sleepwalking, and this was all just a nightmare you're having or that you had amnesia and don't recall any of that conversation so I can tell Coach Haynes you didn't mean any of that."

I sigh, grabbing my water bottle. "I've already confirmed it with Haynes. It's done."

"Like hell it is," Slade growls. "You think this is how you solve your problems? By bailing?"

"I'm not bailing," I say, my voice tight. "I'm doing what needs to be done."

"Who exactly are you doing this for? Cammy? Seven? Because I know for a fact you're not doing this for yourself, and you're sure as hell not doing it for the team that needs you."

"Olsen will get cleared in a couple of weeks. You won't miss me."

Slade shakes his head, his hands on his hips. "This is about something bigger. Isn't it?" he says, shaking a finger at me as I watch him think through it. "You came here to prove something and to get Cammy back. And you ended up doing both. So, I don't get it. What happened?" he asks.

"This isn't about proving anything. It's about making sure Cammy doesn't get dragged down by my shit."

Slade laughs, but there's no humor in it. "You think she's better off without you? That walking away is some noble sacrifice? You're not protecting her, Dumont. You're just proving you're too much of a coward to fight for her."

"That's easy for you to say," I snap. "You don't know what it's like to be compared to someone who ruined everything they touched. You don't know what it's like to see the same patterns in yourself and wonder if you're going to hurt the people you care about."

"You're right," he says, his tone softer but still firm. "I don't know what that's like. But I do know what it's like to lose someone because you were too stubborn to admit you needed help."

I stare at him, my chest heaving. "This isn't the same."

"Isn't it?" he counters. "You think Cammy wants you to leave? You think she'll be happy watching you throw away everything you've built because you're scared?"

"She'll be better off," I say, my voice breaking. "She deserves someone who can give her everything. Someone who doesn't bring trouble wherever they go."

Slade shakes his head, disappointment etched into every line of his face. "You're making a mistake, JP. But if you're determined to blow up your life again, then I can't stop you. Just don't expect me to stand by and watch you throw your life away without saying my piece."

Later that day, Coach Haynes calls me into his office to let me know the transfer request has been submitted. "I still think you're making the wrong choice," he says, his tone heavy. "But I'll respect it."

"Thank you. Do me a favor, though. Don't say anything to anyone about this until you have to," I say, shaking his hand.

I head out of his office and into the locker room. I sit there, in front of my stall for what feels like hours. The room is empty, the usual noise and banter replaced by silence. I stare at the Hawkeyes logo on my gear bag, the memories of this season playing in my mind like a highlight reel. At least I got to play here—train under Coach Wrenley—though it wasn't the experience I expected.

As I leave the facility, it hits me—after tomorrow's home game and the auction the day after, I'll be stepping into the Hawkeyes stadium as a player for the last time.

But not until I give Cammy one last thing.

CHAPTER TWENTY-SIX

Cammy

It's 5:00 a.m. as I stand on my skates with a hockey stick in my hand, my breath creating small clouds in the cold air. It's too early for anyone else to be here, but I couldn't sleep. Not with tomorrow's auction looming and today's home game, where I'll be forced to watch JP take to the ice.

"Always the hero," I mutter bitterly to myself about JP, setting up another puck. The sound of my stick connecting with rubber echoes through the empty arena. The puck hits the back of the net, but it's not good enough. Not nearly good enough to get past JP.

I've been here every morning this week, watching Dad practice his shots. Sometimes helping, sometimes just observing. The weight of what's coming sits heavy on my shoulders —one shot from my dad could change everything, and I still have no idea how much Penelope knows. I suspect she still doesn't know anything, and the guilt I feel for that has been increasing.

Of course, if JP shuts my dad out, maybe she'll never find out. What's the likelihood of that? I have no idea. My dad is a legend in the hockey world, but JP is highly ranked in both his overall career and the start of this season. Who knows where he'll end up if he continues to play professionally.

My phone buzzes in my jacket pocket. For a split second, my pulse jumps at the thought of it being JP, but it's just Brynn.

> **Brynn: I stopped by your apartment this morning to say hi before my yoga class, but you weren't there. Early practice again?**

> **Cammy: Needed to clear my head and get an early start on the auction checklist today, before tonight's game.**

> **Brynn: You've got to stop torturing yourself like this.**

I ignore her last message, and instead wind up and smack the puck, watching it sail into the net. The emerald dress I chose with the girls hangs in my office, a reminder of everything at stake.

The sound of doors opening startles me. Dad walks out onto the ice, still in his street shoes.

"Thought I'd find you here," he says, watching as I collect pucks. "How long have you been at it?"

"Just got here," I lie, but we both know better. The dark circles under my eyes tell a different story.

He studies me for a moment. "You know I'm doing this for you, don't you?"

"Maybe you should let me fight my own battles," I say, though I know he means well.

"What are you asking me to do?" he finishes quietly.

I pause, his question heavy between us. "I want..." My voice catches. "I don't know what I want anymore."

The sound of Angelica's voice when she answered JP's phone flashes through my mind, followed by the way he's been avoiding me at practice. The way his gaze cuts right through me like I'm not even there.

"If you miss, I can't stay here," I admit for the first time out loud to him. "I can't watch him with her, pretending everything's fine. I already have a transfer request drafted to the Hawkeyes farm team in Alberta. It won't be an administration assistant for the GM, but it's a start, and there is a lot of space to move up."

Dad's sharp intake of breath tells me he wasn't expecting that. He's not happy about my decision, but it's still mine to make.

"Wait, Cammy—"

"Please," I cut him off. "I've made up my mind. Either he goes or I do."

"And what about Penelope? She's put years into helping you grow as her administrative assistant. And what about everything you've built here? Milo won't grow up with his sister close by, and what am I supposed to do without our weekly lunches?"

I think about my office upstairs, filled with auction preparations and years of memories. About Everett's trust in me to handle major events. About the players' wives and girlfriends who've become family. But mostly, about my dad, Brynn, and Milo.

"Sometimes you have to make hard choices," I say, echoing words he once told me.

"Is this about choices or about running away?"

Before I can respond, my phone buzzes again. This time it's Penelope.

> **Penelope: Emergency auction meeting in 30 minutes. Catering crisis.**

"Duty calls," I say, grateful for the escape. "The auction won't plan itself."

Dad watches as I gather my gear. "Just remember something, Cam. No matter what you choose to do, I always want the best for you. I'm always in your corner—no matter what."

I carry his words with me as I head upstairs to change. The emerald dress catches my eye as I pass my office, its sequins catching the morning light. I chose it to make JP regret walking away. Now I wonder if I'm the one who needs to remember what I'm fighting for.

The day passes in a blur of last-minute auction details. Seating charts, catering emergencies, sound system checks—it's almost enough to distract me from tonight's game. Almost.

"Earth to Cammy." Brynn waves her hand in front of my face. We're doing final checks on the silent auction displays, but my mind keeps drifting to the ice below. "You went somewhere else for a minute there."

"Sorry," I mutter, adjusting a display card. "Just thinking about tonight."

"About the game or about seeing JP?"

I wince. "Both. Neither. I don't know anymore."

"Have you considered the third option? One where your dad gets a puck past JP, and you leave with him."

"What?" I bark, my eyebrows almost hitting my hairline. "Have you forgotten everything that's happened? The one-night stand in San Diego, the DUI, the return to my stadium and my team, him leading me on and then bringing Angelica back to rub my face in it all? You think I would follow him after everything?"

"Love is complicated and messy. It rarely makes any damn sense, because if it did, your dad and I wouldn't have ended up together. If we had met in Seattle, it never would have worked. It took a phony vacation rental booking and a hurricane to force us to make it work. Maybe what you both need is a new scenario— your own hurricane that forces you together. Maybe the farm team could be that for you two."

"I think you're starting to mix your fictional books with real life. There's no way that works out in the end. Happily-ever-afters are only in novels," I tell her.

There's a glint in her eyes as she stares back. "Yeah, well, we'll see about that."

❧

The home game arrives too soon. Brynn insists I can't hide in my office forever, so here I sit in my dad's seats, with Brynn and Milo beside me, trying to focus on the ice instead of the hollow feeling in my chest. The familiar buzz of pre-game excitement vibrates all around the arena, but I feel disconnected from it all, like I'm watching through someone else's eyes.

Then I see her.

My heart stops, then plummets. Angelica sits in JP's seats. She's elegant in a Hawkeyes jersey, her smile bright as she chats with the other players' families, filling the space I thought would someday be meant for me. Sitting in JP's seats, wearing his jersey like a claim. The stark reality is that JP and I won't ever happen.

"Cammy?" Brynn's voice seems far away as she gives Milo a snack. She sees where my eyes land. "Is that her?"

"Yeah," I barely whisper.

She grabs for the diaper bag as if she's preparing to leave. "We can go. Or head up to the Owner's Box with the rest of the girls. We don't have to sit here."

"No," I manage, but my voice cracks. "I need to be here. I need to see this with my own eyes."

JP skates out for warmups, and something inside me breaks. Not because he looks different, but because he doesn't. He's still the same JP who held me against the broom closet wall, who pulled his jersey over my head like I belonged to him. Who made me believe that I got to keep him forever.

Then it happens. JP glances up toward his seats, toward Angelica. There's something in his expression; a softness I used to think was reserved for me. His eyes drift over to where I sit with Brynn, and for a moment, our gaze locks. There's a sadness in them. Is it for me? Is it for him? I have no idea.

And then I realize... maybe I've seen about as much as I can handle.

"I don't know what I was thinking coming down here. I should go back up and finish my work," I say, my knee bouncing as we watch the puck drop and the game get underway.

"Cammy—"

I turn back to her. I love Brynn more than anything for being the optimist in this situation, but hope is hard to come by when the truth is a blonde in his jersey two aisles away.

"She answered his phone while he was in the shower, Brynn. She was comfortable enough to answer his phone, knowing it was me. And now she's here, in his seats, wearing his team's colors." Each word feels like sandpaper scratching all the way down my throat.

On the ice, JP blocks shots with perfect precision, like nothing in his world is broken. Like my heart isn't shattering in the stands above him.

"I can't watch this," I say suddenly, standing. "I need to go check on the auction preparations for tomorrow."

"The team needs you here, supporting. I already saw everything going on upstairs—you're ready. And Juliet said that this is going to be the best auction ever."

I glance over again, unable to help myself, seeing Angelica's soft blond hair as she laughs with another group sitting behind her.

I feel my heart physically breaking in two. "I've come to a decision. I know exactly what I'm hoping for tomorrow at the auction."

"And what's that?" Brynn asks, holding onto Milo as he waves at the players rushing past.

Angelica catches my eye, and I dart my vision away. "That Dad doesn't miss."

Later that night, I stand alone on the ice, staring out at the empty arena. The silence feels different now, heavier. Tomorrow, everything changes.

If Dad makes the shot, JP leaves.

If Dad misses, I walk away from my home, my family, my whole life here.

Either way, it feels like losing.

For better or worse, tomorrow is the end of something.

I just wish my heart would agree with my head that JP losing is the outcome I want.

CHAPTER TWENTY-SEVEN

Cammy

The arena banquet room shimmers like a winter wonderland, transformed from its usual rugged charm into an elegant gala space. Crystal chandeliers cast warm light across white-draped tables while fairy lights twinkle overhead. I grip my clipboard tighter, using the endless auction details as armor against the emptiness in my chest.

Juliet did an amazing job. This place is stunning. It's my turn to make sure that we raise enough to build the condos.

"Final sound check is done," Juliet confirms, appearing at my elbow. "And the silent auction displays are getting lots of attention."

I nod, scanning the growing crowd of Seattle's elite in their finest evening wear. "Perfect. Has the catering team set up the—"

The words die in my throat as JP walks in.

He's a striking figure in a perfectly tailored tuxedo, the black fabric emphasizing his broad shoulders and athletic build, his hair gelled but only brushed back casually with his fingers. His bow tie sits slightly askew—just enough to make my fingers itch to straighten it. To touch him one last time. To have those mesmerizing blue eyes back on me again.

Our eyes meet across the room, and everything else fades away. The noise of the crowd, the sparkle of the lights, the weight of my clipboard—nothing else exists except for us. For a moment, I see a flicker of something like longing in his expression before he quickly diverts his attention from me again.

But not for long.

Like a magnet, his gaze snaps back, as if he physically can't stop himself. I force myself to look away first, but not before I catch the way his fingers tighten around his whiskey glass, his knuckles going white. His eyes travel slowly—too slowly—making their way from my perfectly manicured toes peeking out from under my dress, to the curve of my hips, the dip of my waist, the corseted bust that lifts just enough to remind him exactly what he lost.

And judging by the way his jaw tenses, the way his throat bobs as he swallows, it's working.

Then someone steps in—Coach Evans from the Seattle football team—shaking JP's hand, momentarily pulling his attention away. The moment between us snaps, but the lingering tension is still there, simmering beneath the surface.

I inhale sharply and grab my phone, my pulse thrumming as I fire off a text before I can talk myself out of it.

Cammy: Stop staring.

I don't expect a response. But my phone buzzes almost instantly.

JP: I can't.

I look up from my phone to see his eyes are back on me. And then another text hits.

JP: You look beautiful tonight.

I read the text over and over again, wishing there was more context to it. Wishing he'd offer an explanation for his actions.

"Cammy?" Brynn touches my arm. "Aria is laying out some additional items on the tables but wants your approval."

"Of course. I'm happy to take a look," I manage, turning toward her to follow her across the room. I feel JP's eyes on me as I walk away.

I throw myself into work, using each task as a shield against JP's presence. Every checklist, every conversation, every auction detail becomes a distraction, a desperate attempt to keep my mind off the fact that he's here.

But no matter how hard I try, my eyes betray me.

JP moves through the room effortlessly, his French charm a well-oiled machine as he shakes hands with donors, leans in just enough to make each conversation feel intimate, and throws out that devastating smile that could melt ice. He's good at this—at making everyone feel special. Like they're the only person in the world when he's looking at them.

I would know.

Because once upon a time, he made me feel that way too.

Right up until he didn't.

The knife twists deeper when she arrives.

Angelica.

She's stunning, of course—elegant in a sleek black evening gown that clings in all the right places, her makeup flawless, her confidence effortless. My stomach churns as JP moves toward her, greeting her with a familiarity that makes my stomach turn and my heart drop.

And then he touches her.

Not in an overt way, not in a way anyone else would think twice about, but his hand settles at the back of her arm as he leans in, guiding her through the crowd with quiet authority. I recognize the way he speaks, the way he gestures, the way his hand lingers just long enough to be noticed.

It's the same way he's touched me.

The same way he led me into Oakley's that night, his hand resting protectively on my back. Though it's not lost on me that his hand settles so much higher on her than it did on me. It's a small victory, but at the end of the day, he's here with her, not me.

A sharp burst of laughter carries across the room—her laughter—and something inside me snaps. I need air. I need space. I need to not be here, standing in the middle of the ballroom, feeling like a damn fool for still caring.

"I need to check in with the sound guy for the slapshot challenge," I tell Brynn, my voice clipped.

Her eyes flick between JP and me, narrowing slightly like she knows exactly what's going through my head. But to her credit, she doesn't call me on it.

"Want me to come with you?" she asks instead, ever the best friend, stepmother, and angel on my right shoulder, always talking me off a ledge.

I shake my head. "I got it."

I move quickly, heels clicking against the polished floors as I put as much distance as possible between myself and the sight of JP and Angelica.

The next few hours pass in a blur of donor conversations, auction logistics, and not looking in JP's direction. The tension in my chest stays put, a constant weight pressing down on me no matter how many smiles I fake or how many hands I shake.

By the time the slapshot challenge nears, the chatter in the arena has reached a fever pitch.

Thank God for Kendall clearing Olsen yesterday, I remind myself. The Hawkeyes' starting goalie is now ready to be put back into the regular season, and with him officially cleared, it means JP won't be the only one in the net tonight. The crowd is practically throwing down donations for a chance to take shots against two professional goalies.

JP and Olsen have already started taking donors down to the players' tunnel, the line shockingly long—way longer than I expected. Men in expensive suits, women in heels they'll regret wearing on the ice, though Juliet thought of this and a red carpet is out on the ice to allow people to walk comfortably in normal shoes.

Kids bouncing on their toes, all itching for their moment to go head-to-head against NHL goalies.

I scan the scene, my clipboard clutched tightly in my hands. Everything is running smoothly. I catch a glimpse of Everett, our eyes meeting briefly, and he nods in approval—he's pleased with the auction. But we'll see how pleased he is with me after my dad and JP go head to head. Will I even have a job if JP leaves, and this whole bet sees the light of day?

My eyes drift back to the ice.

JP stands near the entrance to the tunnel, laughing at something one of the donors said, his mask hanging from his fingertips. His eyes flicker up—to me—like he can feel me watching.

I hold my breath. Then, ever so slightly, his lips quirk.

That damn smirk.

The one that says I see you, Cammy. I know you're watching.

The one that used to wreck me.

The one that still does.

I rip my gaze away and force my attention back to my checklist, ignoring the way my pulse skates wildly out of control. I will not let him get under my skin.

Not tonight.

With the night winding down, I slip away to the office to change out of my dress. My role isn't over yet—there's still cleanup, organizing, and making sure all auction items are accounted for.

And if things don't go the way I want them to during the slapshot challenge, at least I'll be comfortable when I inevitably end up hiding in a bathroom stall, crying my eyes out.

I tug off the emerald gown and slip into something easier—

black leggings, my favorite oversized Hawkeyes hoodie, and sneakers. Something practical. Something safe.

By the time I make it back down to the players' tunnel, the final donor is stepping up to take their last shot. JP and Olsen have been at this for over an hour, effortlessly blocking shots from fans, donors, and even a few local celebrities. The line has finally dwindled, but from the buzz in the arena and the thick stack of donation envelopes, I know we've exceeded expectations.

Everett takes the stage, his voice booming over the speakers as he delivers his closing remarks.

The crowd filters into the arena, where the rink gleams under bright lights. My dad has disappeared into the locker room to change out of his tux and into his gear while I stand at the tunnel entrance, trying to steady my nerves.

"Cammy."

I turn to find my dad approaching, hockey stick in hand. His expression is softer than I expected.

"Dad, I—"

He holds up the stick. "I took a minute to think about it while I was changing, and I realized that this is your shot to take. Not mine."

"What?" I blink at him, confused.

"I've been trying to protect you," he says quietly. "Maybe too much. Someone already took that chance away from me once." His eyes shift toward JP, who's now skating lazy circles in the goal crease. "I think I've been trying to make up for lost time. Maybe I overcompensated a little bit."

He extends the stick. "But this is your decision. The one you have to live with, not me."

With trembling hands, I take the stick. The weight feels right, familiar.

"Ladies and gentlemen," Everett's voice booms through the arena. "Please welcome Cammy Wrenley!"

The crowd cheers as I step onto the ice. I can see in JP's body language that he wasn't expecting this change. He wasn't expecting me to come out and score the goal that sends him packing, and neither was I. There's a flash of hurt in his eyes, but the moment he blinks, it's gone again, replaced with his usual casual confidence.

He skates out to where I'll be shooting from and lays out two pucks, and then reaches into his jersey and pulls out a puck from his chest protector, adding it to the end of the line. Then he skates back to the net.

JP stands tall in the crease, his stance relaxed, his body loose. But I know him. I know that's all for show. Beneath the mask, beneath the cocky swagger, he's locked in, every muscle coiled, his sharp blue eyes tracking my every move.

Waiting.

Watching.

Like he's daring me to come for him.

A flicker of memory flashes through my mind—JP at the rink weeks ago, helping the kids who came in early, lacing up their skates, showing them how to hold a stick properly. He wasn't putting on a show. He wasn't playing a role. He was just JP—the one I keep falling for, the one I keep losing.

Why can't I have that JP? Where did he go?

The thought ignites something deep inside me, fueling the fire burning in my chest as I drop into position, the puck in front of me.

I line up carefully, exhaling slowly through my nose.

Keep it simple. Precise. Controlled, I coach myself.

I draw back and release, the puck slicing cleanly through the air toward the top corner.

But JP barely moves.

His glove snaps up—lightning fast, effortless—snatching the puck mid-air like it's nothing.

The crowd groans in disappointment. A smirk tugs at the corners of JP's mouth beneath his mask, and my stomach knots. He's playing with me.

My jaw tightens as I skate back to the shooting line, rolling my shoulders to shake off the doubt creeping in, because his slapshot isn't just for fun. It will define both of our careers after this moment.

I position myself again, my heart thudding a steady rhythm in my ears.

This time, I don't hold back.

I shift my weight, winding up with every ounce of frustration, every unanswered question, every lingering ache in my chest. I release, sending the puck flying hard and fast toward the lower corner.

JP moves before the shot even lands.

Anticipating. Reading me like a damn book.

His pad sweeps out in a clean, precise motion, deflecting the puck effortlessly.

I curse under my breath, skating a sharp circle before returning to the line. The energy in the arena hums with anticipation, the tension thick enough to choke on. It all comes down to this.

I lift my gaze toward him, my grip tightening on my stick. He's already looking at me.

For a single heartbeat, the world narrows down to just us.

I don't see the crowd. I don't hear the cheers. I don't feel the ice beneath my skates.

It's just JP—his shoulders rising and falling with each breath, his weight shifting slightly, but there's something different this time.

Something off.

His stance isn't as sharp. His shoulders aren't as tense.

And in his eyes, just beneath the steel guard of his mask, there's something that looks an awful lot like defeat.

My pulse is erratic now, my breath uneven as I set up for the final shot.

Everything hinges on this.

I wind up, muscles tingling, tensing as I release and swing through with my hockey stick, the puck flying through the air.

And JP... steps aside.

The puck flies cleanly into the net.

The buzzer sounds. The arena erupts. Confetti cannons explode in a flurry of blue and silver.

But I don't feel like I won.

I stand frozen, my chest heaving, staring across the rink at the black puck in the net. Complete disbelief washes over me. Hot bile bubbles in my stomach, threatening to crawl up my throat with emotion about to boil over. In everything I analyzed, I guess I hadn't been prepared for this scenario.

JP's watching as he lifts his mask. Our eyes collide.

And in that single second, I understand everything.

He let me win.

He's leaving.

And he's doing it on purpose. He's leaving me by choice. The pain of that thought sears so deep that it will probably scar.

His stick clatters to the ice as he dips down to pick up the puck, and then he pushes forward, skating straight toward me. My lips curl into a forced smile for the cameras and the guests all applauding for me, but beneath it, anger simmers like a live wire beneath my skin.

He stops, barely inches from me.

"You let me win," I hiss, breathless.

JP pulls off his mask, his expression unreadable, but his eyes seem sad and yet full of life the moment they meet mine.

"A bet's a bet, Cammy," he says, handing me the puck that I scored against him.

"That's not an answer," I snap, gripping the puck tightly. "Why did you step aside? Did you do it for her?"

He shakes his head. "She's only ever been a friend, Cammy— nothing more." His gaze holds mine, something honest flickering in his eyes. "I'm stepping aside because I'm not fighting you anymore. You're getting what you want. You win."

Before I can respond, he steps closer and reaches up with his bare hand, his thumb brushing over my cheek. His skin is surprisingly warm, despite being out here for that last hour. I wish I was strong enough to step out of his touch—but I can't bring myself to do it. It's probably the last time he'll ever touch me, and I wish I was brave enough to reach out and touch him, too. But the hurt he's put me through demands self-preservation.

His voice drops. "I'm not mad at how this ended. I'm just sorry I couldn't be everything you deserve," he says, pulling his hand back from my skin and dropping his hand to his side. "Je t'aime. I need you to know that."

The words hang in the air, heavy and undeniable. "What does that mean?" I ask. It's significant—I can feel it.

"You're not ready to hear it. Maybe you never will be," he says.

"Tell me? Please," I beg.

He licks his lips, and I almost think he debates it, but then he doesn't. "My apartment key is taped to the puck. Will you drop it off for me in the morning to the property management office?"

I nod, unable to come up with a response. I can't believe he packed up his apartment before all of this. How long ago did he decide that he was going to walk away?

My vision drifts to the green hairband, and he follows my eyes. "Do you mind if I keep it? It would be hard to part with it now," he says.

I nod, staring down at the puck in my hands to keep the tears at bay, but when I look up, the crowd is starting to fill in around us, and JP is already skating away. I can't process all these feelings at once and the image of JP getting farther and farther away has my heart shattering into a million pieces. I knew this would hurt, but it's more painful than I ever imagined it would be.

I feel a presence at my side. "I love you?" Aria says, leaning forward to read something. "Who wrote that on the puck? Kind of a weird place to write it."

Then it dawns on me with Aria's translation.

He let the puck go past him because he loves me.

I turn and race toward the players' tunnel, trying desperately to weave between people without slipping on my ass. The dense crowd makes it harder to get through.

The minute I make it to the tunnel, he's nowhere in sight,

and then I feel a hand reach out and grab me. I spin to see who it is—praying—hoping, it's him. But then I see her.

Angelica.

"We need to talk," she says, her expression stern. "About San Diego. About why he really left that night."

"I don't have time for this, I have to—"

"He won't tell you the truth," she cuts me off. "But I will. It's time you knew everything."

The seriousness of her expression tells me that she has the information I've been begging JP to tell me.

"Everything?" I ask.

"Not here," Angelica says, glancing at the celebrating crowd. "Is there somewhere private we can talk? It's sensitive information that can't get out."

I lead her to my office, my mind racing. The confetti from the challenge still clings to our hair, a glittering reminder of JP's final words before he skated away.

Je t'aime.

I love you.

The words echo in my head as I close the office door behind us. Angelica doesn't sit; instead, she paces near my window.

"I wanted to tell you this when you called two nights ago, but you hung up," she starts. She looks nervous for someone who I suspect thrives on dramatic courtroom moments. "JP and I agreed to keep this a secret, but I think you need to know the truth. But you have to promise to keep our secret."

"Why wouldn't he tell me any of this?" The words come out sharper than intended. This would have cleared up so much.

Angelica turns to face me, and I'm struck by the guilt in her expression. "Because he thinks protecting the people he loves means sacrificing himself. Even if it costs him everything."

She takes a deep breath. "That night in San Diego... I was the one driving the car."

Shock hits me harder than I expect. "What?"

"I had gotten some bad news... a setback on a case I've been working on for years. I was a mess, drinking too much at the party downstairs. This football player wouldn't leave me alone, kept getting handsy..." She wraps her arms around herself, the memory clearly painful. "I called JP in a panic—he was with you."

My throat tightens as pieces start falling into place. "You knew he was with me?"

"He's never shut up about you. He texted me when you showed up to the party. He was so happy. Meeting you all those years ago changed him into a better person. You need to know that."

"So, you two..." I start, hoping she will finish the rest for me.

Her nose wrinkles at the thought of what I'm insinuating. "Listen, I know what you're thinking, but he's not my type and even if he were, I spent a lot of years front row to JP being... well, a man-slut, for lack of a better word. Not to mention that he threw up on me in high school at his mom's third wedding." She grimaces. "There are just some things you never come back from. But we've always been fiercely protective of each other. I spent my life in foster care with no real family, and as you probably know... his family sucks, so we sort of made our own—just the two of us. That's why when I called... he showed up."

My brain is reeling with this new information.

"So, if he wasn't taking you home to..." I can't even say the words out loud.

"He told me he needed to go back up, to let you know what was happening. But I was drunk and scared and stupid." Angelica's voice cracks. "I grabbed his keys and ran to his car. He barely made it into the passenger seat before I took off. I missed the turn, and we ended up hitting the guardrail."

"Oh, my God," I say.

"I still feel guilty about everything. I could have killed us. And then JP called an ambulance for me and moved me into the passenger side so that he would take the fall."

The missed calls, the desperate voicemails, the way he tried to explain but never gave away what happened that night.

"You're the one that got the DUI expunged," I say, piecing it together. "But why would he take the fall?"

"Because I'm working on a huge non-profit court case fighting for foster kids who are stuck in the system, and a DUI would have gotten me dropped from the case I've been working on for years. It's the same case that I was upset about at the party."

I scratch the top of my brow, trying to piece all of this together. "So, why hasn't he said any of this to me?" I ask.

"In the state of California, JP could do ten years in prison for obstruction of justice by moving me out of the driver seat before the police showed up, and I could do ten years for lying to the police to protect him. The statute of limitations is three years. We agreed to wait to tell you until then. But he's lost so much trying to protect us both, and now he's losing it all again after building it back up. I can't let him do this."

Suddenly, everything makes sense.

His secret, their close bond, his DUI getting expunged—her becoming his sports talent agent to help him get back what he lost. Everything is fitting into place. Except for one thing...breaking it off after the bar.

I flash her the puck he gave me. The silver marker visible.

She reads it and gives me a small smile. "He loves you, Cammy—he always has. He called me the first night over four years ago when he tossed you that first puck. He said you turned him down. Do you know what I asked him?" she says, walking over and taking a seat on my desk.

I shake my head. The idea that he would have called her that night and told her about me means something. That night was as significant to him as it was to me.

"I teased him, asking him if you were the one. And his reply was instant. He said 'yes.'" She smiles. "He didn't want to leave you that night. I'm the one that made him. And I promise you that his secrets have only been to protect me. It's been killing him not to tell you."

I sink into one of the reception chairs, the room spinning slightly.

Angelica nods. "He went to jail for me. Lost his spot with the Blue Devils. Lost you." She meets my eyes. "I've spent the last year and a half trying to make it right. Got his record expunged, helped him rebuild his career. But I couldn't fix what mattered most to him—getting you back."

"Then why did he break it off after the fight at Oakley's?" My voice breaks on the question.

She takes in a deep sigh.

"He has this idea that loving him means getting hurt. His mom, me, you..."

"Where is he?" I stand up, suddenly desperate to find him. "I need to—"

"He's gone," Angelica cuts me off gently. "He took the transfer to Canada. His flight is boarding right now."

The words feel like ice in my veins. "No," I shake my head. "He can't be..."

I rush past her, out of my office and through the arena halls. I'm grateful that I changed already as my flats slap against the concrete floors of the stadium as I run for my car—praying I'm not too late.

I make it to The Commons. Maybe Angelica was wrong, and he changed his flight. I unlock the door with the key he left me. Inside, the space is empty except for standard furniture. On the coffee table, a PlayStation 3 sits with a note: For Aleksi.

My eyes blur with tears as I spot another note on the kitchen island. With trembling hands, I unfold it:

Cammy,

You are the most incredible person I've ever met. You're smart, talented, and so much stronger than you give yourself credit for. You're going to do amazing things, and I don't want to be the reason you don't.

You deserve someone who makes your life easier, not

harder. But I'm not strong enough to stay away on my own, not with you only three floors above me. The best thing I can do for you is give you space to move forward with your life.

Je t'aime,

JP

I clutch the note to my chest, tears falling freely now. All this time, I thought he was running away. But he was trying to run toward something better for everyone else, no matter what it cost him.

My phone buzzes—

> **Unknown: This is Angelica. His phone is off, but he's headed to the farm team.**

I wipe my eyes, determination replacing despair.

> **Cammy: Text me the details. All of them.**

> **Unknown: What are you going to do?**

I look down at JP's note, at the words *Je t'aime* written in his messy scrawl. The same words he whispered before skating away.

> **Cammy: I'm going to find him. And then I'm going to bring him home.**

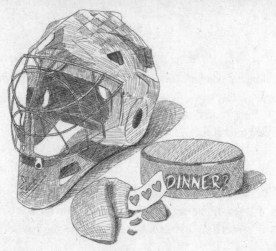

CHAPTER TWENTY-EIGHT

JP

The cold night air bites at my face as I step out of the arena, the distant echoes of cheers and laughter still drifting from inside. Under the glow of the streetlights, my rideshare idles at the curb, its tailpipe sending wisps of smoke into the crisp November night.

I don't know what I expected. Maybe a part of me hoped that Cammy would have chased after me. At least leaving me with a kiss goodbye. Something... Anything, to let me know that what happened between us over the last six weeks meant something to her, too. But her voice isn't echoing through the parking lot of the stadium. There's no clap of her flats behind me as she runs toward me.

She's letting me go.

Like I made it easy for her to do.

I tighten my grip on my bag as I head toward the waiting cab, the slap of my boots on the concrete ringing in my ears. It's done. The puck she made past me is in my pocket, and her smile—bright but edged with confusion—is burned into my memory.

She doesn't understand yet, but she will. This is for her. It has to be.

The cab driver leans out his window. "You the guy heading to the airport?"

"Yeah," I say, tossing my bag into the trunk. I slide into the backseat and slam the door shut. "Sea-Tac, departures."

The driver nods, and the car rumbles to life. I glance out the window as the arena fades into the distance, keeping her with it.

The city lights blur as the cab weaves through the streets. My phone sits heavy in my pocket, off since I walked out of the auction. If I turn it on, I know it'll be lit up with messages. Slade's angry texts, Penelope's demands for an explanation, Angelica's calm but firm instructions to rethink everything. And maybe... maybe a text from Cammy.

I can't afford to see her name on my screen. Not now. Not after tonight.

I glance at the driver, his face lit faintly by the dashboard glow. "Can we pick up the pace?" I ask. "I'm cutting it close for my flight."

He mutters something under his breath about traffic, but the car speeds up.

Leaning my head back against the seat, I close my eyes, replaying the slapshot challenge. She was fierce—every movement confident, every shot deliberate. The way she stared at me when the confetti cannons went off—it was a vision I'll carry with me for the rest of my life.

The puck I gave her with the key and the writing was something I had already planned to hand her after Seven scored a goal, but then when she walked out onto the ice, taking her father's place to send me packing. That's when I knew that I hurt her worse than I will ever recover from because I could have never done that to her. The idea of scoring on Cammy and sending her away from me makes me physically unwell. I had to have done enough to make her resent me that much.

That's when I sent the puck up to be the one she would ultimately score on me. No other outcome would be enough to prove to her what she means to me.

I have no idea if she'll go to my apartment to check on things before she turns in the key, but at least I left a note for her, in case. The words sting, but they're true. Trouble follows me like a shadow—and Seven is right, I won't let it darken her life. She's already been through too much.

Sea-Tac is buzzing when we pull up. I pay the driver and haul my bag out of the trunk, heading for the entrance. The automatic doors whoosh open, and the chaos of the terminal swallows me whole. Travelers rush past, voices blend into a dull roar, and the overhead announcements barely register.

Check-in is a blur. The attendant gives me my boarding pass and wishes me a good flight, and I offer a stiff nod in return. I move through security on autopilot, my thoughts stuck on Cammy. Seeing her tonight in that dress. How it took everything in me not to sweep her up in my arms and carry her away to somewhere private—somewhere to steal her attention—to somehow explain everything. But it's too late for explanations now.

At the gate, I sink into a chair with my phone in my pocket, still turned off. I don't need Angelica cursing me out for this. She can save her wrath for another day.

My flight's boarding call echoes through the speakers, but I don't move right away. Instead, I glance at the hairband around my wrist, pulling it up and letting it snap against my skin.

Finally, I stand as the line starts to dwindle, everyone else loading onto the aircraft. It's time to go.

The flight to Canada is uneventful. The plane's engines lull me into a restless half-sleep. Every time I close my eyes, I see her. The way she leaned in close when we talked, her lips curving into a smile when she teased me. The fire in her eyes when she challenged me on the ice. And the way she whispered my name that night in my apartment. The feeling of her lips against mine.

At least I got to hold her again. One last time that I'll never regret.

I shake the thoughts away, staring out the window as the

plane descends. The snowy expanse of Canada stretches out below, a sharp contrast to Seattle's rain-soaked streets. It feels like I've crossed into another world—one where I'm no longer her problem.

The hotel room is as bare as I expected. A bed, a desk, a chair. The heater hums softly, and I toss my bag onto the floor, sinking onto the edge of the bed. The silence presses in on me, suffocating and hollow all at once.

I pull out my phone, staring at the dark screen. My thumb hovers over the power button, but I don't press it. Not yet. If I turn it on, I'll be tempted to stare at my phone all night, waiting for her to call or text, but I know she won't. This is what she wanted, and I can't blame her for it. I've given her every reason not to trust me.

Instead, I set it on the nightstand and flop back onto the bed, staring at the ceiling. Tomorrow is my first practice with the farm team. I should be focused on proving myself, on working my way back up to where I was. But all I can think about is her. Her smile, her laugh, her fire.

And how I'll never get to hold her again.

"Home sweet home," I whisper to the empty room.

I close my eyes, willing sleep to come, but it doesn't. Not tonight.

Not without her.

CHAPTER TWENTY-NINE

Cammy

It's still dark out as the morning is just starting. I throw another sweater into my duffel bag, along with enough underwear for a few days. I've been up most of the night, my mind racing with everything Angelica revealed about San Diego. The truth about the DUI, about JP protecting her, about everything he sacrificed—it explains so much, yet somehow makes this harder.

My phone buzzes with another text

Angelica: Still no luck with the hotels. His phone's still off. But I'll keep trying.

I reply quickly.

Cammy: Thanks. I got a flight. Leaving in two hours.

The puck from last night sits on my nightstand, JP's key still taped to its surface. His words echo in my mind: *Je t'aime.*

He let me win, sacrificing everything he ever wanted, and then walked away because he thought it was best for me. Just like he did for Angelica—always protecting others he cares about before himself.

A sharp knock interrupts my thoughts, and Brynn bursts in with Penelope right behind her, both still in their workout clothes. Brynn's carrying coffee while Penelope clutches what looks like a file folder.

"You're really doing this?" Brynn asks, setting a coffee cup on my counter. "Going after him?"

"I have to." I stuff my phone charger into the bag. "After everything Angelica told me about what happened that night in San Diego..."

"What happened in San Diego?" Penelope asks, her eyes bulging with new information.

I bite on my lip, realizing that I have a year and a half to hold onto this secret now, too. "Sorry, I can't say. I was sworn to secrecy. It's practically a blood oath, but it connected all the dots for me and explained everything and why he left that night."

I pause, holding JP's note from his apartment. "He thinks he's protecting me by leaving. Just like he protected Angelica. But I don't need protection—I need him."

"Seven's going to lose it when he finds out you're chasing after JP," Brynn warns.

"Dad's part of why JP left in the first place," I say, zipping my bag closed. "That bet he made with JP is why I'm packing a bag to find him."

"That bet we'll get to when you get back," Penelope says with a stern lifted brow. "Coach Haynes wasn't happy with Seven when he found out the real reason JP left last night. Hopefully, you can get JP back before Everett finds out about all of this. Everett has been very vocal about making JP a franchise player. He wants us to sign him right away."

"Then I guess I have my work cut out for me," I say, zipping up my bag.

Brynn steps forward, her expression serious. "Your dad was trying to protect you. Try not to be too hard on him, okay?"

I nod. "I know. But I'm done letting other people decide what's best for me—JP or my father."

Brynn rubs my arm. "I know you are. And what about Thanksgiving? It's in two days."

"I'll be there," I promise, though my voice wavers slightly. "With or without JP. But I have to try."

"Your Dad is counting on you being in Minnesota with us," Brynn reminds me. "It's our first holiday with the Wrenley family back together, and though he won't say it, I think your dad needs you as a buffer."

I chuckle. "I know." I shoulder my bag. "I'll text my mom and grandma that I'll be there Thursday. I just... I have to do this first."

They walk me to the door, and Brynn pulls me into a tight hug. "Go get him."

❧

The airport bustles with early-morning travelers, but I barely notice them. My mind is focused on JP, on everything I need to tell him. About knowing the truth about San Diego. About understanding why he protected Angelica. About how he doesn't need to protect me from himself.

As I move through the terminal, I pull out his note one last time. *You're going to do amazing things, and I don't want to be the reason you don't,* it reads.

No, JP. We'll do amazing things together. And I'm going to prove it.

The airport terminal buzzes, people's excited chatter a stark contrast to the knot in my stomach. As I wait in the security line, my phone vibrates.

Coach Haynes: Just spoke with Coach Miller at the farm team. Thought you should know—JP's spot here is still his if he wants it. I've got paperwork to sign him with the team, officially.

My heart skips. I type back quickly.

Cammy: What do you mean?

Coach Haynes: Never officially processed the transfer. Called in a favor with Miller instead. He owes Slade Matthews from when Slade played for them. Said JP could come up and skate with them for a week or two until he "comes to his senses."

Relief floods through me. JP hasn't lost his spot. He hasn't thrown everything away yet.

Cammy: Thank you. When does he start?

Coach Haynes: Morning skate. 9 a.m. Miller's expecting him.

Coach Haynes: Cammy? Bring our goalie home.

> **Coach Haynes: Before Everett forces me to fire my special team's coach. We're going to need him too.**

I clutch my phone, tears threatening. JP still has a chance—we still have a chance.

I get through security with my shoulders feeling a little lighter after reading Coach Haynes' texts. Knowing that he never processed the transfer makes a huge difference.

The gate area is crowded. A little boy wearing a Hawkeyes jersey runs past, his toy goalie stick dragging behind him. The sight makes my throat tight.

My phone buzzes again.

> **Angelica: Just heard from the farm team's assistant. JP checked into one of the hotels near their practice rink. She's sending me the address and room number.**

My hands shake as I respond.

> **Cammy: Thank you. I owe you.**

> **Angelica: You don't owe me anything. Just... fix this? He deserves to be happy. You both do.**

The boarding call comes over the speakers, and I gather my things, my heart pounding. In less than two hours, I'll be in Alberta. Two hours until I can tell JP everything—about Angelica, about his spot still being open with the Hawkeyes, about how much I love him.

"Now boarding all rows," the gate agent calls.

As I step onto the plane, I have no idea how today will end.

But I hope it ends with JP by my side.

CHAPTER THIRTY

JP

The whistle blows, echoing in the practice rink as I bend over, hands on my knees, catching my breath. The drills are grueling, or maybe it's just me weighed down by everything I've carried here. This place feels foreign—too clean, too quiet, too sterile. Even the ice doesn't feel right under my skates.

Focus, Dumont. You can't screw this up.

I straighten, nodding at the assistant coach when he calls for the next rotation. I push off, forcing my legs to move faster, harder, trying to drown out the noise in my head. The puck ricochets off my pad, and the defense clears it. But my timing is off—half a second slower than it should be.

Every save feels like a battle. Every missed block feels like confirmation that something is off—that I don't belong here. But I have no other choice. The other teams have already filled the spots. Besides, there's only one place that feels like home.

The Hawkeyes, the city, the girl. The only problem is... they're all behind me now. I left it all last night, but I should be grateful that at least I get to play, because it's the only thing I have left.

After an hour of drills, the coach finally blows the whistle for a water break. I skate to the bench, pulling my mask off and dragging my sleeve across my face. The team's chatter fades into the background as I grab my bottle.

The sharp sound of something skidding across the ice draws my attention.

A puck.

It stops near my skate. I frown, leaning down to pick it up. There's writing on it in pink marker.

Dinner?

What the hell?

I glance around the rink, but the players are focused on their break, and the coaching staff are huddled together near the boards.

Then, another puck flies over the plexiglass, landing right in front of me with a soft thud.

I bend down, my breath catching when I see what's taped to it: a crumpled piece of paper. My fingers are shaking as I peel it off and unfold it.

I love you, too.

I glance at the fortune cookie paper taped to it.

An old flame may reignite.

My heart stops.

I look up, and there she is.

Cammy.

She's sitting in the bleachers, bundled in a hoodie with my Hawkeyes jersey stretched on top, her smile bright enough to melt the ice beneath my skates.

I skate toward the plexiglass like a man possessed—because fuck, I am. She waves, her eyes sparkling with something I haven't seen since the night she smiled at me in Oakley's before the fight.

"Where did you get the fortune?" I call out, my voice echoing in the rink.

She leans forward, resting her elbows on the railing. "I lied that night about what it said. I thought you might be interested in what my fortune really was."

I stare at the crumpled slip in my hand, the weight of her words confirming what I had already suspected. *"An old flame may reignite,"* I read aloud, my voice hoarse.

Cammy nods, her smile softening. "You were right. That fortune was very wise... even though I didn't tell you what it said."

The world narrows to just her and me as I skate closer to the boards.

"Why didn't you tell me the truth?" I ask.

She purses her lips and stares down at the paper in my hands. "Because I was scared that it would come true."

"And yet... you came all the way here—wearing my jersey," I say, my voice quieter now, tinged with disbelief. "You don't seem too scared now."

She gets up from her seat and starts walking down the few steps to bring her to the front of the rink.

"I had to come. You weren't answering your phone," she says, her smile faltering for a moment. "And then Angelica told me everything."

My heart sinks. Angelica. Of course she did.

"She told you about the accident?"

"She told me everything," Cammy says firmly. "About the accident. About the DUI. About why you've been running from everyone and everything ever since."

I swallow hard, the words caught in my throat.

Cammy's gaze softens. "You've been carrying that for so long, JP. But you didn't have to. Not alone. I would have kept the secret, but at least now, I understand why you couldn't tell me."

I shake my head, my voice rough. "You don't understand, Cammy. Trouble follows me. It always has. I couldn't drag you down with me."

She moves closer to the boards until we're only separated by the plexiglass. Her hands press against it, her fingers splayed wide.

"Do I look dragged down to you?" she asks, her voice steady.

I blink at her, my throat too tight to speak.

"You're not your father, JP. You're not even close. And you're not alone. Not unless you choose to be."

I press my hands against the glass, mirroring hers. "I got traded, Cammy. I don't even have a team to go back to."

Her lips twitch into a smile. "Actually... this isn't your new team. Coach Haynes never turned in the transfer. You're just here until you come to your senses and come back with me to Seattle. Slade called in a favor with the coach to keep it from you. Your contract paperwork with the Hawkeyes is sitting in the legal department's office, waiting for you to come home and sign it."

I shake my head, the weight of her words slowly lifting. "Slade's a pain in my ass."

"And a genius," she says with a grin. "But Penelope's not thrilled about the whole situation. I probably owe her a month of chai lattes and sticky buns."

The first laugh in days escapes me. "So, you really love me," I say as I move to the section without plexiglass. She follows me, step for step, until there's nothing between us but the boards. I pick her up and pull her over, setting her feet gently on the ice with me.

I keep my hands on her hips as she stares up at me.

"I think I always did," she says.

The next words catch in my throat. "So... what do we do next?"

Cammy's gaze softens, her voice steady. "Well, Thanksgiving is in a couple of days so there's no practice with the team. My grandparents would love to meet you, and honestly," she says, looking down at the ice, timidly pinning a strand back behind her ear, "I know it's a lot to ask you to meet my family, but would you want to come home with me?"

My chest tightens at the thought. "Go home with you? To Minnesota? With Seven and your mom and—"

"And my grandparents," she finishes. "I could really use you. It's going to be a lot, I know. But having you there will make it easier for me."

I nod slowly, the knot in my chest easing as I meet her

gaze. "Your dad's going to kill me, but I'll go anywhere with you, Cammy."

I pull her closer, feeling her body against mine once again.

For the first time in weeks, the world feels like it's shifting back into place.

"I guess I don't have an apartment when I get back, since I already gave mine up," I say, the realization dawning on me.

"I know a girl with a king-size bed three floors up." She gleams.

"We're doing this then. You're mine...finally?"

Her fingers wrap into my practice jersey, pulling me close, her lips full and perfect, making my mouth water. "I've been yours since you threw me that first puck. And I will be yours until the last," she says and then pushes up on her toes to seal her lips with mine.

"We need to find a hotel room right now," I tell her against her lips.

She giggles. "Oh, really? And why would that be?"

"Because... Je vais te lécher des orteils jusqu'aux seins."

A voice comes from Cammy's back pocket, translating what I said.

"I'm going to lick you from your toes to your tits," the voice translates.

Cammy's jaw falls open as we both stare at each other wide-eyed. Other players skate by, chuckling as the translation echoes through the rink.

"What the fuck was that?" I ask.

Cammy snickers as she pulls out her phone from her back pocket. "I believe they call that technology. Now you can't hide your true feelings from me, Dumont. Karma's a bitch."

I laugh. Of course, she won't let me get away with anything. And that's why she's the one, and always has been.

"Je t'aime, mon petit oiseau."

"I love you, my little bird," the translator app says, as I lean down and kiss her again.

CHAPTER THIRTY-ONE

JP

Cammy's hand rests in mine as we drive up the long gravel road to her grandparents' house in the rental car we picked up from the airport. The landscape is a picture-perfect Midwestern winter—a light dusting of snow blankets the ground, a string of smoke curling from the chimney, and the faint glow of lights in the windows. It's cozy, idyllic.

Everything I'm not.

"My grandparents are going to love you," she says, squeezing my hand as if willing me to believe it.

I glance at her, her soft smile doing little to calm the churning in my stomach. "How did Seven take it when you told him that I was coming?"

Cammy falls silent, not looking in my direction, but her finger twitches the moment I ask.

"Cammy..." I say, quickly glancing over at her while keeping a sharp eye on the road. "You told him I was coming with you, right?"

Finally, her eyes drift over to mine. "Not in so many words, but..."

My head falls against the headrest as I let out a groan.

"He knew I flew out to Alberta to bring you back. He had to know that this was a possibility."

"Does he know that we're officially together?" I ask. I have a feeling I already know the answer, and it's not in my favor.

Cammy plasters on an encouraging smile that's tinged with nerves. "He'll warm up. It might take some time, but he will. He doesn't have much of a choice. I'm not giving you up a third time for anyone."

Hearing her say that is encouraging, but I still grip the steering wheel tighter with one hand as the house comes into full view. I pull her hand up to mine and kiss the back of it. "I hope you're right, because we're about to find out."

The front door swings open, and my worst fears are confirmed. Seven storms out like a man on a mission, his jaw set, his eyes locked on me. Right behind him is a guy almost as big as he is—must be Cammy's uncle Eli.

Brynn trails after them, Milo perched on her hip, grinning ear to ear. Behind her, a woman who could be Cammy's twin if she were twenty years older steps out. That must be her mom.

"Shocking...Seven doesn't seem thrilled," I mutter, trying to keep my voice steady.

Cammy squeezes my hand again, her voice firm. "It's going to be fine. Just... be yourself."

I snort. "That's what I'm afraid of."

The car barely comes to a stop before Seven yanks the door open.

"Cammy," he says, his voice low but commanding. "Go inside."

She stiffens, her fingers tightening around mine. "Dad, no—"

"Cammy," he repeats, his tone leaving no room for argument. "Go. Inside."

I glance at her, giving her a small nod. "It's okay. I've got this, mon amour."

"Don't call her that," Seven warns.

I stare back at him. I'm not scared of the man, but he and I are going to have this out so Cammy and I can move on with our lives. I'm not letting her go this time, and if he thinks that leaving the Hawkeyes is the best I can do to prove how much I love her, then he has no idea what I'm capable of giving up for her.

I glance back at her and give her another reassuring nod.

Her eyes dart between us, reluctant, but she finally climbs out of the car. Brynn meets her halfway, wrapping an arm around her shoulders and steering her toward the house.

I climb out of the car next, and Seven comes around to my side.

He waits until they're inside before turning to me, his expression hard as steel.

"JP," he says, his voice dangerously calm.

I stand tall despite the weight of his glare. "Coach."

Seven crosses his arms over his chest, Eli standing just behind him like backup. "I warned you to stay away from her."

"And I tried," I admit, my voice steady. "But I can't. I'm not going to give her up. Not for you. Not for the Hawkeyes. Not for anything."

Seven's eyes narrow, his jaw ticking, but I press on.

"I respect you, Seven," I say, my voice firm. "As my coach, as one of the best goalies to ever play the game, and as Cammy's protector. But loving your daughter isn't something I can turn off or walk away from. And just like Cammy isn't a product of who raised her... neither am I."

Seven's silence stretches, heavy and taut, his eyes boring into mine.

Finally, he exhales a slow breath, shaking his head.

"She deserves everything this world has to offer."

I nod. "And I swear to God that Cammy won't ever want for anything. She'll have whatever she asks for—you have my word."

He blows out a breath. He knows his daughter is just as stubborn as he is, and I'm too stupid to back down.

"You know I'm going to be watching every step," he says, his voice low. "If you screw this up—"

"I won't," I cut in, meeting his gaze. "Not this time. I'd rather lose everything else than lose her."

For a moment, I think he's going to hit me—his fists ball at his side, his jaw is tight enough that he looks like he might break a tooth. But finally his eyes lighten just a little, another exhale softening his tense shoulders... just barely.

"It's Thanksgiving. Come inside," he says gruffly, turning on his heel and heading toward the house. Eli gives me a once-over before following.

I let out a breath and head up the steps.

Inside, the warmth of the house is a stark contrast to the tension outside. Cammy is standing by the fireplace, her cheeks pink, her smile bright as she talks to her mom. Brynn and who I presume to be her grandmother are setting the table while Milo plays in his highchair.

Seven brushes past me, clapping a hand on Eli's shoulder. "Let's get that turkey carved."

Cammy's eyes meet mine. Her smile softens, and in that moment, the world feels like it's shifting into place.

She walks over, slipping her arms around my waist. "You okay?"

I nod, pressing a kiss to her forehead. "Your dad's intense."

She laughs, tilting her head up to look at me. "He just wants to make sure I'm happy."

"Well," I say, wrapping my arms around her, "I'll just have to prove that I'm the man for the job."

"I made up a room for you two upstairs," Cammy's grandma calls out to her from the kitchen.

"Oh, thanks, Gram, but I got us a hotel room just down the street. I hope that's okay," she tells her, as her eyes find mine.

I pull her into my arms and plant a kiss on her lips. She giggles against my mouth. "I thought you might need a break from my dad," she whispers.

"Have I told you today how much I love you?" I tease.

"Only a couple dozen times." Her hazel eyes stare up at mine, that warm amber color that tells me she's happy.

"Then, let me tell you again in case you forgot. Je t'aime, Cammy. Tu es mon amour."

Her smile widens, and she pulls me toward the table. "Come on. Let's eat."

As we sit down to dinner, surrounded by warmth and laughter, I realize something.

I've been searching for the place where I fit, where I'm home.

I looked for it in my father, in the long line of stepfathers, stadiums, and coaches. And before Cammy found Seven, she was searching for that, too.

But, finally, we've both found it.

Cammy's the place I belong.

And I want to be that for her.

I'll never let her down.

CHAPTER THIRTY-TWO

Cammy

The roar of the crowd fills the arena as I stand just outside the tunnel, gripping my hockey stick. My heart pounds but not from nerves. This isn't like last year when everything felt make-or-break. This time, it's just fun—well, mostly.

I take a deep breath and glance toward my dad. Seven stands beside me, arms crossed, watching the ice with his usual intensity. When he looks down at me, though, his expression softens.

"You ready, kid?" he asks, his voice rough with emotion.

I nod, adjusting my gloves. "Always."

He exhales a quiet laugh, then sits down beside me on the bench, the weight of his presence grounding me. "I was thinking about the first time I taught you to skate," he says, shaking his head with a small smile. "You were stubborn as hell."

I grin. "Wonder where I got that from?"

"Must've been your mother," he quips, but his smile fades into something softer. "Cammy... I want you to know that no matter what happens out there tonight, I'm proud of you. Not just for this"—he gestures toward the ice, where the slapshot challenge is about to take place—"but for everything. For standing your ground, for following your heart, for knowing what you want and fighting for it."

Emotion tightens my throat, and I blink rapidly to keep it at bay. "You really mean that?"

Seven nods. "I do. And I know I gave JP a hard time, but... he's proven himself. Not just as a player, but as a man. The way he looks at you, the way he takes care of you—I see it now. And I see the way you take care of him, too."

I reach for his hand, squeezing it. "Thanks, Dad."

His lips twitch. "Now don't let him win out there."

A laugh bursts from my chest as I stand, giving my skates one last adjustment. "Oh, I don't plan on it."

I skate toward center ice, my eyes immediately locking onto JP, everything else fades away. He stands tall in full goalie gear, tapping his stick against the ice, that familiar cocky smirk hidden behind his mask. His eyes, though, tell me everything—they're full of warmth, pride, and just a little bit of mischief.

"Ladies and gentlemen, let's hear it for Cammy Wrenley, our defending champion! Can she score again this year?"

The crowd cheers as I take my spot at center ice. This year's slapshot challenge has drawn even more attention than last year's—thanks to the millions raised. Autumn wasn't on maternity leave this year, and she and Juliet outdid themselves, transforming the event into a spectacle with a light show, live music, and a packed arena filled with die-hard hockey fans and supporters of the cause.

Of course, JP and I helped with the live auction items again.

JP stands in the crease, leaning on his stick, casual and cocky, waiting for me like he always does.

The last year flashes through my mind—the off-season in Cancun with my dad, Brynn, and Milo, where JP fit into our family like he was always meant to be there. Lazy beach mornings, JP hoisting my little brother onto his shoulders and letting him "play hockey" with a stick twice his size. Nights filled with laughter, with whispered promises, with learning each other in ways that go beyond words.

We'd come back to Seattle as more than just a couple. We were a team. And when we decided to upgrade to a bigger two-bedroom apartment in The Commons, it wasn't just about space—it was about building something permanent together. A life, a home, a future.

JP taps his stick against the ice, drawing me back to the present. The challenge. The bet we made before the season started—one shot, just like last time. But this time, there's nothing on the line except our pride and maybe, just maybe, the kind of competitive tension that would lead to some truly great sex later tonight.

I roll my shoulders back, watching the way his stance shifts, the way his body readies for me. He's studying me, anticipating me, the way he always does.

"You ready for this, Dumont?" I call, raising a brow.

"Don't go easy on me, Wrenley," his voice echoing through the mic on the arena speakers, teasing, full of challenge.

"I wasn't planning on it."

He chuckles, low and knowing. "Good. Because we both know you like it when I make you work for it."

Heat rushes through me, but I smirk, keeping my expression playful. "Talk all you want, Dumont. You still have to stop me."

"I will, and then I'm changing that last name," he teases.

He told me he wants the name on my game day jersey to match his all of last season. It's a comment I've become accustomed to, but it never ceases to pull butterflies from my belly.

I line up the puck, taking a deep breath, letting every memory of every shot I've ever taken against him flood my mind. The ones he's blocked. The ones I've scored. The ones that led to playful fights that turned into something much, much hotter behind closed doors.

The first puck skates down the ice with a sharp crack of my stick. He blocks it effortlessly, flashing the crowd with a dramatic glove save. The arena oohs and aahs, eating up his theatrics.

The second puck? Same result. This time, he lets it bounce off his chest protector, skating out just a little to smack it back toward me with his stick.

He's toying with me. And I love it.

By the time I line up for my third and final shot, the crowd holds its breath. I wind up, putting every ounce of force and precision I have into the shot. The puck slices through the air, hurtling straight for the top corner of the net.

JP dives—but he's too slow.

The puck hits the back of the net with a satisfying clang, and the stadium erupts. Confetti cannons go off, showering the ice in blue and silver. I throw my arms up in victory, laughing as the players walk out onto the ice from the tunnel, each holding a single red rose.

Twenty-two roses. Twenty-two players. By the time JP skates up to me, my arms are overflowing with long stems.

He stops in front of me, holding the puck I scored on him in his glove. He pulls his goalie helmet off and drops it to the ice. The air between us shifts, the playful teasing giving way to something deeper.

When he speaks, his voice carries even through the deafening noise. "I have a question to ask you."

At that moment, I know what he's going to ask. My throat clogs—emotions quickly bubbling to the surface with his surprise.

He drops to one knee right there on the ice, in front of a stadium full of friends, family, donors, and fans, flipping the puck over to reveal the words written in a silver Sharpie.

Marry Me?

My breath catches, and tears prick my eyes—I clutch the roses with one arm as my free hand reaches up to cover my mouth. I had no idea—no inkling—but the signs were there... I should have seen them. The bigger apartment he pushed for, the wedding venue in Cancun that he claimed he *accidentally* stumbled upon one day, the private dinner he and my dad went to weeks ago that he said I wasn't invited to—JP was asking my dad for his blessing.

He had to have been. It all makes sense now.

The world blurs, narrowing down to just him, kneeling before me with that lopsided grin that made me fall in love with him in the first place. With that first puck he tossed me years ago. I feel like I barely know those two people anymore. JP and I have changed—grown—and we did it together.

"Yes," I whisper, then louder, "Yes!" I yell as I drop all of the roses to the ground and leap into his arms, laying a kiss on his lips.

The crowd roars, but it all fades away as JP slips the ring onto my finger. He stands, pulling me into his arms, and kisses me like we're the only two people in the world.

The cheers swell again, and when we pull apart, I see Seven skating out onto the ice, a jersey in his hands. He stops in front of JP, holding it out with a small, rare smile. They share a hand shake as if this was all planned—but of course it was.

"Here," he says, his voice gruff. "This is for you."

JP takes the jersey and unfolds it. The back reads *Mrs. Dumont* in bold letters, with the number one printed beneath.

Seven leans down and presses a quick kiss to my head. "Congrats, kiddo," he says softly before turning and skating off.

JP holds up the jersey, his grin widening as he drapes it over my shoulders.

"You're my number one, Cammy," he says, his voice thick with emotion. "Nothing will ever change that."

I laugh through my tears, standing on my tiptoes to kiss him again as the crowd cheers.

In this moment, with JP by my side and our future stretched out before us, I know I've finally found my forever.

Later tonight, in our apartment, we'll have our own version of a rematch. And something tells me, win or lose, we'll both come out on top.

THE WEDDING

Cammy

Two Years Later

"Hold still," Brynn orders, wielding a curling iron in one hand. "Unless you want singed-off hair in your wedding photos that will last the rest of your life."

The gravity of her words hit me—"*the rest of your life.*"

She means that I will spend the rest of my life with JP, and suddenly the moment where everything we've planned and done to get to this day—our wedding day—finally kicks in.

I thought it would the moment I picked up my dress after my last fitting. Or the moment that JP and I boarded our flight four days ago to Cancun for our wedding that we've been planning for the last two years. But that overwhelming feeling of the weight of today never came.

I've been calm and cool. Not even the flowers showing up late this morning rattled me, because somehow, this entire thing—marrying JP in a beach wedding in my favorite place on earth—it's just felt ordained since the moment he dropped to one knee and asked me to marry him in the Hawkeyes stadium.

The anxious or nervous butterflies never came, and I think it's because I've never felt so sure about anything in my life the way I'm sure about JP. He showed me what I mean to him that day that he gave up his dreams of playing for the Hawkeyes for me, and every day since.

Staring at my wedding dress hanging from the floor-to-ceiling window casing in this gorgeous bridal suite with all my bridesmaids scurrying around getting ready, my belly fills with butterflies. In a matter of hours, JP and I will say our "I do's," in front of close friends and family. And by tonight, my last name will officially match the jersey I've been wearing for the last three years.

Mrs. Dumont.

I fidget away from Brynn as she comes closer, earning an exasperated sigh from my stepmom. Through the windows of our beachfront suite, the Cancun sunrise paints the sky in shades of pink and gold that reflect off the crystal-clear water.

The warm breeze carries the salt-tinged air through the open balcony doors, mixing with the scent of hairspray and the fresh flowers scattered around the room.

Suddenly, a small object comes flying up and over the balcony.

A hockey puck rolls on its side into the suite, catching everyone's attention. Instant giggles ensue as every one of my bridesmaids know exactly what it is.

My mom walks over and picks it up, glancing over the side of the balcony to verify the offender, but I can already guess the culprit.

"Get out of here. You can't see her until she walks down the aisle," my mom scolds him.

I can already imagine JP's gorgeous smirk. He doesn't believe in bad luck. Not when we've been through so much and still ended up coming out on the other side.

Besides, he asked me to wear my old green hairband for a week before the wedding to make sure its luck was fully recharged.

"Make sure she gets it," I hear him call out to her.

She saunters over with it in her hand—a smile on her lips. "This is for you, from your impatient groom."

I take it from her, the weight of the puck heavy in my hand as I read JP's messy scrawl, I DO written in silver marker. The newest message he's been writing on the puck and tossing to me at every home game since he proposed.

"It's just a reminder that no matter what happens on the ice, I will always choose you first over everything else," he told me, the first time he tossed it to me.

A soft knock interrupts Brynn's concentration with the curling iron. Penelope, looking radiant in her pale-blue bridesmaid dress, crosses to answer it. Slade stands in the doorway, holding an elegant white box tied with a silver ribbon.

"For the bride," he says, but his eyes are locked on his wife. "You look gorgeous, Pen," he murmurs, just loud enough for me to hear.

Penelope's cheeks flush as she accepts the box, rising on her toes to kiss him quickly. "Go on, get back to the guys," she shoos him away with a smile.

She brings the box to me, and I open it, recognizing JP's handwriting on a card that lies on top of white tissue paper: *To my bride, my soul, my life. On our wedding day.*

My hands shake slightly as I lift the card off the paper. Underneath, nestled in white tissue paper, in a signature blue box, lies a Tiffany tennis bracelet that takes my breath away.

I turn it over, reading the inscription etched into the diamond-studded plate: *You're mine to love, and I'm yours to keep.*

"That boy." Brynn laughs, leaning over my shoulder. "Who knew JP Dumont was such a romantic?"

"I did," I whisper, blinking back tears as Penelope helps me fasten it around my wrist. "I always did."

My fingers brush gently over the bracelet.

I should have known he would do something today while we're apart, to let me know he's thinking of me.

"Remember when you used to dodge his pucks?" Brynn teases, pinning another curl in place. "Now look at you—marrying the guy you swore was just another player with a reputation."

I catch her eye in the mirror, unable to stop my smile. "Remember when Dad threatened to trade him if he didn't stay away?"

We smile back at one another. All of that feels like a lifetime ago.

Now JP is a well-beloved and respected player of the Hawkeyes, and Penelope just promoted me from Administrative Assistant to Assistant General Manager. A lot can happen in three years.

"And now they're golfing buddies." She laughs. "Though, I'm pretty sure Seven only invites him to lay the pressure on thick that he wants grandkids someday."

"I heard that." My dad's voice carries from the doorway. We turn to find him leaning against the frame, already in his tux. My dad's eyes are suspiciously bright as he takes me in, though I'm still in only my white bridal robe, but it's enough to pull emotions from him. He looks different than the man who once bet JP to leave the team—softer somehow, like the edges have been smoothed by time and understanding.

"Dad," I say, knowing that this day could have gone differently, but instead, both my father and Eli gave JP their blessing to marry me.

My dad is dressed to walk me down the aisle, and I couldn't be happier.

He crosses the room in three strides, then presses a kiss to my forehead. "You look beautiful, kiddo. Like you could score on any goalie in the league."

"Don't make me cry," I warn, fanning my face. "Brynn put a lot of work into my makeup. If my mascara runs, she's going to kill you."

"Damn right I will," Brynn mutters, but she's smiling too.

My dad's hearty laugh fills the air.

A knock at the door announces my grandparents and Eli, all dressed and looking elegant. The sight of us all together still feels surreal sometimes—years of tension dissolved into something peaceful, something whole.

"Oh, Cammy," my gran breathes, her hand flying to her chest. "You look..."

"Like a champion," Eli finishes, his smile proud. "A true Wrenley."

"And soon to be a Dumont," Dad adds, his voice gruff but warm. "JP's proven himself—on and off the ice. Took overtime, but... he won fair and square."

I blink rapidly, determined not to cry. "Thank you for being here to support me. I wouldn't have wanted to do this without your blessing, but I would be marrying JP today, either way."

He laughs, then grows serious. "I know you would. That night JP came to ask for my blessing. He didn't just ask about marrying you. He asked me to help him be the kind of man you deserve— the kind of father his kids deserve." Dad's voice catches. "That's when I knew. He's nothing like his old man. He's better. You gave him a reason to dig deep and find the man he could be."

My dad reaches out for Brynn's hand and squeezes it for a moment, as if Brynn is his reason for doing the same.

The door bursts open before I can respond, and Milo races in, his tiny tux slightly askew, the ring pillow clutched in his hands like a prized puck.

"Cammy!" he shouts, running straight for me. He's not little any more at five years old and already taking after my dad— towering over other kids his age. "Look! I practiced with JP! He showed me the butterfly position for carrying the rings!"

I struggle to scoop him up onto my lap, but I manage, ring pillow and all, pressing kisses to his cheeks. "My perfect ring bearer. Did JP teach you any other moves?"

"He said I have to protect these like they're Game Seven of the Stanley Cup Finals," Milo says proudly. "No turnovers allowed!"

Penelope appears in the doorway, stunning in her bridesmaid

dress. "Face-off in five minutes," she says softly.

My heart skips, then settles into a steady rhythm. This is it—the biggest game of my life.

As we make our way down to the beach, I think about that first puck JP tossed me, how I rolled my eyes at his dinner invitation. About all the pucks that followed, each one a piece of our story. About San Diego, about finding our way back to each other, about building something real.

The wedding march begins, and I grip Dad's arm. Through the gauzy curtains of the beach pavilion, I catch glimpses of our guests—teammates in suits instead of jerseys, family, friends. And at the end of the aisle, standing tall in his tux with that infuriating smirk I fell in love with, is JP.

My MVP.

My forever.

The music changes, and my heart stops mid-beat.

The curtains part, and there she is—my Cammy, on Seven's arm, looking like every dream I've ever had come to life. Her form-fitting dress catches the sunlight, making her glow like an angel against the backdrop of turquoise water and white sand. My lucky charm, mon petit oiseau, my everything.

"Breathe, Dumont," Slade mutters from beside me.

I take a deep inhale, taking his advice. I didn't realize that I held my breath the moment I saw her.

She glides down the aisle, and memories flood my mind: that first game when I spotted her across enemy lines, every puck I tossed, hoping to make her smile, the night in San Diego when I thought I'd lost her forever, the day she showed up at the farm team's practice rink to bring me home.

Seven stops at the altar, and for a moment, we share a look—one of understanding, of respect, of family. He places Cammy's hand in mine, and everything else fades away like crowd noise during sudden-death overtime.

"Hi, goalie," she whispers, her eyes bright with tears.

"Bonjour, mon amour," I whisper back, my voice rough with emotion. My thumb brushes over her knuckles, feeling her pulse race beneath her skin, the rhythm matching my own.

The ceremony passes in a blur of promises and rings, but when it's time for our vows, the world narrows to just us—like it's just the two of us alone on center ice.

"Cammy," I start, my hands steady now as I hold hers. "Before you, I was just playing defense, protecting my net but never really living. But you? You made me want to be better. To be worthy. You're my home-ice advantage, my lucky charm, my everything. I promise to spend every day proving that betting on us was the best play we ever made."

She laughs through her tears, squeezing my hands. "JP," she says, her voice steady, despite the emotion in her eyes. "You threw a lot of pucks my way before I caught one. But now? Now I'll catch every one. I promise to be your teammate, your biggest fan, and your forever. Je t'aime, mon gardien de but."

The reception is a whirlwind of laughter and celebration. Seven's toast brings tears to everyone's eyes when he admits that having me as a son-in-law is better than having me as a starting goalie—but now he's stuck with both.

Later, much later, I carry Cammy across the threshold of our honeymoon suite, her laughter echoing off the walls as I set her down gently.

"Alone at last," I murmur, pulling her close. The moonlight streaming through the windows catches on her ring, sending prisms dancing across the walls and reminding me that she promised me forever, today.

She runs her hands up my chest, her touch igniting every nerve ending. "Think you can score tonight, Dumont?"

I growl, backing her toward the bed. "Oh, I plan on it, Mrs. Dumont. Multiple times."

Her breath catches at the name, and then my mouth is on hers, hungry and desperate. We fall onto the bed together, hands exploring familiar territory that somehow feels brand new. Every touch, every kiss, every whispered promise feels deeper, more meaningful.

"Je t'aime," I whisper against her skin as I trail kisses down her neck. "Mon coeur, mon âme, ma vie."

She arches into me, her fingers threading through my hair. "Show me," she demands softly.

It doesn't take long before I'm inside her, pulling orgasm after orgasm from her body, claiming her as my wife, until she can't take anymore. Until we're both breathless and sated, tangled in each other and the sheets.

Later, as we lie in the quiet darkness, Cammy traces patterns on my chest. "Hey," she says softly. "I have something for you."

She reaches for her bag beside the bed, pulling out something small. A puck.

I take it, turning it over in my hands. Written in her neat script: *Game On, Dumont.*

My heart swells as I pull her close, pressing a kiss to her temple. "Game on, Mrs. Dumont. Forever."

Because some games aren't meant to end—they're meant to be played for a lifetime.

Acknowledgements

To my incredible readers—your patience, enthusiasm, and unwavering support mean everything to me. Through delayed releases, unexpected plot twists (both on and off the page), and the occasional typo I swear wasn't there before 😊 —you're still here. And that? That makes you my MVPs, my ride-or-die book family.

Your sweet Insta DMs, emails, and our chats in my Facebook reader group have been the absolute highlight of this journey. Keep them coming—I love hearing from you! 🖤 And to everyone who has fallen in love with the Hawkeyes boys as much as I have, thank you for taking this ride with me

To my phenomenal team—Michelle, Erin, Julie, and Madeline—thank you for keeping me on track, polishing my words, and handling my last-minute chaos with grace. Mikaela Brown, Chasing Books PR, my PR wizard, you've been in my corner since the beginning, making sure I can focus on what I love most—writing. I couldn't do this without you.

To my beta readers—Chelsea, Hosana, Julia, Caitlin, Taylor, Alicia, Stephen, and so many others—thank you for your sharp eyes, honest feedback, and for saving me from my own mistakes more times than I can count. You are lifesavers!

And to my family—who has endured takeout nights and my writing marathons—I appreciate you beyond words. To my husband, who has stepped in whenever I needed to lose myself in these stories, you are my rock, my sanity, and the reason I get to chase this dream.

Want to stay connected? Let's keep in touch!

📩 Newsletter: https://www.kennaking.com
📚 Facebook Reader Group: Kenna King's MVPs
📷 Instagram: @kennakingbooks

ABOUT THE AUTHOR

Author of "spice on ice" romance novels.

As an avid reader myself, and a Westcoast girl, I love two things: swoon-worthy pro athlete book boyfriends, and writing stories about them living in the beautiful Northwest where I'm blessed to call home.

I do my best work late at night after I've tucked in my three littles, and my hard-working husband.

Learn more at: kennaking.com